RONIN 47 is unlike other books. In fact, it is an interactive science fiction novel, inspired by the Legend of the Forty-Seven Ronin from 18th century Japan. And rather than reading it from cover to cover, you will discover that at the end of each narrative section you will be presented with a series of choices that allow you to control the course of the story.

As well as the book itself, you will need two dice (or a standard pack of playing cards), a pencil and an eraser. Using these tools, and a simple set of game rules contained within the book, you will undertake a dangerous mission to avenge a terrible wrong, whilst piloting a twenty-metre-tall robot war-machine.

YOU decide which route to take, which perils to risk, and which of the monstrous creatures and rogue mechs you will meet along the way to fight. But be warned – whether you succeed in your quest, or suffer a terrible fate yourself, will be down to the choices YOU make.

Proudly Published by Snowbooks in 2022

Snowbooks Ltd.
email: info@snowbooks.com
www.snowbooks.com

British Library Cataloguing in Publication Data
A catalogue record for this book is available from the British
Library.

Hardcover 9781913525200
Paperback 9781913525187
eBook 9781913525194

Play-testers

Paul 'Moggie' Morrough • Fabrice Gatille • Pete Wood •
Ashley Hall • Emma Owen • Anton Killin • Nicholas Chin •
Dan Kaiwarrior Schell • Judykins • Jason Lenox •
Stephane Bechard • Benjamin Wicka • Y. K. Lee •
Our Games Trading Co Ltd • Andrés Rodríguez •
Victor Cheng • Lin Liren
With special thanks to Anthony England and Paul Simpson.

WRITTEN BY JONATHAN GREEN
ILLUSTRATED BY NEIL GODGE

SNOWBOOKS

Also by Jonathan Green

ACE Gamebooks

Alice's Nightmare in Wonderland
The Wicked Wizard of Oz
NEVERLAND – Here Be Monsters!
Beowulf Beastslayer
'TWAS – The Krampus Night Before Christmas
Dracula – Curse of the Vampire

Snowbooks Fantasy Histories

You Are The Hero – A History of Fighting Fantasy Gamebooks
You Are The Hero Part 2

Snowbooks Anthologies

Sharkpunk (edited by Jonathan Green)
Game Over (edited by Jonathan Green)
Shakespeare Vs Cthulhu (edited by Jonathan Green)

Fighting Fantasy Gamebooks

Spellbreaker
Knights of Doom
Curse of the Mummy
Bloodbones
Howl of the Werewolf
Stormslayer
Night of the Necromancer

Sonic the Hedgehog Adventure Gamebooks

Theme Park Panic (with Marc Gascoigne)
Stormin' Sonic (with Marc Gascoigne)

Doctor Who Adventure Gamebooks

Decide Your Destiny: The Horror of Howling Hill
Choose The Future: Night of the Kraken

Star Wars: The Clone Wars – Decide Your Destiny

Crisis on Coruscant

Gamebook Adventures

Temple of the Spider God

Warlock's Bounty

Revenge of the Sorcerer

Path to Victory

Herald of Oblivion
Shadows Over Sylvania

Dedicated to the memory of
Oishi Yoshio and the rest of the Forty-Seven Ronin.

A BRIEF HISTORY OF THE FUTURE

2021 – A new hottest-ever temperature is recorded in the southern polar region of Antarctica.

2030 – Global emissions of greenhouse gases peak after policy makers fail to curb climate change.

2040 – Global warming continues, resulting in widespread droughts and rising sea levels.

2051 – With the world facing the 'Hothouse Earth' scenario, the United Nations sign the Gaia Treaty.

The people of Earth combine their scientific knowledge in an attempt to restore balance to the natural world. Plans are put into action to ensure the relentless destruction of the biosphere ceases for good.

In many parts of the world, Mother Nature needs a helping hand to repair the damage done to the planet by the human race, and so Project Proteus is born, with geneticists and marine biologists developing the K-Compound to restore the coral reefs.

At first, it is hailed as a success, as the corals quickly return, and the seas around them soon teem with life. But the genetically-modified *Corallium novum* continues to grow and multiply, laying claim to coastal communities. Growing in size all the time, it evolves to combat whatever obstacles stand in its way.

Those creatures that feed on the coral also begin to absorb enough K-Compound to start mutating. The beneficial properties of the unintentionally created bio-weapons pass up the food chain, and the kaiju are born.

A 'Scorched Earth' policy is adopted, but in the long term, this only serves to make the situation worse. Bombing runs, or attacks against the creatures utilising heavy ordnance, help to spread the

K-Compound farther afield. Something is needed that can get right to the heart of the problem, meeting the kaiju head on in single combat.

In Japan, this dire need leads to the development of the Guardian Programme – building giant robots that can resist the monsters – which is subsequently copied by other nations. But it is too little too late. The islands of Japan are among the first to fall to the kaiju, and Tokyo itself is destroyed.

Those Guardians that survive go their separate ways, some banding together to seek vengeance against the kaiju.

THE WAY OF THE WARRIOR

Introduction

The year is 2121, and the apocalypse has been and gone. Amidst the ruins of the old world, the human race fights for survival against the gigantic, hyper-evolved kaiju. Humanity's most effective weapons against the monsters are the colossal mechs developed by the Guardian Programme.

In *RONIN 47* you take on the role of Commander Oishi, a Samurai-class mech pilot and leader of Phoenix Squad, operating out of Ako Base in the Philippine Sea. You decide which route to take, which perils to risk, and which of the monstrous creatures and rogue mechs you will meet along the way to fight.

Success is by no means certain, and you may well fail to complete the adventure at your first attempt. However, with experience, skill, and maybe even a little luck, each new attempt should bring you closer to your ultimate goal.

In addition to the book itself, you will need two six-sided dice, or a conventional pack of 52 playing cards, a pencil, an eraser, and a copy of the *RONIN 47* Adventure Sheets (spare copies of which can be downloaded from **www.acegamebooks.com**).

Playing the Game

There are three ways to play through *RONIN 47*. The first is to use two six-sided dice. The second is to use a conventional pack of 52 playing cards. The third is to ignore the rules altogether and just read the book, making choices as appropriate, but ignoring any combat or attribute tests, always assuming you win every battle and pass every skill test. (Even if you play the adventure this way, there is still no guarantee that you will complete it at your first attempt.)

If you are opting to play through *RONIN 47* using the game rules, you first need to determine your strengths and weaknesses.

Your Attributes

You have three attributes that you need to keep track of during the course of the adventure. Some of these will change frequently, others less so, but it is important that you keep an accurate record of the current level for all of them.

- *Agility* – This is a measure of how athletic and agile you are. If you need to leap across a chasm or dodge a deadly projectile, this is the attribute that will be employed.

- *Combat* – This is a measure of how skilful you are at fighting, whether it be in unarmed combat, wielding your keen-edged katana, or using a blaster.

- *Endurance* – This is a measure of how physically tough you are and how much strength you have left. This attribute will vary more than any other during your adventure.

Unlike some adventure gamebooks, in **RONIN 47** your strengths and weaknesses are not determined randomly. Instead, you get to decide what you are good at and, conversely, what you might not be so good at.

Your *Agility* and *Combat* attributes start at a base level of 6. Your *Endurance* score starts at a base level of 20. You then have a pool of 10 extra points to share out between *Agility*, *Combat* and *Endurance* as you see fit, but you can only add up to 5 points to each attribute. Therefore, the maximum starting score for *Agility* and *Combat* is 11, and the maximum starting score for *Endurance* is 25. (You must apportion all 10 points one way or another and cannot leave any unused.)

For example, you might choose to add nothing to your *Agility* score, 5 points to your *Combat* score, and allocate the remaining 5 points to your *Endurance* score, making you a mighty warrior and giving you the following starting profile for the game:

Agility = 6, *Combat* = 11, *Endurance* = 25.

Alternatively, you might want to add 4 points to your *Agility* and *Combat* scores, and the remaining 2 points to your *Endurance* score, making you more of an all-rounder, and giving you this starting profile:

Agility = 10, *Combat* = 10, *Endurance* = 22.

Having determined where your strengths and weaknesses lie, record the value of each attribute in the appropriate box on your

Adventure Sheet in pencil, and make sure you have an eraser to hand, as they will doubtless all change at some point as you play through the adventure.

There are limits on how high each of your attributes can be at the start of the adventure, but there are also limits on how high they can be raised during the course of the adventure, dependent upon bonus points you may be awarded. Neither your *Agility* score nor your *Combat* score may exceed 12 points, while your *Endurance* score may not exceed 30 points. However, should your *Endurance* score ever drop to zero, or below, then your adventure is over, and you should stop reading immediately; if you want to tackle the quest again, you will have to start from the beginning, determining your attributes anew and starting the story from section 1 once more.

Testing Your Attributes

At various times during the adventure, you will be asked to test one or more of your attributes.

If it is your *Agility* or *Combat* that is being tested, simply roll two dice. If the total rolled is equal to or less than the particular attribute being tested, you have passed the test; if the total rolled is greater than the attribute in question, then you have failed the test.

If it is your *Endurance* score that is being tested, roll four dice in total. If the combined score of all four dice is equal to or less than your *Endurance* score, then you have passed the test, but if it is greater, then what is being asked of you is beyond what you are capable of and you have failed the test.

Restoring Your Attributes

There are various ways that you can restore lost attribute points or be granted bonuses that take your attributes beyond their starting scores, and these will be described in the text.

However, an easy way to restore lost *Endurance* points is to consume Rations or use a Medi-Pack. You begin the adventure with 5 Ration Packs and 3 Medi-Packs. One Ration Pack will restore up to 4 *Endurance* points, while one Medi-Pack will restore up to 6 *Endurance* points.

Sometimes you may find a way to replenish your Rations or Medi-Packs. Make sure that if you do find any supplies of this nature you record them on your Adventure Sheet.

Combat

You will repeatedly be called upon to defend yourself, during the course of your adventure. Sometimes you may even choose to attack an enemy yourself. After all, as they say, the best form of defence is attack.

When this happens, start by filling in your opponent's *Combat* and *Endurance* scores in the first available Oishi Encounter Box on your Adventure Sheet.

Whenever you engage in combat, you will be told in the text whether you or your enemy has the initiative; in other words, who has the advantage and gets to attack first.

1. Roll two dice and add your *Combat* score. The resulting total is your *Combat Rating*.

2. Roll two dice and add your opponent's *Combat* score. The resulting total is your opponent's *Combat Rating*.

3. For each Combat Round, add a temporary 1 point bonus to the *Combat Rating* of whichever of the combatants has the initiative for the duration of that round.

4. If your *Combat Rating* is higher than your opponent's, you have wounded your enemy; deduct 2 points from your opponent's *Endurance* score and move on to step 7.

5. If your opponent's *Combat Rating* is higher, then you have been wounded; deduct 2 points from your *Endurance* score and move on to step 8.

6. If your *Combat Rating* and your opponent's *Combat Rating* are the same, roll one die. If the number rolled is odd, you and your opponent deflect each other's attacks; go to step 10. If the number rolled is even, go to step 9.

7. If your opponent's *Endurance* score has been reduced to zero or below, you have won; the battle is over, and you can continue the adventure. If your opponent is not yet dead, go to step 10.

8. If your *Endurance* score has been reduced to zero or below, your opponent has won the battle. If you want to continue your adventure you will have to start again from the beginning. However, if you are still alive, go to step 10.

9. You and your opponent have both managed to injure each other; deduct 1 point from both your *Endurance* score and your opponent's *Endurance* score. If your *Endurance* score has been reduced to zero or below, your adventure is over; if you want to play again you will have to start again from the beginning. If you are still alive but your enemy's *Endurance* has been reduced to zero or below, you have won; the battle is over, and you can continue the adventure. If neither you nor your opponent are dead, go to step 10.

10. If you won the Combat Round, you will have the initiative in the next Combat Round. If your opponent won the Combat Round, they will have the initiative. If neither of you won the Combat Round, neither of you will gain the initiative bonus for the next Combat Round. Go back to step 1 and work through the sequence again until either your opponent is dead, or you are defeated.

Fighting More Than One Opponent

Sometimes you may find yourself having to fight more than one opponent at the same time. Such battles are conducted in the same way as above, using the ten-step process, except that you will have to work out the *Combat Ratings* of all those involved. As long as you have a higher rating than an opponent you will injure them, no matter how many opponents you are taking on at the same time. Equally, any opponent with a *Combat Rating* higher than yours will be able to injure you too.

However, if you are fighting two or three opponents simultaneously, you must deduct 1 point from your *Combat Rating* for the duration of the battle. If you are facing four or five opponents at the same time, you must deduct 2 points from your *Combat Rating*. And if you ever have to fight six or more opponents at the same time, deduct 3 points from your *Combat Rating*!

For example, if you find yourself having to fight two Giant Spider Crabs, for the duration of that fight you must deduct 1 point from your *Combat Rating*. If you were fighting three Giant Spider Crabs at the same time, you would still only have to deduct 1 point from your *Combat Rating*. But if there were four Giant Spider Crabs attacking you at the same time, you would have to deduct 2 points from your *Combat Rating*, for the duration of the battle.

Please note, if even just one of your opponents makes a successful strike against you during a Combat Round, you will not have the initiative against any of them in the following Combat Round – if you are still alive!

Ranged Combat

As well as a sword, your katana, you are also armed with a gun, in the form of an energy blaster.

If you find yourself in battle, and you have the initiative in the opening Combat Round, you may choose to fire your gun before engaging in hand-to-hand combat. *Take a Combat test* and if you pass the test, you cause your opponent 3 *Endurance* points of damage; if you fail the test you have simply wasted your shot.

If you hit your opponent, you may take a second shot, by *Taking another Combat test*, but no more after this.

When facing multiple opponents, you must choose which one you want to target in ranged combat. However, if you pass the initial *Combat test*, you may target a different opponent with your bonus second shot.

An Alternative to Dice

Rather than rolling dice, you may prefer to determine random numbers during the game using a pack of playing cards.

To do this, when you are called upon to roll dice, simply shuffle a standard 52-card deck (having removed the Jokers) and draw a single card. (If you are asked to roll four dice, draw two cards.) Number cards are worth the number shown on the card. Jacks, Queens and Kings are all worth 11, and if you draw an Ace, it counts as being worth 12 (for example, if you are engaged in Combat), and is an automatic pass if you are testing an attribute – any attribute.

After drawing from the deck, you can either return any cards you have drawn or, using the Pontoon method, leave those drawn cards out of the deck. Both styles of play will influence how lucky, or unlucky, you may be during the game, when it comes to determining random numbers.

If the text asks you to roll one die, simply pick a card and if its face value is greater than 6, or it is a picture card, it still counts as a 6.

Your Mech's Attributes

In *RONIN 47*, you do not only have to keep track of your own attribute scores, you also need to keep an accurate record of the stats for your Samurai-class mech. These are as follows:

- *Speed* – This is a measure of how quickly the mech is able to move. The more heavily-armoured a robot is, the slower it will be.

- *Artillery* – This is a measure of how powerful the robot's long-range, heavy ordnance weapons are. However, the more artillery weapons a mech has, the less effective it will be in hand-to-hand combat.

- *Melee* – This is a measure of how effective the mech is in close combat.

- *Upgrades* – This is actually an inventory of the items carried by the Samurai-class mech.

- *Reactor* – This is a measure of how effectively the mech's nuclear power core is operating.

- *Armour* – This is a measure of how heavily-armoured the robot is.

- *Integrity* – This stat keeps track of how much damage the mech has suffered.

As with your own attributes, your mech is fully customisable; you decide whether it is faster, or more heavily-armoured, whether it is better at long-range combat or at close-quarters fighting. While the machine's *Reactor* and *Integrity* starting scores are fixed, you determine everything else. However, balance is the name of the game when it comes to customising your mech, as certain stats work in pairs.

Speed and *Armour* work as one pair, based on a sliding scale, but you must have a minimum of 1 point in each attribute.

Look at the example below:

SPEED							ARMOUR

Three blocks have been shaded in at the *Speed* end of the scale. This means that the mech has a *Speed* score of 3 and an *Armour* score of 3, which would be typical of a standard Samurai-class mech.

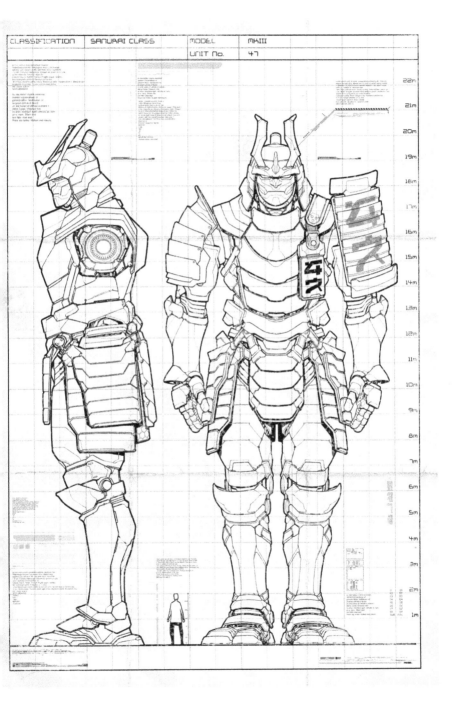

CLASSIFICATION	SAMURAI CLASS	MODEL	MKIII
		UNIT No.	47

Now consider this example:

SPEED							ARMOUR

This would better suit a Ninja-class mech, which is much faster and more agile, with a *Speed* score of 5, but which is also much less well-armoured, with an *Armour* score of only 1.

Equally, *Artillery* and *Melee* also work as a pair on the same sliding scale. Once again, you must have at least 1 point in each attribute.

MELEE							ARTILLERY

The example above would be best suited to an Oni-class heavy ordnance mech since it has an *Artillery* score of 4 but a *Melee* score of just 2.

Using the sliding scales on your mech's Adventure Sheet, work out your war-machine's *Speed, Armour, Artillery* and *Melee* scores, and then record them in the appropriate boxes.

Your mech's *Reactor* score starts at zero and may not drop below this level. However, if the *Reactor* score reaches 3 points, the nuclear core will suffer a catastrophic failure that will destroy your mech and you along with it. If this happens you must stop reading immediately; if you want to try to complete your quest again, you will have to start from the beginning once more, determining the strengths and weaknesses of you and your mech anew.

Your mech's *Integrity* score starts at 50. If its *Integrity* drops to zero or below, your war-machine has been destroyed and you have been killed. If you want to continue your adventure you will have to start again from the beginning, determining your own strengths and weaknesses, as well as those of your mech, all over again. It is much harder to recover lost *Integrity* points than it is to recover lost *Endurance* points, so make sure you take care of your mech.

All of your mech's *Speed, Armour, Melee, Artillery,* and *Integrity* scores may rise above their starting level, under certain circumstances. However, please note that its *Speed, Armour, Melee, Artillery* scores may never exceed 5 points, or drop below zero points.

Testing Your Mech's Attributes

At various times during the adventure, you will also be asked to test one or more of your mech's attributes.

If it is the mech's *Speed, Armour, Melee* or *Artillery* that is being tested, simply roll one die. If the total rolled is equal to or less than the attribute being tested, your mech has passed the test; if the total rolled is greater than the attribute in question, then it has failed the test.

If it is your mech's *Integrity* score that is being tested, roll one die and multiply the number rolled by 10. If the total is equal to or less than your mech's current *Integrity* score, your mech has passed the test; but if it is greater, then the robot has failed the test.

Restoring Your Mech's Attributes

There are various ways that you can restore lost attribute points or be granted bonuses that take your mech's attributes beyond their starting scores, and these will be described in the text.

Mech Combat

Fighting other mechs or kaiju with *Samurai 47* is more complicated than determining the outcome of battles you are involved in without your mech being present and takes place in two distinct phases; the Long-Range Combat phase followed by the Close Combat phase.

Start by filling in your opponent's *Speed, Armour, Melee, Artillery,* and *Integrity* scores in the first available Mech Encounter Box on your Adventure Sheet.

Next, before Long-Range Combat can commence, you must determine how far away you are from your opponent.

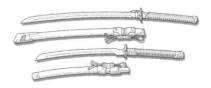

Determining Distance

Long-Range Combat is worked out over a number of Combat Rounds, and you need to start by determining how many, based on how close *Samurai 47* is to your opponent.

1. Roll one die and add 5. (Alternatively, pick a card, and if it is a 7 or higher, it is worth 6, and then add 5.) The total is the measure of the *Distance* between you and your opponent.

2. Add your mech's *Speed* score to your opponent's *Speed* score. (If you are fighting more than one opponent, use the *Speed* score that is the highest of all your opponents.)

3. Deduct the combined *Speed* scores from the *Distance*. This is how many Combat Rounds of long-range combat you need to fight before commencing Close Combat.

4. If, having deducted the combined *Speed* scores from the *Distance,* the total is zero or a negative number, go straight to the Close Combat phase.

The Long-Range Combat Phase

Long-Range Combat is conducted using *Samurai 47*'s artillery weapons and heavy ordnance.

1. Roll two dice and add your mech's *Artillery* score. The resulting total is your mech's *Artillery Rating*.

2. Roll two dice and add your opponent's *Artillery* score. The resulting total is your opponent's *Artillery Rating*.

3. For each Combat Round, add a temporary 1 point bonus to the *Artillery Rating* of whichever of the combatants has the initiative for the duration of that round. (In the first Combat Round, this will be the mech or monster with the highest *Speed* score, unless your mech's *Speed* score is that same as its opponent's, in which case no bonus point is awarded.)

4. If your mech's *Artillery Rating* is higher than your opponent's you have wounded your enemy; determine

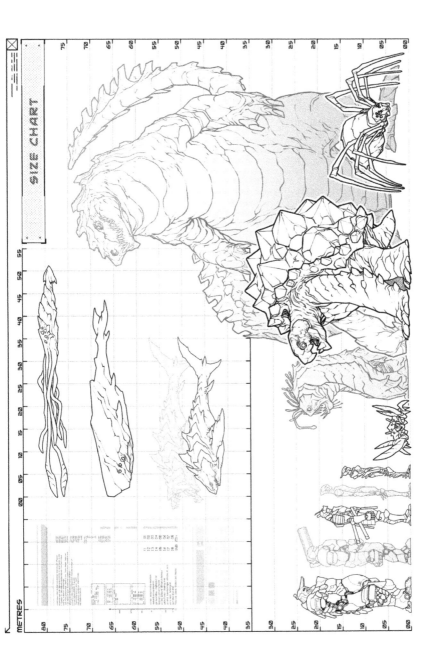

how much damage your mech has caused (as described under Determining Damage on page 28), and then move on to step 7.

5. If your opponent's *Artillery Rating* is higher, then you have been wounded; determine how much damage has been inflicted against your mech (as described under Determining Damage on page 28), and then move on to step 8.

6. If your *Artillery Rating* and your opponent's *Artillery Rating* are the same, your mech and your opponent have both managed to injure each other; determine how much (as described under Determining Damage on page 28). If your opponent's *Integrity* score has been reduced to zero or below, you have won the battle and can continue on your way, but if your opponent is not yet dead, go to step 10. If your mech's *Integrity* score has been reduced to zero or below, your opponent has won the battle and your adventure is over, but if your mech is still operational, go to step 10.

7. If your opponent's *Integrity* score has been reduced to zero or below, you have won; the battle is over, and you can continue on your way. If your opponent is not yet dead, go to step 10.

8. If your mech's *Integrity* score has been reduced to zero or below, your opponent has won the battle. If you want to continue your adventure you will have to start again from the beginning, determining your attributes anew. However, if you are still alive, go to step 9.

9. If there are no more Long-Range Combat Rounds left to fight, and your opponent is still alive, the battle now moves to the Close Combat phase. However, if you still have more Combat Rounds of Long-Range Combat left to conduct, go to step 10.

10. If you won the Combat Round, you will have the initiative in the next Combat Round. If your opponent won the Combat Round, they will have the initiative. If neither of you won the Combat Round, neither of you will gain the

initiative bonus for the next Combat Round. Go back to step 1 and work through the sequence again.

The Close Combat Phase

Close Combat works in a similar way to battles fought by Commander Oishi without the aid of a 20-metre tall mech. Sometimes, the text will tell you to go straight to the Close Combat phase.

1. Roll two dice and add your mech's *Melee* score. The resulting total is your mech's *Melee Rating*.

2. Roll two dice and add your opponent's *Melee* score. The resulting total is your opponent's *Melee Rating*.

3. For each Combat Round, add a temporary 1 point bonus to the *Melee Rating* of whichever of the combatants has the initiative for the duration of that round. (In the first Combat Round, this will be the mech or monster with the highest *Speed* score, unless your mech's *Speed* score is the same as its opponent's, in which case no bonus point is awarded.)

4. If your mech's *Melee Rating* is higher than your opponent's, you have wounded your enemy; determine damage (as described under Determining Damage on page 28) and go to step 7.

5. If your opponent's *Melee Rating* is higher, then you have been wounded; determine damage (as described under Determining Damage on page 28) and go to step 8.

6. If your mech's *Melee Rating* and your opponent's *Melee Rating* are the same, roll one die. If the number rolled is odd, your mech and your opponent deflect each other's attacks; go to step 10. If the number rolled is even, go to step 9.

7. If your opponent's *Integrity* score has been reduced to zero or below, you have won; the battle is over, and you can continue on your way. If your opponent is not yet dead, go to step 10.

8. If your mech's *Integrity* score has been reduced to zero or below, your opponent has won the battle. If you want to continue your adventure you will have to start again from the beginning, determining your attributes anew. However, if you are still alive, go to step 10.

9. Your mech and your opponent have both managed to injure each other. If your opponent's *Integrity* score has been reduced to zero or below, you have won the battle and can continue on your way, but if your opponent is not yet dead, go to step 10. If your mech's *Integrity* score has been reduced to zero or below, your opponent has won the battle and your adventure is over, but if your mech is still operational, go to step 10.

10. If you won the Combat Round, you will have the initiative in the next Combat Round. If your opponent won the Combat Round, they will have the initiative. If neither of you won the Combat Round, neither of you will gain the initiative bonus for the next Combat Round. Go back to step 1 and work through the sequence again until either your opponent is dead, or your mech has been defeated.

Determining Damage

You determine damage caused during Long-Range Combat and Close Combat in the same way.

Roll as many dice as the winner of the Combat Round has *Artillery* points (in the case of Long- Range Combat) or Melee points (in Close Combat). Only those dice that have a score that is equal to or higher than the loser's *Armour* score cause damage. Each damaging dice does 2 points of *Integrity* damage.

Alternatively, pick as many cards as the winner of the Combat Round has *Artillery* points (in Long-Range Combat) or Melee points (in Close Combat). Any that have a score that is equal to or higher than the loser's *Armour* score cause 2 points of *Integrity* damage.

Fighting More Than One Opponent in Mech Combat

Occasionally you may find yourself having to fight more than one opponent at once. Such battles are conducted in the same way as above, using the ten-step process, except that you will have to work out the *Artillery/Melee Ratings* of all those involved. As long as you have a higher rating than an opponent you will injure them, no matter how many opponents you are taking on at the same time. Equally, any opponent with a *Artillery/Melee Rating* higher than yours will be able to injure you too.

In mech combat, there are no penalties applied for fighting more than one opponent at the same time. However, initiative bonuses do not apply either.

Quick Mech Combat

If you wish to reduce the amount of time taken by mech combat, you can use the Quick Mech Combat rules instead. In this case, ignore the rules about determining distance and the Long-Range Combat and Close Combat Phases. Instead, follow this ten-step process.

1. Roll two dice and add your mech's *Artillery* and *Melee* scores. The resulting total is your mech's *Combat Rating*.

2. Roll two dice and add your opponent's *Artillery* and *Melee* scores. The resulting total is your opponent's *Combat Rating*.

3. For each Combat Round, add a temporary 1 point bonus to the *Combat Rating* of whichever of the combatants has the initiative for the duration of that round. (In the first Combat Round, this will be the mech or monster with the highest *Speed* score.)

4. If your mech's *Combat Rating* is higher than your opponent's, you have wounded your enemy; determine damage (as described under Determining Damage on page 28) and go to step 7.

5. If your opponent's *Combat Rating* is higher, then you have been wounded; determine damage (as described under Determining Damage on page 28) and go to step 8.

6. If your mech's *Combat Rating* and your opponent's *Combat Rating* are the same, roll one die. If the number rolled is odd, your mech and your opponent deflect each other's attacks; go to step 10. If the number rolled is even, go to step 9.

7. If your opponent's *Integrity* score has been reduced to zero or below, you have won; the battle is over, and you can continue on your way. If your opponent is not yet dead, go to step 10.

8. If your mech's *Integrity* score has been reduced to zero or below, your opponent has won the battle. If you want to continue your adventure you will have to start again from the beginning, determining your attributes anew. However, if you are still alive, go to step 10.

9. Your mech and your opponent have both managed to injure each other. If your opponent's *Integrity* score has been reduced to zero or below, you have won the battle and can continue on your way, but if your opponent is not yet dead, go to step 10. If your mech's *Integrity* score has been reduced to zero or below, your opponent has won the battle and your adventure is over, but if your mech is still operational, go to step 10.

10. If you won the Combat Round, you will have the initiative in the next Combat Round. If your opponent won the Combat Round, they will have the initiative. If neither of you won the Combat Round, neither of you will gain the initiative bonus for the next Combat Round. Go back to step 1 and work through the sequence again until either your opponent is dead, or your mech has been defeated.

Double Damage

This is an optional rule that you can use to speed up Mech Combat, or make Quick Mech Combat even quicker.

If you roll a double when calculating your mech's *Combat Rating*, your machine automatically causes its opponent a severe wound; deduct 10 points from your enemy's *Integrity* score.

Upgrades

Your mech is armed with a ten-metre-long Electro-Katana and various rocket batteries. However, it also comes with a number of customisable Upgrades. When determining your war-machine's strengths and weaknesses, you may also choose one Upgrade from each of the three categories below.

Combat Computer Upgrades

Enhanced Interface – *adds 1 point to your Melee Rating when the mech is in close combat*.*

Enhanced Targeting – *adds 1 point to your Artillery Rating when engaged in long-range combat*.*

Enhanced Scanners – *deducts 1 point from your opponent's Armour score when engaged in close com*bat*.

Robot Upgrades

Upgraded Actuators – *adds 1 point to your Melee Rating when the mech is in close combat*.*

Upgraded Stabilisers – *adds 1 point to your mech's Speed score.*

Upgraded Hull – *adds 1 point to your mech's Armour score and 5 points to its Integrity score.*

Deployable Upgrades**

Depth Charges – *anti-submarine underwater explosives.*

Drones – *unmanned aerial vehicles used primarily for reconnaissance.*

Flares – *pyrotechnics that produce bright light and intense heat.*

* These bonuses apply to Quick Mech Combat as well, and also when determining damage.

** Your chosen upgrade from this category may be used up to 3 times during an adventure.

Please note that the effects of Upgrades are cumulative. For example, if you selected the Enhanced Interface and the Upgraded Actuators, you will be adding 2 points to your *Melee Rating* when your mech is in close combat.

Record the Upgrades you have selected on the Samurai-class mech's Adventure Sheet, along with the Electro-Katana, in the Upgrades box.

Equipment

You start your adventure wearing a protective, Kevlar-weave, armoured bodyglove, and carrying a blaster. You are also armed with a Katana; the iconic curved sword of the Japanese Samurai warrior class, famed for its keen cutting edge. During your quest, you will no doubt acquire other items that may be of use to you later on. Anything that you do collect should be recorded on your Adventure Sheet, including any clues, as well as weapons, provisions, and other miscellaneous objects.

Any items that provide bonuses for any of your attributes, or those of your mech – such as a weapon that adds 1 point to the giant robot's *Melee* score – only provide those bonuses when the item in question is in use.

And don't forget, you also begin the adventure with 5 Ration Packs and 3 Medi-Packs.

Hints on Play

There is more than one path that you can follow through *RONIN 47*, to reach your ultimate goal, but it may take you several attempts to complete the adventure successfully. Make notes and draw a map as you explore. This map will doubtless prove invaluable during future attempts at completing your quest and will allow you to progress more speedily, in order to reach unexplored regions.

Keep a careful eye on your attributes throughout the game. Beware of traps and setting off on wild goose chases. However, it would be wise to collect useful items along the way that may aid you later on in your quest.

Ending the Game

There are several ways that your adventure can end. If your *Endurance* score ever drops to zero or below, your trials have exhausted and overcome you. If this happens, stop reading at once.

There may also be occasions where you are prevented from progressing any further thanks to the choices you have made, or if you meet a sudden and untimely end. In all of these cases, if you want to have another crack at completing the adventure you will have to start again with a new Adventure Sheet and begin the story afresh from the beginning.

There is, of course, one other reason for your adventure coming to an end, and that is if you successfully complete your quest, the very same quest that awaits you now...

ADVENTURE SHEETS

COMMANDER OISHI

AGILITY	COMBAT	ENDURANCE

EQUIPMENT	RATION PACKS	MEDI-PACKS

NOTES AND CODE WORDS

OISHI ENCOUNTER BOXES

OPPONENT =	OPPONENT =
COMBAT =	COMBAT =
ENDURANCE =	ENDURANCE =

OPPONENT =	OPPONENT =
COMBAT =	COMBAT =
ENDURANCE =	ENDURANCE =

OPPONENT =	OPPONENT =
COMBAT =	COMBAT =
ENDURANCE =	ENDURANCE =

OPPONENT =	OPPONENT =
COMBAT =	COMBAT =
ENDURANCE =	ENDURANCE =

OPPONENT =	OPPONENT =
COMBAT =	COMBAT =
ENDURANCE =	ENDURANCE =

OPPONENT =	OPPONENT =
COMBAT =	COMBAT =
ENDURANCE =	ENDURANCE =

OPPONENT =	OPPONENT =
COMBAT =	COMBAT =
ENDURANCE =	ENDURANCE =

SAMURAI-CLASS MECH

SPEED								ARMOUR

MELEE								ARTILLERY

INTEGRITY

REACTOR

UPGRADES

				DEPTH CHARGES
				DRONES
				FLARES

MECH ENCOUNTER BOXES

OPPONENT =		DISTANCE =
SPEED =	ARMOUR =	INTEGRITY =
MELEE =	ARTILLERY =	☒

OPPONENT =		DISTANCE =
SPEED =	ARMOUR =	INTEGRITY =
MELEE =	ARTILLERY =	☒

OPPONENT =		DISTANCE =
SPEED =	ARMOUR =	INTEGRITY =
MELEE =	ARTILLERY =	☒

OPPONENT =		DISTANCE =
SPEED =	ARMOUR =	INTEGRITY =
MELEE =	ARTILLERY =	☒

OPPONENT =		DISTANCE =
SPEED =	ARMOUR =	INTEGRITY =
MELEE =	ARTILLERY =	☒

OPPONENT =		DISTANCE =
SPEED =	ARMOUR =	INTEGRITY =
MELEE =	ARTILLERY =	☒

OPPONENT =		DISTANCE =
SPEED =	ARMOUR =	INTEGRITY =
MELEE =	ARTILLERY =	☒

MECH ENCOUNTER BOXES

OPPONENT =		DISTANCE =
SPEED =	ARMOUR =	INTEGRITY =
MELEE =	ARTILLERY =	⊠

OPPONENT =		DISTANCE =
SPEED =	ARMOUR =	INTEGRITY =
MELEE =	ARTILLERY =	⊠

OPPONENT =		DISTANCE =
SPEED =	ARMOUR =	INTEGRITY =
MELEE =	ARTILLERY =	⊠

OPPONENT =		DISTANCE =
SPEED =	ARMOUR =	INTEGRITY =
MELEE =	ARTILLERY =	⊠

OPPONENT =		DISTANCE =
SPEED =	ARMOUR =	INTEGRITY =
MELEE =	ARTILLERY =	⊠

OPPONENT =		DISTANCE =
SPEED =	ARMOUR =	INTEGRITY =
MELEE =	ARTILLERY =	⊠

OPPONENT =		DISTANCE =
SPEED =	ARMOUR =	INTEGRITY =
MELEE =	ARTILLERY =	⊠

2121

The scream of the dropship's thrusters, and the hum of your mech's reactor, are reduced to almost nothing by the audio dampeners operational in the cockpit of the Samurai.

As the Tatsu maintains position over the atoll, you instinctively check your harness straps one more time, and put a hand to the hilt of the katana clamped to the side of your seat.

"Commander Oishi," the voice of the dropship's pilot crackles over the comm, "we are over the drop zone."

"Understood, Lieutenant Tsunenari," you respond and then, broadcasting on all channels, address your team. "Phoenix Squad, sign in!"

One by one, the five other members of Phoenix Squad do as you command.

"Takanao reporting, Commander. *Samurai 16* is ready to deploy."

"Masatane. *Samurai 23* is also ready, Commander."

"Norikane, Commander! *Samurai 39* is good to go!"

"Sadayuki. *Samurai 41* firing on all cylinders, Commander."

"The supreme art of war is to subdue the enemy without fighting," Shigemori's voice echoes within the cockpit. "*Samurai 52* is primed for battle."

"Let your plans be dark and impenetrable as night, and when you move, fall like a thunderbolt," you reply, quoting Sun Tzu's *The Art of War* back at him.

"Weapons hot!" you bark into the comm, bringing both your own mech's long-range artillery and close combat weapons online. "The Tengu Array had pinpointed this location as a hotspot of kaiju activity, so stay alert."

The doors in the belly of the dropship yawn open and an alert starts to chime on the helm-display in front of you.

"Release docking clamps on my mark," you say, your hand hovering over the touchscreen control panel. "Mark!"

Tapping a virtual button on the screen, you feel the vibration as the docking clamps holding the great war-suit in place snap open, and a split second later your stomach is in your mouth as the Samurai freefalls from the belly of the hovering Tatsu.

Turn to **1**.

Even though you brace yourself, the jolt, when it comes – as the Samurai splashes down in the shallows – still rocks you within your pilot's cradle. It is a sensation you think you will never entirely get used to, no matter how many assault drops you make, just as you will never quite get used to feeling like a god when you stride across land and sea at the controls of *Samurai 47.*

The mech's metal toes immediately anchor themselves in the ground as the rest of Phoenix Squad lands around you. You sweep the island, the war-machine's Combat AI registering each of the other five Samurai in turn, and the Tatsu dropship departs.

Tactical data streams across the helm-display in front of you, overlaying your view of the coral atoll, the brilliant azure sky, and white-armoured mechs, with cascading crimson characters.

Despite all having the same basic Samurai-class chassis, on closer inspection, each giant robot has its own distinctive differences, whether it be the different armaments options they have been fitted out with, or because of the scars left by previous battles with the kaiju, the proliferation of which has brought humankind to its knees.

The island – which the mech's onboard computer informs you is called Hitode Atoll, via an alert in the top left corner of the HUD – is little more than a ring of coral reefs surrounding the hypnotically deep ultramarine waters of a blue hole – a giant marine sinkhole that could be hundreds of metres deep and hide who knows what secrets.

There is no obvious sign of the kaiju activity the Tengu Satellite Array detected four hours ago, but that is why you have been deployed to this precise location.

What do you want to do? Will you:

Deploy Drones (if you have them)?	Turn to **21**.
Perform a long-range sensor scan with your Enhanced Scanners (if you have them)?	Turn to **519**.
Deploy Depth Charges into the blue hole (if you have them)?	Turn to **437**.
Descend into the blue hole yourself?	Turn to **82**.
Maintain a defensive position on the atoll and wait?	Turn to **41**.

Tokyo lies 500 clicks almost due north of the coral atoll, but how do you want to travel there?

If *Ronin 47* is equipped with a Booster Rocket, and you want to use it to reach Honshu Island, turn to **60**. If not, or you would prefer not to use the Booster Rocket at this time, you will have no choice but to travel by sea – turn to **590**.

You suddenly become aware of something moving in the dark depths of the sea-hole, at the same time as a proximity alarm starts to sound within the cockpit.

In the next moment something bursts from the water in front of you. As the pixelated distortion on the screen resolves itself, the image is revealed to be that of a monstrous creature. Its body is a thick column of supple flesh, as if some abyssal worm has risen from the depths, but one of gargantuan proportions.

The column of flesh ends in a gaping maw, full of razor-sharp fangs, each one as long as your arm. The de facto head of the creature is ringed by vast starfish-like limbs that twitch and writhe independently of one another, as if possessed of a will of their own. More of these limbs emerge from the side of the creature's body, like tentacles, and the monster reaches for your Samurai with these pseudo-limbs.

A prompt on the HUD informs you that this particular kaiju has the designation Oni-Hitode, or 'Devil-Starfish.' And it is not alone; more of its kind have attacked *en masse*, forcing the entirety of Phoenix Squad to engage in battle.

At least as long as your mech is tall, the kaiju attacks.

ONI-HITODE				
SPEED	ARMOUR	MELEE	ARTILLERY	INTEGRITY
3	1	3	1	10

If you manage to defeat your kaiju attacker, turn to **560**.

The blaring klaxon of the *Ronin 47's* proximity alarm brings you to full alertness and has you scrambling to access the data feed from the mech's AI to find out what is happening.

You pull up images from the war-suit's ocular arrays on the screen in front of you. Appearing as glowing, multi-coloured blurs on the screen, thanks to the mech's infra-red cameras, you are horrified to see three monstrous crab-like creatures, each the size of a tank, scuttling towards you over the rocks, their powerful pincers snapping in expectation.

Doubtless drawn to this rocky outcrop by the scent of the Gumyocho's bodily fluids that have been draining into the sea for the last however-many hours, while others of their kind pick the bird's flesh from its carcass, these Kani-Oni have gone in search of other prey.

Do you want to:

Launch some Flares (if you can)?	Turn to **380**.
Launch a Hunter-Killer Missile (if you have one)?	Turn to **409**.
Activate a DNA Bomb (if you have one)?	Turn to **50**.
Fire up a Booster Rocket (if your mech is fitted with one)?	Turn to **434**.
Fire up *Ronin 47's* jump-jets?	Turn to **465**.
Attack the Kani-Oni?	Turn to **493**.

In only a matter of minutes, every room and passageway in the facility becomes filled with seawater. Reaching Airlock 2, you open it and swim inside, as it also fills with water, and then, having sealed the hatch behind you, wait for it to drain again before you attempt re-entering your mech.

If you have the code word *Modified* recorded on your Adventure Sheet, turn to **177**. If you have the code word *Untested* recorded on your Adventure Sheet, turn to **203**. If you have neither code word recorded on your Adventure Sheet, turn to **417**.

Taking the metal cylinder from where it is stored in the mech's chest cavity, you hurl it at the colossal spider-like monster. The canister tumbles end over end through the air, emitting a thick gas from vented openings in each end as it does so. The cloud expands rapidly, enveloping the Tsuchigumo in a toxic green fog.

It is an anxious wait as you wonder if the compounds you selected to make the DNA Bomb will have any effect on the eight-legged horror at all!

Double the number you have associated with the DNA Bomb and then turn to the section which is the same as the total to see what effect the gas has.

If you do not have a number associated with the DNA Bomb, turn to **205**.

7

The ruined city is soon many kilometres behind you and you begin your ascent of Mount Fuji, every colossal stride taking you higher up the sloping side of the dormant volcano.

If your mech is equipped with a Cloaking Device, and you want to activate it now, turn to **23**. If not, turn to **51**.

8

Having checked that your seat-harness is secure, you power up the mech's engines and set off for the surface.

If you have the code word *Hunted* recorded on your Adventure Sheet, turn to **29**. If not, turn to **55**.

9

You take a moment to initiate a long-range sensor scan and await the outcome.

Roll one die (or pick a card). If the number rolled is odd (or the card is red), turn to **527**. If the number rolled is even (or the card is black), turn to **69**.

10

A hissing sound draws your attention to a row of vents at both floor level and where the walls meet the ceiling. The corridor is starting to fill with gas, while the door by which you entered is starting to slide shut.

Before you really know what is happening, you inhale some of the toxic fumes and immediately feel light-headed and start to cough. (Lose 4 *Endurance* points.)

Do you want to sprint for the door by which you entered, hoping to reach it before it closes (turn to **84**), or do you want to attempt to break through the door by which the security drones entered but which is already closed (turn to **145**)?

11

You succeed in shooting down the incoming missiles before any of them can make contact with your mech. Turn to **95**.

12

As automated systems connect the airlock in the back of your Samurai-class mech with the unused one located in the trench wall, you don your helmet and check that the in-built aqualung is functioning correctly, just in case. Once pressures have equalised, you access the airlock via the hatch behind your seat, taking your katana with you as well, just in case...

****

You emerge from the airlock into a brightly-lit octagonal corridor. You follow it until it turns sharply left and find yourself at an intersection, and the proof that you are not the only one here. The passageway continues ahead of you before turning sharply left, and no doubt leads to the other airlock. You can see multiple sets of wet footprints on the floor coming from the direction of the other airlock and heading off along the new corridor to your right. To your left, facing this new passageway, is an octagonal door.

Do you want to try to open the door (turn to **39**), head along the corridor that you believe leads to the other airlock (turn to **276**), or follow the passageway to the right (turn to **332**)?

13

The men dead, you turn your attention to the control room. As you realised as soon as you entered the building, the traitors have successfully destroyed every terminal and screen that could have given you access to the array or seen what the satellites can see.

The most frustrating thing is that the array is still there, two thousand kilometres above the surface of the Earth, and operational, it's just that there is no way for you to access the data it has acquired... or is there?

The control room might be gone, but the traitors didn't think to destroy the satellite dish itself. You could use *Ronin 47*'s computer to download the data from the Tengu Array, but only if the uplink is working, of course.

If you have the code word *Connected* recorded on your Adventure Sheet, turn to **594**. If not, turn to **568**.

14

Ronin 47's Combat AI alerts you to the presence of something descending from the azure sky on jets of flame. The mech automatically trains its long-range weapons on the target, but you do not activate them when you see through the HUD that it is another Samurai-class war-machine.

The mech lands fifty metres away from you, throwing up a great cloud of dust and debris as it does so. But when the cloud clears again, you see the stylised sun decoration on the robot's hull and are relieved when it is Kanesada's voice you hear over the comm.

"Commander Oishi!" Kanesada declares.

"It is good to be reunited with you and *Rising Sun* again," you reply. "But what are you doing here?"

"I was able to escape after you initiated that breakout at the Wrecker arena. All the mech-pilots were, and after sending that supertanker to the bottom of the ocean we went our separate ways. I thought about what you told me, when we were incarcerated together, and I thought you could probably do with a hand."

"But what of Okinawa Prefecture?" you ask. "Are you not needed there?"

"I am the last of my kind," Kanesada explains, his tone sombre, "and there is work to be done here. Honourable work. Deaths to be avenged. Besides, I think I may be able to help."

"I am sure you will," you say. "Two mechs are definitely better than one."

"No, I mean I can offer more immediate help. There is one who I believe still survives in this ruined city, one who may be able to give us an advantage even against a foe as terrible as this Shogun-class mech you have told me of."

This is an intriguing offer, but do you have time to indulge in a search for someone who may not even be alive anymore? When you accessed the Tengu Satellite Array, you saw what looked like mechs active in the city. One of them may even be the Shogun you are hunting.

So how will you respond to Kanesada's offer?

"Take me to them!"   Turn to **56**.

"There is no time to delay, we have mechs to hunt!"   Turn to **31**.

15

You shut off the audio alarm, whilst leaving the reactor infographic on the screen, and, avoiding the island, continue your journey north.

Add 1 point to the mech's *Reactor* score and then turn to **429**.

16

The roar of rockets overhead, and the plethora of hazard markers that appear on the HUD, as the Combat AI tracks the incoming projectiles, alerts you to the fact that you are under fire.

Roll one die (or pick a card). If the number rolled is odd (or the card is red), turn to **68**. If the number rolled is even (or the card is black), turn to **47**.

"Ivan thought you Samurai were all about honour," the big Russian growls, the smile vanishing from his face in a second. "Where is the honour in being a bad loser?"

"All warfare is based on deception," you come back at him. But he's right; in refusing to settle the bet you have brought dishonour on all Samurai. (Deduct 1 *Combat* point.)

"And there is honour in besting oath-breakers in battle!" Ivan declares, and, biceps bulging, goes for you. (In this battle, your opponent has the initiative.)

IVAN 'THE BEAR' BUKOVSKI   COMBAT 10   ENDURANCE 10

If you reduce Ivan's *Endurance* score to 4 points or fewer, or if you are still alive after 6 Combat Rounds, turn to **413** at once.

Entering the fortress, you initiate a full sensor sweep, *Ronin 47* using the information it receives to plot a route through the complex, locking onto the Shogun's energy signature as its objective.

Entering what you take to be a mech hangar, you expect to find yourself confronted by a guard patrol, or at least some form of defensive measures set up by Kira's retinue. But it would appear that everyone and everything that might have stood against you was in the force that attacked you outside the fortress walls.

And then you enter an even bigger, vaulted space, filled with noise, and you realise you have found the fully automated factory that lies at the heart of the pagoda complex. It is already fully operational, and *Ronin 47* calculates that there are twelve of the titanic Shogun-class war-machines at various stages of completion.

Passing through another set of gates, you find yourself on the lower slope of the dormant volcanic crater. Before you, a colossal gantry rises from reinforced concrete footings and berthed beside it, looking like some robotic warrior god, is the prototype Shogun-class mech the traitor stole from Ako Base, dooming the whole of Tokugawa Island so that he could make off with it, for his own egocentric purposes.

The Shogun suddenly shakes itself and takes a step forward, leaving the security of its gantry-berth. But then the image of the gigantic, black war-machine on the screen in front of you flickers and is distorted by a wash of static interference. As you watch in horror, the image becomes pixelated, random lines of code scrolling across it, or flicking from left to right, in a confusion of kanji characters. What is going on? It is as if *Ronin 47*'s machine soul is under attack.

If you have the code word *Protected* recorded on your Adventure Sheet, turn to **32**. If not, turn to **54**.

19

Both Ninja-mechs are now lying stricken in the shallows of the sunken reef. One of them has been utterly obliterated by your attack, but the other still has its cockpit intact, even if it is missing both its arms. Chances are the pilot is still alive inside.

Assuming your mech's proximity alarms are fully functional, the Ninjas must have employed some kind of cloaking technology in order to remain hidden from *Ronin 47*'s sensors. But who would send two cloaked mechs to ambush you and take you down? Surely there can only be one answer: former Deputy Director Kira.

If you want to pull the pilot from the mech, so that you can interrogate the villain, turn to **511**. If you would rather not waste your time and be on your way, seeing as how you are sure you already know the answer to your question, turn to **436**.

20

You realise that the spiny protuberances covering the submersible are not just intended to discourage larger, submarine kaiju from attempting to eat the craft, there are also torpedo launchers!

TOMOKAZUKI-SUB				
SPEED	ARMOUR	MELEE	ARTILLERY	INTEGRITY
5	4	1	4	20

If you win, turn to **45**.

Hatches open on the Samurai's back and a cluster of Drones takes to the air. (Cross off one use of the Drones from your Adventure Sheet.)

Rapidly gaining height, the Drones spread out and assume a hexagonal formation, relaying what their optic arrays can 'see' to the visor-screen in front of you in the cockpit.

The image that your Samurai's battle computer pieces together for you gives you a top-down view of the drop zone Phoenix Squad has deployed into. But, other than for the mechs and the ring of coral reefs, all you can see is square nautical kilometre after square nautical kilometre of sea, and nothing else.

Their energy reserves depleted, the Drones return to their roost within the Samurai. Turn to **3**.

Ronin 47's AI is still shaking off the malign influence of whatever jamming signal the control room was broadcasting to keep its artillery weapons offline. As a result, it doesn't manage to achieve target-lock before launching the Hunter-Killer.

The missile streaks from the mech's shoulder and across the chamber, passing straight between the two Wrecker mechs that are approaching you, and detonates against the back wall of the echoing iron chamber. (Strike the Hunter-Killer Missile from your Adventure Sheet.)

As the smoke starts to clear, you see that the missile has blasted a hole into what appears to be a mech weapon storage vault.

If you want to run towards the vault, in the hope of recovering a weapon you can use against the Wrecker robots, turn to **239**. If you would prefer to simply fight the mechs using those weapons the Samurai-class mech is already equipped with, turn to **43**.

Eventually you pass beyond the treeline and find yourself scaling the steeper snowy slopes, as *Ronin 47* makes for the coordinates you programmed into its nav-systems.

The HUD suddenly starts to light up with all manner of potential hostiles, as *Ronin 47*'s Combat AI constantly revises its ongoing threat assessment.

And then you spot something that the mech's sensors appear to have missed: two angular mounds under the snow that speak of something man-made to you, hidden under the form-deadening white blanket.

You bring *Ronin 47* to a complete stop and consider what could be lurking under the snow. Could it be a hidden gun emplacement, or might it be something more akin to your own walking war-machine.

A persistent gust of wind blows across the mountainside, causing the snow to shift from where it has settled over the angular shapes and, in that moment, you glimpse matte-black metal and the glowing red eye-sensor of a mech. There must be two of them hiding here, ready to ambush anyone entering their territory.

But it is at that moment that your Cloaking Device fails and in a flurry of activity – their pilots suddenly realising *Ronin 47* has entered their killzone – two lithe, matte-black mechs burst from their hiding place under the snow, armed with ten-metre-long Electro-Katanas.

(Strike the Cloaking Device from your Adventure Sheet; you will not be able to use it again.)

What do you want to do? Will you:

Launch a Hunter-Killer Missile at one of the mounds (if you can)?	Turn to **293**.
Trigger an EMP Device (if you have one)?	Turn to **232**.
Engage the enemy?	Turn to **309**.

While you are making your selection, Mototoki activates the Vault's automated assembly line. A huge blast door slides up at the far end of the chamber and *Ronin 47* enters the armoury, suspended from a colossal winch assembly. Reaching the middle of the armoury, the mech is lowered, and a series of robotic arms emerge from holes that open in the floor, which then prepare to secure your selection to the Samurai war-machine.

"So, what's it to be?" Mototoki asks.

Choose one of the seven upgrades and record it in the relevant space on your Adventure Sheet, noting down any special rules or bonuses it confers.

When you are done, if you have the code word *Wrecked* recorded on your Adventure Sheet, turn to **575**. If not, turn to **528**.

You dread to think what could have spun the colossal webs that cover the buildings here. They certainly don't look like they are intended to catch flies!

Record the code word *Bugged* on your Adventure Sheet and then turn to **582**.

The Hunter-Killer is as effective underwater as it is above. It streaks from its shoulder launcher and hits the giant fish before exploding, a cloud of inky blood pluming in the freezing water of the abyssal trench.

Strike the Hunter-Killer Missile from your Adventure Sheet and turn to **63**.

You come at last to an atoll and what is clearly the aftermath of an epic battle. You identify the remains of three different war-machines – two Ninja-class mechs and a Daimyo war-suit. The Ninjas are painted a matte black, while the Daimyo mech – which is slightly larger than a Samurai but still significantly shorter than the prototype Shogun – is painted a bright orange with a yellow lightning bolt. You recognise the colours as those of Honjo Base, another isolated colony, independent from Ako Base, but one that is allied to it.

Ronin 47 is not reading any human life-signs on board any of the mechs and none of them are pilotable anymore. However, while the mechs might no longer be operational, that doesn't necessarily mean that their weapons systems or other tech won't still be in working order.

If you want to see what you can salvage from the mechs, turn to **80**. If you would rather leave the atoll without further delay, turn to **2**.

28

You activate the Yurei Corporation-made 'ghostware' Cloaking Device, not knowing how long it will remain operational before either its circuits burn out or the reactor core itself suffers burnout.

As *Ronin 47* strides slowly through the sea, negotiating a path between the drifting bombs, they ignore it. The Cloaking Device is working! As long as the mech doesn't accidentally come into contact with one of the mines, you should be able to make it all the way to Tokyo Bay unharmed. But it's going to take a steady hand on the controls to ensure that that nothing untoward happens.

Take an Agility test and a Speed test. If you pass both tests, turn to **238**. If you fail either test, turn to **278**.

29

Just as you start to pull away, the monster that has been circling the wreck while you were exploring its flooded interior makes its move. But you are ready for it.

As the Isonade powers towards you, you catch sight of the savage injuries you have already dealt it and know you can finish the kaiju.

If you have some Depth Charges, and want to deploy them now, turn to **97**. If your mech is equipped with Flares and you want to launch those instead, turn to **164**. If you are unable to use either of these deterrents, or do not want to, turn to **77**.

30

You assume a fighting stance, as you prepare to defend yourself against the monstrous Kaijin. You suspect that no matter how tough its leathery hide is, it will be no match for the sharpness of your katana's blade. (In this battle, you have the initiative.)

KAIJIN   COMBAT 9   ENDURANCE 10

If you slay the hideous hybrid, knowing that you cannot let anything delay you further in your search for the traitor, you hurry through the door on the other side of the lab – turn to **230**.

31

"Then let us split up," Kanesada suggests. "We have a better chance of tracking them down that way." And so that is what you do.

Make a note that your starting grid square is A1 and turn to **420**.

32

Kira is attacking your mech's very operating system, hoping he can take it out before even engaging you in battle. The traitor knows *The Art of War* as well as you do: *"The supreme art of war is to subdue the enemy without fighting."*

But *Ronin 47*'s computer brain is defended by Nozomi's 'Worm-Killer' software, which immediately starts to fight back against the invasive malware Kira is trying to use to take control of your machine, using the robot's repaired uplink against you.

If you have the code word *Triggered* recorded on your Adventure Sheet, turn to **224**. If not, turn to **588**.

As you sneak into the room, you step on a piece of broken glass, which cracks as you put your weight on it. The traitors turn, but you are on your feet in seconds and spring at them. You manage to dispatch two of them before they can even bring their weapons to bear. That leaves just two more, but they are ready for you now. (In this battle, your opponents have the initiative.)

	COMBAT	ENDURANCE
First TRAITOR AGENT	8	8
Second TRAITOR AGENT	8	7

If you win the fight, turn to **13**.

34

The missile hits the Oni to your left, detonating the instant it impacts against the hull of the heavy ordnance mech. (Strike the Hunter-Killer Missile from your Adventure Sheet.)

When the smoke clears, you see that the Hunter-Killer has done some serious damage, blowing a great hole in the robot's torso and taking out one of its rocket-battery arms altogether.

Now all that remains is for you to put the demon-engine out of its misery. (You must fight the two Oni-mechs at the same time.)

First ONI-MECH				
SPEED	ARMOUR	MELEE	ARTILLERY	INTEGRITY
2	3	2	2	15

Second ONI-MECH				
SPEED	ARMOUR	MELEE	ARTILLERY	INTEGRITY
2	3	2	4	25

If you win the battle with the heavy artillery mechs, turn to **290**.

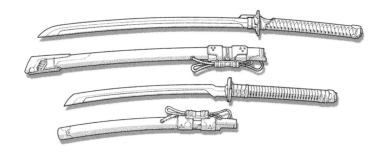

35

"We should do this again some time, wanderer," the Russian says with a chuckle. "Never let it be said that Ivan doesn't play fair."

(Deduct the Rations you put up as a bet from your total.)

Record the code word *Trusted* on your Adventure Sheet and then turn to **387**.

36

There is simply not enough time to shoot down every single missile.

Roll one die and add 3; deduct this many *Integrity* points from your mech. (Alternatively, pick a card and deduct its face value from your mech's *Integrity* score, unless it is a 10 or a picture card, in which case deduct 9 points from the Samurai's *Integrity* score; if it is less than 4 you must deduct 4 *Integrity* points.)

If *Ronin 47* has lost 7-9 *Integrity* points, you must also deduct 1 point from its *Armour* score.

If you are still alive and *Ronin 47* is still standing, turn to **95**.

37

If *Ronin 47* is fitted with Enhanced Scanners, turn to **143**. If not, turn to **64**.

38

Bringing your katana to bear, you leap at the droids, your blade singing as it slices through the air. (You must fight the Security Drones at the same time, but you have the initiative in this battle.)

	COMBAT	ENDURANCE
First SECURITY DRONE	8	8
Second SECURITY DRONE	8	7

If you manage to destroy the robotic guards, turn to **10**.

39

The instant you touch the door's controls, it slides open with a soft pneumatic hiss and you enter what is quite clearly a laboratory of some kind. A layer of cryogenic mist is drifting across the floor from a disconnected rubber hose.

Against one wall stands a number of large cylindrical tanks. Each one is three metres tall and filled with a sludgy, yellow-green liquid. However, there is a gap where one is missing, and the hose appears to have previously been connected to this missing cylinder.

As you make your way along the line of intact tanks, you realise that there are things floating in the sickly soup that fills each one. You make out the odd flipper, tentacle and even an arm, but you have no idea what the creatures could be. You do not even know if they are alive or dead.

Nearby stands a stainless steel dissection table. Pinned out on a board, with its chest cavity open, is a hideous monstrosity that appears to be half monkey and half fish. Lying on the table next to the specimen is a curious device that looks like a cross between a blaster and a loud hailer.

If you want to take a closer look at the strange device, turn to **83**. If you would rather leave the lab without touching anything, turn to **149**.

As the robotic arms set about making the necessary upgrades to *Ronin 47*, the Spider is placed into a recharging bay to restore its battery core to full power.

By the time the alterations to your mech are complete, and you are ready to leave, the Spider will have enough charge to carry out 6 sets of repairs. Each time it repairs the mech, roll one die and multiply the result by 5; this is the number of *Integrity* points restored to the mech by the repair droid's work. (Alternatively, pick a card and if it is a 7 or higher, it counts as a 6; then multiply the result by 5 and restore this many *Integrity* points.)

Each time the Spider repairs the mech, you may increase *one* of the war-machine's following stats – *Armour*, *Speed*, *Melee*, or *Artillery* – by 1 point. The Spider droid can even make repairs in the midst of battle!

Turn to **575**.

At your command, the Samurai of Phoenix Squad take up positions around the island-reefs, their weapons trained on the shadowy blue depths of the submarine sinkhole. Turn to **3**.

As cataclysmic tremors continue to rock Ako Base, you push past the tide of administrative staff and base personnel, who all appear to be heading in the opposite direction from you. But at last, you make it to the large, octagonal control room at the heart of the facility, only to be met by a terrible sight.

The place is in a state of ruin. Many of the great screens that surround the room are either cracked and broken, or the dull black of 'No Signal Received.'

Those that are working, and aren't broadcasting snowy static, provide you with your first glimpse of the kaiju attacking the base. There must be at least two dozen and they are not all of one type. You can see lumbering Kappas and crustacean-like Kani-Oni, as well as Oni-Hitode and giant fish-jawed Shachihoko.

You turn your horrified gaze slowly from the screens to the workstations that would normally be occupied by staff monitoring the progress of Samurai squads out in the field, as well as scrutinising the data being relayed from the Tengu Satellite Array in geostationary orbit over the Philippine Sea.

The only personnel left inside Operations HQ are either dying, or already dead. You find Director Asano lying at the foot of a computer console. The older man's face is almost as white as his hair, while his uniform is dark with blood oozing from a fatal wound he has sustained to his stomach.

You hurry over to the Director and kneel beside him, cradling his head. His eyes flick open – there is still life in him yet – and he opens his mouth to speak. But in the very next moment his words are drowned out by a deafening roar as a great rift appears in the ceiling of the domed chamber, a kaiju's claw tearing through the structure as if it were made from paper.

Daylight suddenly floods the chamber. Through the hole in the roof, you can see the brilliant azure sky and, silhouetted against it, the titanic form of a monster that appears to have both piscine and simian heritage – a kaiju classified as Anko-Oni, or 'Devil Fish.'

The monster gives voice to a roar that reverberates around the command centre – causing more debris to shake loose and come crashing to the ground – as a swarm of late-launched combat drones engage the kaiju. As the Anko-Oni bats at its attackers with huge, taloned forelimbs, it stumbles into the side of the building,

dislodging a number of parasites that were previously lurking in its gills, which then drop into the Operations room.

Many species of fish play host to parasitic isopods – creatures related to the humble woodlouse. Usually, these aquatic crustaceans grow to no more than six millimetres in length. But those that make their home within the mouth cavities of the Anko-Oni have feasted on their mutated host's blood, which has caused them to undergo their own K-Compound growth spurt, and they are now classified as their own species: Gusoku.

The isopods that have been deposited in the control room are each as long as a human being is tall. Three of them have landed in front of you, and they are hungry.

Unsheathing your katana in one fluid action, you prepare to dispatch the mutated isopods as quickly as possible.

You must fight the three Gusoku at the same time, but at least you have the initiative in this battle.

	COMBAT	ENDURANCE
First GUSOKU	6	6
Second GUSOKU	7	5
Third GUSOKU	5	6

If you manage to kill all the overgrown parasites, turn to **62**.

43

The Wreckers aren't interested in capturing you this time. This is going to be a fight to the death! (You must fight the Wrecker-mechs simultaneously.)

	First WRECKER-MECH			
SPEED	ARMOUR	MELEE	ARTILLERY	INTEGRITY
2	4	4	2	20

Second WRECKER-MECH				
SPEED	ARMOUR	MELEE	ARTILLERY	INTEGRITY
2	4	3	2	25

If you defeat your two opponents, turn to **319**.

44

Suddenly, a feline Bakeneko launches itself out of the toxic cloud straight at you. The only measurable effect the compounds have had on the kaiju is to make them more aggressive.

Before you can do anything to defend yourself, a red-haired, ape-like Shojo leaps from the edge of the crater onto *Ronin 47's* back, knocking the colossal mech to the ground. You are soon overwhelmed by the sheer number of monsters that Kira's kaiju-call has drawn to the top of Mount Fuji.

You are oblivious to the traitor's fate as the kaiju swarm over *Ronin 47*, crushing the mech under their combined weight, and soon you are oblivious to all as it is crushed like a tin can inside a trash compactor.

Your adventure, like your life, is over.

THE END

45

Your attack triggers a series of explosions that ripple through the vessel, the chain reaction destroying not only the sub but the airlock it was attached to as well.

As the wreckage of the submersible disappears deeper into the abyss, seawater rushes in through the airlock even as the cliff-face itself starts to collapse. Whatever secrets Yokai Base might have held are lost to you now.

You have no choice but to return to the surface and set a course for Tokyo – turn to **231**.

46

Two matte-black mechs suddenly burst from the sea on either side of you, while *Ronin 47*'s proximity alarms remain stubbornly silent. Could they have developed a fault?

Each of the new arrivals is slightly shorter than *Ronin 47*, and less well-armoured to boot, but they are also markedly more agile.

Take a Speed test. If you pass the test, turn to **88**. However, it you fail the test, turn to **66**.

47

You guess that whoever is firing on you only has an approximate idea of where you are, as the rocket barrage misses you and strikes a skyscraper on the other side of the street, demolishing the top twelve floors.

How will you respond?

Deploy a flight of Drones, if you can?	Turn to **92**.
Engage a Cloaking Device, if you have one?	Turn to **121**.
Perform a long-range sensor sweep, if *Ronin 47* has Enhanced Scanners?	Turn to **9**.
Keep moving, in the hope that whoever is targeting you will lose your position?	Turn to **582**.

48

Protected from the effects of the mech-killing weapon, under your guidance, *Ronin 47* sets off across the now disarmed minefield, heading for Tokyo Bay. Turn to **288**.

49

The black-robed figures are too busy indulging their destructive urges to notice your arrival. They don't even know your mech is standing right outside, since they've already destroyed the facility's scanner displays and data readout screens.

The first one dies with your sword in his back; the second, a moment later when you slice open his throat with one deft sweep of your katana. Hearing the gargling cry he makes as he falls, the other two stop firing and turn to face you. But it's already too late for the one on the right, as the tip of your blade plunges into his stomach. That leaves just one. (In this battle, you have the initiative.)

TRAITOR AGENT   COMBAT 8   ENDURANCE 8

If you kill the last of Kira's lackeys, turn to **13**.

50

Taking the metal cylinder from where it is stored in the mech's chest cavity, you hurl it at the crabs and watch with bated breath as the device lands on the rocks with an anti-climactic clang.

There is an audible click, and a thick gas starts to escape the container, through vented openings that have appeared in each end. Hugging the ground, the gas soon swallows the crab-kaiju in a toxic green cloud.

You watch through the cockpit screen, wondering if you chose the correct combination of compounds to ensure that the bomb is effective against the Kani-Oni.

Add the number you have associated with the DNA Bomb to this section and then turn to that new section to see what effect the gas has on the crustaceans.

If you do not have a number associated with the DNA Bomb, turn to **493**.

51

Eventually you pass beyond the treeline and find yourself scaling the steeper snowy slopes, as *Ronin 47* makes for the coordinates you programmed into its nav-systems.

The HUD starts to light up with all manner of potential hostiles, as *Ronin 47*'s Combat AI constantly revises its ongoing threat assessment. But it completely fails to detect the most serious and immediate threat.

Two lithe matte-black mechs suddenly burst from their hiding place under the thick blanket of snow, each armed with a pair of Electro-Wakizashi swords, and one of them manages to lay a blow against *Ronin 47* before you have time to react to their unexpected appearance.

(Deduct 6 *Integrity* points.)

If your mech is still capable of fighting back, that is what you are going to have to do now (turn to **309**), unless *Ronin 47* is equipped with an EMP Device, and you want to activate that instead (turn to **232**).

52

As you enter the last of the four numbers into the keypad, you hear the whirring of servos, and the door opens.

As you swim past the tanks of invertebrates and crustaceans, you feel a hundred eyes following your progress.

One large computer console attracts your attention. Judging by what is still displayed on the screen, it looks like the scientists here were analysing genetic material taken from creatures mutated by the K-Compound to see if there was a way they could reverse its effects, testing various new compounds on kaiju cells and assessing their effects. While the compounds themselves have doubtless dissipated into the ocean long ago, the geneticists' findings are still displayed on the screen.

Compound	Taxonomic Class Affected
Amabie	Arachnida
Byakko	Aves
Chochinbi	Crustacea
Datsue-ba	???

Having memorised this potentially valuable information (write it down on your Adventure Sheet if you need to), you exit the lab.

Checking your chronometer, you see that you have just ten minutes of oxygen remaining.

Turn to **550**.

"Bad luck, you lose!" Ivan declares, a broad, broken-toothed smile splitting his bearded face. "Pay up!"

If you want to give the Russian the Rations you wagered on the fight, turn to **35**. If not, turn to **17**.

Kira is attacking your mech's very operating system, hoping he can take it out before even engaging you in battle. The traitor knows *The Art of War* as well as you do: *"The supreme art of war is to subdue the enemy without fighting."*

If *Ronin 47* has an Enhanced Interface, turn to **118**. If not, turn to **98**.

As you are pulling away from the spot where the *Gojira* sank, something rockets up out of the pelagic abyss, taking you completely by surprise, its blunt nose smashing into your mech with savage force. (Deduct 5 *Integrity* points.)

The shark-kaiju is clearly not done with you yet. Conclude your battle with the Isonade, and if you manage to slay the beast, turn to **132**.

Rising Sun sets off through the devastation that was once the most technologically advanced city on the planet.

You pass overturned cars, toppled streetlamps, and broken bridges on your journey through the ruins until you enter an empty plaza. You can't help noticing that the structures around the square appear to be covered by long, thick strands of what looks like sticky cobwebs.

Rising Sun comes to a halt and kneels down in the street. A moment later, Kanesada exits the cockpit and climbs down to the ground, constantly eyeing the surrounding buildings as he does so.

Following his lead, you park *Ronin 47* and join Kanesada out in the open. You feel very exposed, outside of your mech, and your heartrate starts to quicken.

"This way," your companion says, setting off across the plaza.

It is then that you see the concrete bunker on the other side of the square. Once the two of you are in the shade of the bunker's entrance, Kanesada picks up a broken piece of pipe, and uses it to bang on the steel hatch that is set into the concrete at your feet three times.

You wait as the clanging echo dies away and then hear two knocks come from the other side of the hatch. Kanesada strikes the hatch another four times, and then you hear the creaking of a wheel-lock being turned. Slowly the hatch opens from underneath.

A face appears in the gap, and a voice hisses, "Quick, inside, if you're coming in!"

Kanesada leads the way once more and you follow, closing the hatch behind you. You climb ten metres down a circular shaft set with iron rungs to a dimly-lit passageway and pass through another steel door into somebody's cramped living quarters. It is crammed with pre-K-Day tech and clearly has its own independent power supply, since various computer screens are aglow with views of the plaza and the surrounding city blocks.

Your host is a young woman with bright pink hair. You also can't help but notice that the irises of her eyes are different colours.

"Oishi-san, let me introduce you to Nozomi," Kanesada says, bowing his head respectfully. "Nozomi, this is Oishi-san."

The girl bows too and then says, "Kane, what are you doing here?"

"I owe Oishi-san my freedom," Kanesada says, and then proceeds to tell the girl about what happened on board the Wreckers' supertanker as well as filling her in regarding the incident at Tokugawa Island.

When he is done, it is Nozomi's turn to speak.

"You say this Kira took out the island's security systems and all the other mechs using a virus?" You nod in confirmation. "It sounds like an assassin virus, in which case, if you are planning on going up against him, you are going to need to protect your mech to make sure it doesn't suffer the same fate as that of your former companions."

"Can you help?" says Kanesada.

"Of course, I can," Nozomi replies, "but it's going to cost you. I don't give away my genius for free, you know."

"What is it going to cost me?" you ask.

"The only currency that's worth anything in this post-K-Day world," she says. "Rations and Medi-Packs. Two, to be precise."

If you have 2 lots of Rations or 2 Medi-Packs, or at least one of each, and are prepared to give them to the girl in exchange for her help, turn to **78**. If not, turn to **109**.

57

One of the hovering maintenance droids homes in on the shoulder of the mech and starts to remove the protective cover housing the uplink unit with its manipulator-digits.

Record the code word *Connected* on your Adventure Sheet and then turn to **575**.

58

And then the question of what made the webs is answered when something truly terrifying clambers over the ruins of a skyscraper in front of you.

You know it is impossible for a spider to grow this large, but this is of course not actually an arachnid, but an eight-legged kaiju that just happens to look like a gigantic spider. But that doesn't make the encounter any less terrifying, particularly since the monstrous arachnoid kaiju is now picking its way over the ruined tenements towards you, either seeing *Ronin 47* as a potential threat or a potential meal.

Ronin 47's database classifies it as a Tsuchigumo, but how do you want to tackle the brute? Will you:

Launch a Hunter-Killer Missile, if you can?	Turn to **142**.
Detonate a DNA Bomb, if you have one?	Turn to **6**.
Fire up *Ronin 47*'s weapons and attack the kaiju?	Turn to **205**.

59

The droids start to glide towards you as their weapons go hot. You have no choice but to defend yourself, as best you can, with your katana. (The Security Drones have the initiative in this battle, and you must fight them at the same time.)

	COMBAT	ENDURANCE
First SECURITY DRONE	8	8
Second SECURITY DRONE	8	7

If you manage to destroy the droids, turn to **10**.

60

Ronin 47 rises from the sea on a column of coruscating flame. You see the view beneath you projected on the HUD, the visible landmasses transforming into the recognisable pattern of the islands of Japan, as if seen in a satellite photograph.

The Booster Rocket carries you over the Sagami-nada Sea and, as its fuel supply rapidly runs out, you land among the shattered skyscrapers and devastated ruins of Tokyo.

Cross the Booster Rocket off your Adventure Sheet and turn to **370**.

61

Knowing that a cold death awaits you at the bottom of the ocean if you don't get yourself out of this dire situation soon, thanks to your piloting skills, the mech finally manages to break free of the kaiju's clutches. But you are not out of danger yet. Turn to **376**.

62

The giant isopods are dead!

Flicking your blade clean of the horrors' blood before sheathing it in one fluid motion, you take in the scene before you. It quickly becomes apparent that the people who have died here were not killed by the destruction wrought on the base by the attacking kaiju; their corpses bear evidence of gunshot wounds and lethal blade strikes.

"Who did this?" you ask. Director Asano has been like a father to you since the rise of the kaiju and the fall of humankind.

"It was Kira and his traitors!" he splutters, blood bubbling from his lips.

"Deputy Director Kira?" you gasp. You cannot believe what you are hearing. Kira Yoshinaka is a legend among the Samurai squads, for he was one of the first to pilot a war-machine mech in battle against the kaiju and the record of his victories over the beasts is legendary in and of itself.

"Yes, it was Kira. He has betrayed us all! He intends to steal the Shogun and is making his way to the main hangar even now. Hurry, you must stop him… Avenge our deaths."

"I will!" you declare. "I swear it! Kira's life is now forfeit, as a result of what he has done here this day."

But Director Asano does not reply. He is with the ancestors now.

"Rest easy, my master," you say, closing his eyelids with your fingertips, "you will be avenged."

There's not a moment to lose if you are going to stop Kira stealing the Shogun prototype. Not only that, but from the terrible groaning and creaking sounds besetting the command centre, you get the very strong impression that the roof might come crashing down at any moment.

However, if you could access Ako Base's computer systems, via one of the terminals in this room, you might also be able to learn more about what Kira has done and what he intends.

Do you want to head straight for the Shogun hangar (turn to **402**), or do you want to try to access the base's computer systems first (turn to **85**)?

63

The monstrous Shachihoko turns tail and, as quickly as it first appeared, darts away again into the darkness, heading towards the bottom of the trench. Turn to **305**.

Using the craggy rocks to aid the mech's exit from the ocean, you climb to the central ridge of the island before putting *Ronin 47* into standby mode.

Now would be a good time to see to your own wellbeing, eating some rations or tending to any wounds with a Medi-Pack (if you have some left).

If you have an operational Spider repair droid on board, turn to **93**. If not, turn to **116**.

You charge at the Russian robot, the mech's melee weapon in hand. But as you do so, the hulking war-machine hunkers down, ramming its knuckles against the oily floor to give it purchase.

You make an almighty leap and, as your robot lands on the Russian robot's back, the mighty *Volos* pushes upwards, sending *Ronin 47* flying into the air.

Your outstretched weapon connects with the squat metal box of the control room, tearing it in two. A series of electrical explosions ripples through the suspended chamber and gasps of disbelief rise from gamblers, Wreckers, and prisoners alike.

You come to ground again on the other side of the gladiatorial arena, a great clang reverberating around the chamber as *Ronin 47* lands in a crouch.

At the same time, static washes through the HUD and then the lights within the cockpit rise to full brightness, while markers on the screen indicate that the mech's artillery weapons are back online.

It is not only *Ronin 47*'s ordnance weapons that are active again. With a whoosh of rockets, *Volos* launches a barrage of missiles at the gallery where the gamblers were whooping and jeering only moments ago.

The gallery vanishes in a series of explosions that send blackened bodies flying in all directions. As the echo of the devastating fusillade fades, the sound of the explosions is replaced by the screams of the dying and the desperate, who are already attempting to flee.

You are about to turn your attention to freeing your fellow prisoners, when four Wrecker mechs charge into the arena, ready to take you both down.

How do you want to deal with the Wreckers?

Trigger an EMP Device (if you can)?	Turn to **280.**
Launch a Hunter-Killer Missile (if you can)?	Turn to **22.**
Engage the robots in battle?	Turn to **43.**

66

Where *Ronin 47* is armed with a single melee weapon, the Ninjas are each armed with a pair of Electro-Wakizashi swords – mech-swords similar in design and function to the standard Electro-Katana, but with a shorter blade and packing slightly less of a punch.

Both your ambushers make unopposed strikes against *Ronin 47*, which sends your war-machine reeling. (The Ninja-mechs both have a Melee score of 5 points, so determine damage from their two attacks and deduct the appropriate number of *Integrity* points.)

Pressing home their advantage, the Ninjas come for you again, as your weapons go hot.

Take a Melee test. If you pass the test, turn to **108**. However, it you fail the test, turn to **411**.

67

The EMP weapon is devastatingly effective, and *Ronin 47*'s systems and Combat AI are just as susceptible to its effects as Tokyo's defences. The mech is dead in the water.

Not only that but, with the power off, you are unable to open any hatches and the war-machine's life support systems will be offline too.

Ronin 47 has become your tomb. All that awaits you is a slow death by suffocation, or a swift one by means of seppuku and a katana to the belly. The choice is yours, but whatever you choose, your adventure is over.

THE END

68

The rocket barrage just misses your mech and impacts against the ruined façade of a building next to you. However, the explosion brings down the already weakened structure on top of *Ronin 47*.

Roll one die and add 3. Deduct this many *Integrity* points from your mech. (Alternatively, pick a card and deduct its face value from your mech's *Integrity* score, unless it is a 10 or a picture card, in which case deduct 9 points from the Samurai's *Integrity* score; if it is less than 4 you must deduct 4 *Integrity* points.)

If you are still alive and *Ronin 47* is still standing, how will you respond?

Deploy a flight of Drones, if you can?	Turn to **92**.
Engage a Cloaking Device, if you have one?	Turn to **121**.
Perform a long-range sensor sweep, if *Ronin 47* has Enhanced Scanners?	Turn to **9**.
Keep moving, in the hope that whoever is targeting you loses your position?	Turn to **582**.

Unfortunately, there is too much interference – either caused by the ruined buildings themselves or by whatever devices were detonated here during the Battle of Tokyo in the desperate weeks after K-Day – for *Ronin 47*'s sensors to detect anything with any confidence further than five blocks away.

Turn to **420** and resume your exploration of the city.

The Shogun pushes *Ronin 47* right to the edge of the widening crack.

There is a horrendous tearing of metal, that you can hear from your place inside the cockpit, and then, through the HUD, you see the other mech take a step back. It is holding something in its right hand: a silver metal box trailing a tangle of sparking wires and sheared circuits. Kira has ripped out the Samurai's control systems.

The haptic controls refusing to respond to your instructions, and with the mech's flight systems offline too, there is nothing you can do as *Ronin 47* teeters at the edge of the fissure before toppling over the edge and into the seething lava below.

Your adventure is over, as is your life.

THE END

You succeed in taking out all of the missiles before any of them can make contact with *Ronin 47*.

Turn to **172**.

Tightening your grip on your katana and keeping low, you creep into the devastated control room.

Take an Agility test. If you pass the test, turn to **49**. If you fail the test, turn to **33**.

"While the automated assembly line does its thing, I can programme the droids to make some minor repairs, or I can recharge the mech's maintenance Spider, if you like."

If *Ronin 47*'s uplink unit is still damaged, and you want to have it repaired, turn to **57**. If you want Mototoki to recharge *Ronin 47*'s Spider maintenance droid, turn to **40**.

"Congratulations," says Ivan begrudgingly, a pair of sycophantic cronies behind him looking like they're squaring up for a fight. The big Russian tosses you some Rations. "Enjoy your winnings. Never let it be said that Ivan 'The Bear' Bukovski isn't a gracious loser."

(Increase the total number of Rations you have by the number you bet on the mech-fight.)

Record the code word *Trusted* on your Adventure Sheet and then turn to **387**.

The last Ninja falls, throwing up a great cloud of snow that obscures your view as surely as a wash of snowy static would, as it passes across the cockpit screen.

And then, as the powder settles again, you catch sight of your objective for the first time, close to the peak of Mount Fuji. It looks like an outcropping of black rock, but then you are able to make out the stacked, sloping, butto-style roofs and you realise then that the vast structure is man-made. Facing you is a wall a hundred metres tall. But before you can even attempt to breach the walls of the fortress, you are going to have to deal with the red-hulled Oni-mechs that are trudging towards you across the snowfield, their artillery weapons primed.

If you have the code word *Allied* recorded on your Adventure Sheet, turn to **154**. If not, turn to **438**.

Suddenly, a Kappa launches itself out of the toxic cloud straight at you. The only demonstrable effect the combination of compounds you used in the bomb has had on the kaiju is to make them more aggressive.

Despite your desperate situation, you have no choice but to defend yourself against the Kappa, as a gigantic, snake-like Uwabami attempts to wrap the Shogun in its constricting coils.

KAPPA				
SPEED	ARMOUR	MELEE	ARTILLERY	INTEGRITY
2	4	3	2	25

If you win, turn to **321**.

Conclude your battle with the Isonade, and if you manage to slay the beast, turn to **132**.

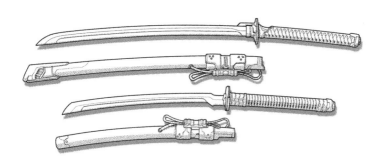

You hand over the payment. (Cross off the appropriate number of Rations and/or Medi-Packs.)

Nozomi immediately gets to work, sitting down in front of one of her numerous computer terminals, her fingers flying over the keyboard as lines of code appear on the screen in front of her.

While she works, you and Kanesada make yourselves comfortable and wait, but the enforced rest does you good. (Restore up to 2 *Endurance* points.)

"Done!" Nozomi suddenly exclaims, spinning round in her chair. Jumping to her feet, she takes a flash drive from a port in her computer and scrawls 'Worm-Killer' on it in permanent marker pen, before handing it to you.

As soon as you are back on board your mech, you will be able to download Nozomi's anti-virus software into *Ronin 47*'s tactical computer.

Record the code word *Protected* on your Adventure Sheet and then turn to **432**.

79

The second drone drops to the steel floor with a clang, joining its broken fellow and emitting a final burst of sparks from a shattered scanner lens.

A voice, distorted by electronic static, suddenly addresses you from a speaker grille set into the ceiling: "State your name and purpose!"

"I am Commander Oishi of Ako Base," you reply, "and I need your help."

"Who sent you?" the voice asks.

How will you respond?

"Director Asano sent me."   Turn to **188**.

"Deputy Director Kira sent me."   Turn to **10**.

Alternatively, you could exit the corridor the same way you entered and return to *Ronin 47* (turn to **84**).

It appears that the three mechs died fighting each other, with the damage they caused each other proving fatal, so that no one was going to be walking away from this fight.

Which of the machines do you want to strip first?

The Ninja-mechs?   Turn to **113**.

The Daimyo-mech?   Turn to **286**.

You know what you have to do now, and that's get out of here as fast as possible. It clearly isn't safe to remain on Tokugawa Island now that Ako Base has been compromised.

A tremor passes through the hangar, and then another. They bear all the hallmarks of seismic footfalls. Unable to help yourself, you bring your mech to a halt and turn to see something truly monstrous entering the hangar through the rift opened up by the crashing Kirin.

It is one of the kaiju that is in the process of attacking the facility. Twenty-five metres tall, it has an almost simian build and bipedal gait, while its hide is covered in tough scales, and it has a shell-like dome on its back. It is a Kappa, a deadly, amphibious kaiju species!

What do you want to do? Will you:

Turn and face the Kappa in battle?	Turn to **117**.
Flee from the colossus?	Turn to **137**.
Deploy Flares (if your mech is equipped with them)?	Turn to **157**.

Through a combination of cerebral impulses, and thanks to you taking hold of the mech's haptic controls, *Samurai 47* steps off the coral reef and drops into the blue void of the submarine sinkhole.

As the ocean waters close over the top of the machine and the sunlight rapidly fades above you, you rely on the HUD more than ever to alert you to what is below.

Then you see them, as a proximity alarm starts to chime inside the cockpit; pallid shapes worming their way up from the depths, cnidarian limbs curling and uncurling as they search for prey. And they are heading straight for you.

Take a Speed test. If your mech passes the test, turn to **123**. However, if it fails the test, turn to **102**.

Picking up the device, you cannot resist pulling the trigger. Just at the edge of hearing, you make out a high-pitched whine. It doesn't have any effect on you, but the same cannot be said for the specimen pinned out on the dissecting board.

The creature, that you believed was dead, suddenly jerks into life. It opens its mouth – exposing sharp, fish-like teeth – and emits a mewling cry as it twists in agony, but it cannot free itself from the pins and clamps holding it in place. However, it also lashes out with one of its monkey paws, scratching your hand and causing you to release the trigger at once. (Lose 2 *Endurance* points.)

The horrible hybrid immediately becomes as still and lifeless as it was before.

(If you want to take the Sonic Emitter with you, record it on your Adventure Sheet.)

Not wanting to spend a moment longer in this macabre lab, you leave the same way you entered.

Turn to **149**.

You sprint for the door and slip through it sideways before it snaps shut.

It looks like your trip to the Vault has been a waste of valuable time. You certainly can't afford to spend any more of it here. As you are wondering how you are going to get out again, with a jolt, the floor starts to ascend. You quickly climb back into your waiting mech, and upon reaching the surface once more, exit the bunker. You make for the shore at once and re-enter the ocean.

Turn to **216**.

Entering your login details into one of the still-working terminals, you run a systems diagnostic test and pull up the base's status feed.

It quickly becomes clear that someone intentionally turned off the defence grid, shutting down the sensor nets and early warning alarm system. But who would do such a thing?

Not only that but you can see that the base is actually broadcasting a subsonic pulse, with a range of over a hundred kilometres. Could this be what has brought so many kaiju to this one spot at this particular time?

(Make a note of this on your Adventure Sheet and that the pulse has a frequency of 5 Hertz.)

Suddenly the text and graphics on the terminal display jerk and stutter, and streams of nonsensical characters begin to cascade down the screen, destroying the data displayed beneath. Is this a result of the damage the computer systems have suffered due to the kaiju attack, or has someone uploaded a virus?

As you are staring at the screen in confusion, you hear the rending of metal above you as the bolts holding a lighting rig to the ceiling shear through and the whole metal framework starts to fall.

Take an Agility test. If you pass the test, turn to **105**. If you fail the test, turn to **135**.

86

"Listen to me, Ivan!" you shout over the comm. "Remember the ancient proverb: the enemy of my enemy is my friend!"

The Russian mech raises a heavy, pile-driver fist, but the expected punch doesn't come.

"I have another saying for you," Ivan's voice comes over the comm at last. "Without effort, you won't even pull a fish out of a pond. So, let's catch ourselves a fish!"

Turn to **65**.

87

As you trigger the weapon, a pulse of electromagnetic energy ripples out across the Sagami-nada Sea, with *Ronin 47* at its epicentre. One by one the blinking lights on the bobbing mines go dark, as their internal circuitry is fried by the EMP weapon.

(Cross the EMP Device off your Adventure Sheet; you will not be able to use it again.)

If *Ronin 47* is fitted with EMP Shielding, turn to **48**. If not, turn to **67**.

88

Where *Ronin 47* is armed with a single melee weapon, the Ninjas are each armed with a pair of Electro-Wakizashi swords – mech-swords similar in design and function to the standard Electro-Katana, but with a shorter blade and packing slightly less of a punch.

As the Ninjas land in the shallows, they each attempt to strike you with their charged blades. While you manage to dodge one of them, the other manages to make contact.

The Ninja-mech has a *Melee* score of 5 points; determine damage from its attack and then turn to **108**.

89

Taking the emitter from a utility pouch, you point it at the creature and pull the trigger. Although you cannot see anything coming out of the device, you can see its effects. The Kaijin throws its hands to its head – it does not have any external ears – its body contorting in obvious pain.

The way onward, it would appear, lies through a door on the other side of the lab. Keeping the prototype sonic weapon trained on the Kaijin, you make for the door. The moment you are through, you sabotage the controls so that you won't become the victim of any nasty surprises later, if the monster decides to follow you.

Turn to **230**.

90

Assisted by Mototoki's drones, the assembly line continues to upgrade *Ronin 47,* but you are aware that it will take longer than if you had chosen fewer upgrades.

Record the code word *Delayed* on your Adventure Sheet and then turn to **73**.

91

Your blood boiling in anger, you can do nothing other than charge into the room, blade in hand, and cut down the nearest, black-robed figure before they even know what is happening.

That leaves three, but even though they also already have their guns in hand, you have the advantage. (Fight the Traitor Agents at the same time but note that you have the initiative in this battle.)

	COMBAT	ENDURANCE
First TRAITOR AGENT	8	8
Second TRAITOR AGENT	8	7
Third TRAITOR AGENT	7	7

If you win your righteous fight, turn to **13**.

92

The Drones deploy from their ports in *Ronin 47's* back, and quickly rise into the air.

As they spread out over the ruined city, in search of the source of the rocket assault, an aerial view of Tokyo forms on the HUD in front of you. But before they can pinpoint the attacker's position, a second fusillade of rockets takes them all out.

(Cross off one use of the Drones from your Adventure Sheet.)

As far as you tell, the rocket strike did not come from anywhere nearby. But clearly, it's not safe to stay where you are, so you get moving again.

Turn to **582.**

93

While you look after yourself, the Spider droid carries out maintenance on the overheating reactor core.

Deduct 1 point from your mech's *Reactor* score and turn to **116**.

You are not interested in placing bets on the outcome of a mech-battle, like some dishonourable gaijin! You are only interested in finding a way out of your prison and reclaiming your mech. After all, you have a mission to complete; the souls of all those who died during the Ako Incident are crying out for revenge.

However, the clamour of battle coming from the adjacent arena soon draws you back to the barred slot. You might not want to bet on the outcome, but you might learn something from watching the two combatants.

Despite *Suhosin's* balletic poise and grace, the heavier, more powerful *Devastator* soon gains the upper hand, although you notice that the servos in its right leg appear to be slow to respond. Nonetheless, the American machine soon pummels the Korean mech into submission. It is about to perform the *coup de grâce*, when the klaxon sounds, and the bout is halted. The *Devastator* punches the air with its clawed fists, as its pilot soaks up the adulation of the crowd, before finally turning and leaving the arena. A pair of Wrecker-mechs enter and together remove the shattered *Suhosin* from the fighting chamber.

Record the code word *Forewarned* on your Adventure Sheet and then turn to **387**.

Clearly your attacker is nearby, so how do you want to respond?

Deploy a flight of Drones, if you can?   Turn to **213**.

Engage a Cloaking Device, if you have one?   Turn to **121**.

Perform a long-range sensor sweep,
if *Ronin 47* has Enhanced Scanners?   Turn to **241**.

Keep moving, in the hope that your
attacker loses your position again?   Turn to **582**.

Now that you know where Kira and the stolen Shogun-mech have gone, you see no point in doing anything other than travelling to Tokyo as fast as you can.

If *Ronin 47* has been fitted with a Booster Rocket, turn to **119**. If not, turn to **140**.

You deploy the Depth Charges into the path of the monstrously mutated shark, and seconds later they detonate.

Cross off one use of the Depth Charges from your Adventure Sheet; roll 1 die and double the result, then deduct that many points from the Isonade's *Integrity score*, then turn to **77**.

You are utterly helpless as the invasive programme spreads rapidly throughout the AI's neural network, replicating itself over and over again, corrupting *Ronin 47*'s operating system in the process.

With your mech incapacitated by the insidious virus, you find yourself locked out of its controls entirely. There is absolutely nothing you can do to defend yourself as the Shogun powers up its weapons and cuts *Ronin 47* down where it stands.

Your adventure is over.

THE END

The levitating droids hover slowly towards you, looking like a pair of robotic jellyfish or octopi, as they scan you with sweeper beams of red laser light.

A voice, distorted by the speakers through which it is being broadcast, comes from both drones simultaneously: "State your name and purpose."

"I am Commander Oishi of Ako Base and I need your help," you explain.

"Who sent you?" the voice asks.

How will you reply?

"Director Asano sent me."	Turn to **188**.
"Deputy Director Kira sent me."	Turn to **59**.

Alternatively, you could attack the droids (turn to **38**).

100

The toxic cloud briefly smothers *Ronin 47* before it starts to dissipate on the wind. As it clears, you realise that the DNA Bomb hasn't had any effect on the vast majority of the kaiju.

Before you can do anything to defend yourself, a red-haired, ape-like Shojo leaps from the edge of the crater onto *Ronin 47*'s back, knocking the colossal mech to the ground. You are soon overwhelmed by the sheer number of monsters that Kira's kaiju-call has drawn to the top of Mount Fuji.

You are oblivious to the traitor's fate as the kaiju swarm over *Ronin 47*, crushing the mech under their combined weight. A split second later, the remnants of the gas-weapon are burned away as the mech's ruptured reactor core detonates with the force of a nuclear warhead.

Your adventure, like your life, is over.

THE END

101

When was the last time you ate? You are not even sure what time it is or how long has passed since the attack on Ako Base.

Deduct 1 *Endurance* point and turn to **420**.

102

In their natural environment, the kaiju are too quick for you. One of the monsters makes a lunge for you, grabbing *Samurai 47* with its writhing arms. All you can see on the HUD now are the millions of tubular feet that cover the underside of the starfish-limbs of the creature.

With your Samurai in its clutches, the kaiju turns and heads for the bottom of the ocean.

Even though the mechs' arms are pinned to the sides of its body-hull, straining at the controls, you try to break free of the monster's crushing clutches.

Take a Combat test. If you pass the test, turn to **153**; if you fail the test, turn to **184**.

103

Ignoring you, the Russian machine barrels into *Ronin 47* again.

Roll one die and add 3. Deduct this many *Integrity* points from your mech. (Alternatively, pick a card and deduct its face value from your mech's *Integrity* score, unless it is a 10 or a picture card, in which case deduct 9 points from the Samurai's *Integrity* score; if it is less than 4 you must deduct 4 *Integrity* points.)

If *Ronin 47* is still standing, continue your battle with the *Volos* mech.

After another 5 Combat Rounds, if you have not been defeated yet, or if you reduce *Volos*'s *Integrity* score to 15 points or fewer, turn to **86**.

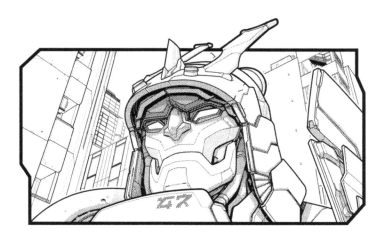

104

The first inkling you have that the device might have worked is when you hear the appalling shrieks and primeval screams coming from the stricken kaiju as the gas-weapon begins to break down their bodies at a cellular level. As the toxic cloud starts to dissipate, you catch glimpses of the odd writhing tentacle, snapping claw, and gaping maw as the monsters struggle to breathe.

Confident that the kaiju are no longer a threat, you turn your attention to the Shogun, as the towering mech steps away from the gantry tower to deal with you once and for all.

How do you want to respond?

Fire a salvo of Flares (if you can)?	Turn to **352**.
Launch a flight of Drones (if you can)?	Turn to **381**.
Target the Shogun with a Hunter-Killer Missile (if you have one)?	Turn to **408**.
Trigger an EMP Device (if you have one)?	Turn to **495**.
Engage your enemy in battle?	Turn to **446**.

105

You throw yourself out of the way of the plummeting rig just in time, but hit the concrete floor hard, badly bruising your shoulder.

(Deduct 2 *Endurance* points and 1 *Combat* point.)

Knowing that you have to get out of here as quickly as you can, you pick yourself up and head for the exit.

Turn to **402**.

106

As soon as you activate *Ronin 47*'s weapons, the sub's running lights flicker into life as its pilot prepares to fight back.

If *Ronin 47* is carrying a Hunter-Killer missile, and you want to use it now, turn to **161**. If not, turn to **20**.

Reducing the mech's drive systems to half power, you advance slowly towards the minefield, wondering if you can possibly chart a course between the lanes of open water that lie between the bobbing bombs.

If your mech is equipped with a Cloaking Device and you want to activate it now, turn to **28**.

If not, but *Ronin 47* is equipped with an EMP Device, and you want to use it now, turn to **87.**

If your mech is equipped with neither of these devices, turn to **548**.

108

You have no choice but to defend yourself against these Ninja-class mechs. (In this battle, go straight to the Close Combat phase.)

First NINJA-MECH

SPEED	ARMOUR	MELEE	ARTILLERY	INTEGRITY
5	2	5	2	20

Second NINJA-MECH

SPEED	ARMOUR	MELEE	ARTILLERY	INTEGRITY
5	2	5	2	18

If you manage to defeat both Ninjas, turn to **19**.

109

"Then we're done here!" Nozomi says, bluntly.

There's no point in threatening her. Not only would it be a dishonourable thing to do, but you suspect Kanesada would leap to her defence.

If you want to change your mind, and you are able to make the necessary 'payment', turn to **78**. If not, turn to **432**.

As you fight to maintain your balance, there is a horrendous tearing of metal, that you can hear from your place inside the cockpit, and the Shogun abruptly stumbles away from you, towards the widening fissure.

Through the HUD, you see an exposed section of the mech, where you have managed to rip something away. Raising *Ronin 47*'s left-hand, you see that the Samurai is holding a silver metal box trailing a tangle of sparking wires and sheared circuits. You have managed to wrench out the Shogun's flight system controls, ensuring that Kira won't be able to escape you again.

Deduct 1 point from the Shogun's *Speed* score and 5 points from its *Integrity* score, and then turn to **136**.

The tarantula-like defence droids eliminated, you continue your ascent of the central peak until you reach the highest point of the island and bring *Ronin 47* to a halt at the foot of the satellite dish.

You are perturbed to find that the defences appear to be down, and your presence here goes unchallenged as well.

However, it turns out you are not alone, when your mech's scanners detect human life-signs inside the facility. You hope it is the facility staff, but you would have thought there would be more than four of them working here.

But what you find upon reaching the summit has your guard up in an instant. Bodies litter the ground in front of the facility, and they are all wearing the uniforms of technical staff. There are also scorch-marks in the turf, as if a landing craft touched down here, while the walls of the building bear the marks of gunfire. The doors leading to the interior of the facility have been blown off their hinges.

Disembarking from *Ronin 47*, having set the Combat AI to overwatch mode, you approach the building, your katana and blaster already in your hands. Stealthily making your way inside, sounds of gunfire draw you to the main control room. Peering through a broken glass panel, you are horrified to see four figures, dressed entirely in black, firing upon the computer consoles and data-screens with their energy blasters. How are you supposed to access the Tengu Array now?

You can only assume that these blackguards are agents of the traitor Kira. Honour demands that you take vengeance on them for what they have done. But will you charge in with weapons in hand and a war-cry of retribution on your lips (turn to **91**), or will you sneak into the control room and try to take down as many of them as you can before they even realise they are in peril for their lives (turn to **72**)?

112

Slowly the blackness abates, and you wake up.

The first thing you become aware of is the fact that you have been separated from your mech. The second thing you notice is... the noise, the low lighting, the smell...

You have a throbbing headache and, as you sit up, a wave of nausea passes through you. Swallowing hard to suppress the desire to vomit, you slowly take in your surroundings.

You appear to be in a large cell, and you are not alone. In fact, you haven't seen so many people together in one place since Ako Base fell. There are men and women here, the representatives of many different races. Most are wearing hard-wearing combat fatigues of some kind or other, and all of them look like they have had their spirit beaten out of them.

The walls of the chamber are rust-red and appear to be constructed from steel. Set into the back wall is a heavily reinforced security door, which is closed, while running the entire length of the wall in front of you is an open slit, set with thick bars.

You and the others present are all quite clearly prisoners. You pat down your bodyglove and check your utility pouches. Your heart sinks still further when you realise you are also without your katana or your blaster.

Curiosity getting the better of you, rising to your feet you stagger over to the slit in the wall. Grasping the bars to support yourself, you peer through into the space beyond.

It appears to be a cavernous vault, its walls streaked with rust and oily effluent. The floor and steel plate walls are pitted and gouged as if they have been subjected to attacks by massive metal warriors.

A blaring klaxon sounds, and powerful arc-lights come on, illuminating the vast chamber. Your fellow prisoners start to join you at the slit, some of them cheering, others giving voice to insults.

It is then that you realise there are others watching the battle and jeering from another caged block to your left. But these people are not prisoners; they have come here to bet on the outcome of the mech fight. They are the ne'er-do-wells – wreckers, scavengers, and pirates – who have proliferated across the seas since the fall of civilisation.

And then, with a heavy grinding of gears, a huge set of doors on the opposite side of the vault are winched open and you watch in amazement as a colossal robot strides into the chamber. It is a shining steel giant and, even though its hull is marked by all manner of battle damage, you can still make out a red, white and blue pattern of stars and stripes on its torso. Along with the flag of the United States of America, a name has been stencilled across its chestplate in English letter-forms: *Devastator*. You cannot help but notice the rocket launcher mounted on one shoulder and the pulse cannon on the other.

The cheers and hollering increase in volume as the *Devastator* strikes a dramatic battle pose.

Moments later, a second giant robot joins the American mech in what you now realise is an arena. This second combatant is more slightly built and less broad across the shoulders. It also doesn't carry anything like as much heavy ordnance as the *Devastator*, but is armed with a long, thin mech-blade.

You recognise the characters painted in red on the robot's carapace as being Korean. They spell out the word *Suhosin*, meaning 'Guardian Spirit'.

As the Korean mech takes its place on the other side of the combat arena, opposite the American robot, it performs a balletic pirouette that ends with a flourish of its elongated sword. The cheers become deafening, and you realise several of your fellow prisoners are placing bets on the outcome of the battle.

"What do you say, wanderer?" says a broad-chested Caucasian in stilted English. He has a shaved head and bushy beard, and his thick Slavic vowels suggest that he is from Russia. "Do you want to make a wager on the outcome of the fight?"

"For what currency?" you ask. Your command of English is more assured, one of Director Asano's dictates having been that everyone who operated out of Ako Base should be fluent in more than one language.

"Rations! What else?" laughs the Russian.

If you have some Rations left and agree to place a wager on the outcome of the imminent mech-battle, turn to **393**. If you do not want to place a bet on the fight, or you do not have any Rations to use as currency, turn to **94**.

It quickly becomes apparent that the Ninjas' systems were fried by what you imagine was a massive burst of electromagnetic energy, such as might be released by a focused nuclear explosion – not that you've seen any evidence of one. This EM pulse has rendered all the mechs' weapons and other tech unusable, and so it is utterly worthless to you.

If an EMP took out the Ninjas, chances are the same thing shutdown the Daimyo's systems.

If you want to take a look at the Daimyo, to see if there is anything you can salvage from the dead titan, turn to **134**. If you would prefer not to waste your time, and want to leave the atoll instead, turn to **2**.

Several hours later, you reach the last recorded position of the *Gojira* that is stored in your mech's databanks, but there is no sign of the research vessel. There is nothing but empty sea as far as *Ronin 47* can scan.

But then a thought strikes you. Perhaps Kira had covert operatives working aboard the *Gojira* too, who might have triggered a similar kaiju beacon in order to put it out of action. Or maybe the ship simply fell foul of a kaiju attack that was nothing to do with Kira's betrayal. Either way, the ship could be at the bottom of the ocean.

If your mech is fitted with Enhanced Scanners, turn to **171**. If not, turn to **126**.

Crimson hazard lights fill the cockpit with their ruddy glow, and an alarm starts to sound as the Combat AI tracks the missile barrage that is incoming.

Activating the mech's heavy ordnance, you open fire, as the AI achieves firing solutions, in the hope that you can shoot down as many of the projectiles as possible before they hit you.

Take an Artillery test. If you pass the test, turn to **71**, but if you fail the test, turn to **133**.

Several hours later, which, you feel, is a sufficient amount of time to allow the reactor to cool down, with the sun beginning its descent towards the horizon, you power up the mech once more. The AI initiates a diagnostic check that reveals what you already suspected that the reactor is operating within acceptable parameters once more.

Ronin 47's gyroscopic stabilisers are abruptly put to the test when a tremor passes through the ground beneath its feet.

What was that? A seaquake?

Seconds later there comes another tremor, more powerful than the first, and you bring all the mech's systems online as you fear that it could lose its footing altogether.

And then, before you can do anything else, the world turns upside down and *Ronin 47* is thrown backwards into the sea as the crags rise from the waves.

Turn to **315**.

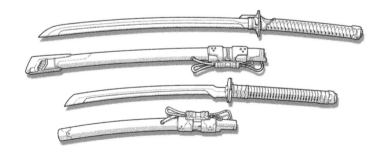

As you activate the Samurai's weaponry, the Kappa announces its intentions with an aggressive bellow, which echoes from the cracking walls of the devastated hangar, and attacks.

KAPPA				
SPEED	ARMOUR	MELEE	ARTILLERY	INTEGRITY
2	4	3	2	25

If you are victorious against the Kappa, turn to **179**.

The Enhanced Interface enables the mech to respond more quickly to your commands, at literally the speed of thought, effectively transforming you and the giant robot into a twenty metre-tall cyborg. But just as it can help the war-machine's AI to process what you want it to do, it can work the other way too.

Closing your eyes, through your mind's eye you 'see' what the AI 'sees', and observe the battle that is occurring between the combat computer and the virus, the interface reinterpreting the endless strings of zeros and ones as something you might better understand...

****

You are standing on an infinite plain of mirror-smooth obsidian. Above you, streams of glowing green numbers rush across the equally black sky in cascading waves, like a digital aurora borealis.

On the perfectly flat plain directly in front of you is an endlessly coiling and uncoiling worm, which looks like some horrible denizen of the abyssal depths. Looking down at your own body, you see that it is that of a Samurai-class mech.

Instinctively knowing what you must do, in your digitally-rendered robot form, you attack the virus. (In this battle, you have the initiative.)

WORM   COMBAT 8   ENDURANCE 12

If you succeed in defeating the worm, turn to **147**. However, if you lose the battle, turn to **98**.

With a subsonic roar, *Ronin 47* blasts into the sky. The island and the satellite dish control station vanish beneath you, an emerald pearl amidst the endless sapphire blue of the Pacific Ocean, as the mech heads into the stratosphere.

As you climb higher, and the curvature of the Earth allows you to see ever further, you observe bank after bank of white swirling cloud, and realise that a tropical cyclone is heading your way. However, the Booster Rocket carries the mech high above the typhoon, until you are able to see the becalmed zone at its heart.

You are glad you didn't run into the storm at sea level; even a 200-tonne war-machine like *Ronin 47* would have been tossed about like a ragdoll by the typhoon's 200 kilometre per hour winds.

However, while the Booster Rocket is far more effective than the mech's built-in jump-jets, it is still not designed to turn *Ronin 47* into a plane, and it doesn't have the range to carry you all the way to mainland Japan. On top of that, it is strictly one use only. (Strike the Booster Rocket from your Adventure Sheet; you may not use it again.)

As the rocket rapidly burns through its fuel supply, you realise you are going to have to find somewhere to land. The good news is that wherever you do set down will be on the other side of the storm.

Consulting a combination of the battle-computer's memory banks, the map downloaded from the Tengu Array, and the mech's own scanners, you find two locations that pique your interest.

Yokai Base, a secretive scientific research facility, lies to the west, while to the east lies what you can only describe as a large sensor anomaly. Alternatively, you could just set down directly below, on the same northerly line of longitude as Tokyo.

So, what's it to be?

East?   Turn to **259**.

West?   Turn to **513**.

North?   Turn to **27**.

The monster has the distinctive, elongated profile of a shark, but one that is thirty metres long, with two dorsal fins, rather than just one, and its hide is covered with an array of vicious-looking spines.

It is an Isonade, a class of kaiju that developed from sharks and manta rays, although it looks like some sea-urchin DNA entered the mix somewhere along the line.

As it makes its attack run, the monstrous shark-kaiju opens its jaws wide and you see a second set of jaws emerge from within.

ISONADE				
SPEED	ARMOUR	MELEE	ARTILLERY	INTEGRITY
5	2	4	1	20

If you are still alive after 5 Combat Rounds, or you reduce the Isonade's *Integrity* score to 15 points or fewer, whichever is sooner, turn to **253**.

121

You activate the Yurei Corporation-made 'ghostware' Cloaking Device – not knowing how long it will remain operational before either its circuits burn out or the reactor core suffers burnout – and set off again through the devastated city.

You explore the ruins for several hours before your Cloaking Device eventually gives up the ghost…

Turn to **215**.

122

Bringing your katana to bear, you leap at the droids, your blade singing as it slices through the air. (You must fight the Security Drones at the same time, but you have the initiative in this battle.)

	COMBAT	ENDURANCE
First SECURITY DRONE	8	8
Second SECURITY DRONE	8	7

If you manage to destroy the robotic guards, record the code word *Wrecked* on your Adventure Sheet and turn to **79**.

123

The mech responds almost instantaneously, the huge machine twisting out of the way as one of the kaiju makes a grab for the Samurai with its five-metre long arms. As the rest of the hunting pack continues to make for the surface, two of the hag-worm-like horrors turn at speed, almost tying themselves in knots as they change direction, and attack. Turn to **376**.

124

The skies above are clear and blue, while the streets you are exploring are grey and dark.

Turn to **435**.

125

Even though your bombardment of the minefield takes out numerous mines, there are still many more where they came from. Not only that but the sentient explosive devices have pinpointed your position now and are on the move. Turn to **548**.

126

If the *Gojira* is lying on the seabed, then it is out of range of *Ronin 47*'s scanners. While your mech is capable of submerging to a considerable depth, go too far down and its hull will start to buckle, compromising the integrity of its superstructure.

If you want to risk piloting the mech towards the bottom of the ocean in search of the *Gojira*, turn to **148**. If you think the risks involved outweigh the possible benefits – if the ship is even down there at all! – turn to **195**.

127

It seems to you that the Russian mech is about to take a step forward and then hesitates.

"What is it, Wanderer?" the Russian's voice comes over the comm.

"Never let it be said that Ivan doesn't play fair," you say, repeating his own words back to him.

"That's right! Never let it be said!"

"For there is no honour in not playing fair," you say, your mech indicating its artillery weapons with a jerk of a gigantic robotic thumb and then pointing to the control room high above the arena.

"No honour at all!" Ivan bellows.

Turn to **65**.

128

Unfortunately, *Ronin 47*'s melee weapons are not strong enough to penetrate the reinforced hull of the research vessel. In fact, they are damaged by the ablative armour. (Deduct 1 *Melee* point.)

You are going to have to try a different approach, but what will it be?

Bombard the shipwreck with heavy ordnance?   Turn to **322**.

Exit the mech, in order to enter the sunken ship?   Turn to **451**.

Abandon the *Gojira* and return to the surface?   Turn to **8**.

129

As you initiate the Konnichiwa protocol, the sentinels continue to process their firing solutions regardless. Clearly someone has re-programmed the Kyojin gun-towers regarding what constitutes a friend and what constitutes a foe.

Note that in the battle to come, the gun-towers will get in an unopposed strike, winning the first Combat Round, before *Ronin 47* can fight back.

Turn to **525**.

And then suddenly the mech's scanners register a return and the AI projects a wireframe image of Yokai Base on the screen, overlaid on top of the gloomy image that the robot's cameras are transmitting.

As you draw nearer, *Ronin 47*'s running lights pick out details from the darkness. The facility appears to have been built into the wall of the abyssal trench and only a pair of airlocks project from the submarine cliff face. Already latched onto one of these airlocks is a submersible that looks like a cross between a limpet and a sea urchin. But how long has it been there? Is it a recent arrival like yourself, or has it been docked here since before Ako Base fell?

Do you want to dock *Ronin 47* at the other airlock so that you can enter the facility yourself (turn to **12**), or do you want to open fire on the sub (turn to **106**)?

131

Your far superior Samurai-class mech takes out the opportunistic Wreckers, leaving their broken carcasses to remain here with the rest of the detritus that has collected within the Pacific waste vortex.

From here your target destination lies to the northwest and so you set off once more, thoughts of revenge hot inside your head.

Turn to **566**.

132

The scourge of the deep dead at last, its huge carcass slowly sinks into the depths, thousands of small fish and other submarine creatures emerging from the preternatural gloom to feast on the tyrant's flesh.

Returning to the surface, it is a relief to see clear blue skies through the HUD once more. But there's no time to lose, and so you set off northwards again, in pursuit of the stolen Shogun.

Turn to **141**.

133

It is insanity to think you can take out every single incoming rocket, and several do indeed make it through your defence screen.

Roll one die and add 3; deduct this many *Integrity* points from your mech. (Alternatively, pick a card and deduct its face value from your mech's *Integrity* score, unless it is a 10, or a picture card, in which case deduct 9 points from the Samurai's *Integrity* score; if it is less than 4 you must deduct 4 *Integrity* points.)

If your mech has lost 7-9 *Integrity* points, you must also deduct 1 point from its *Armour* score.

If *Ronin 47* is still standing, turn to **172**.

134

As you turn to examine the downed Daimyo-mech you almost physically recoil in revulsion as something slides over its arm, dragging a shell behind it that is as big as a house.

It is a Sazae-Oni, a colossal kaiju sea snail. The massive mollusc is composed of a fleshy pink body, and its huge shell, which is covered with elongated spikes, is as hard as rock. The teeth-covered tongue of a Sazae-Oni is strong enough to grind through the armour plating of a mech to get at whatever tasty morsels are hidden within, making it more than a match for *Ronin 47*.

The sea-snail colossus rears up before you in a threat posture of un-mollusc-like aggression.

Disgusted by its protruding eye-stalks, waving tentacles, and rippling mantle, do you want to leave the atoll, abandoning the mech to the monster snail (turn to **155**), or do you want to attack the mollusc-monster (turn to **175**)?

135

Before you can throw yourself out of the way, the lighting rig comes down on top of you. You cry out in pain as your legs become trapped under the heavy metal framework.

(Lose 4 *Endurance* points and 2 *Agility* points.)

All the signs indicate that the roof could come down at any moment. But do you have the strength to free yourself before it's too late? Getting your hands under the metal bar trapping your legs, you grit your teeth and start to heave.

Take an Endurance test. If you pass the test, turn to **166**. If you fail the test, turn to **196**.

136

Continue the battle between the two mechs, starting again with the Long-Range Combat phase.

If you manage to get the better of the prototype Shogun-class mech, turn to **343**.

137

The great robot turns and starts to run for the exit that leads to the launch pad, in response to your commands, its own pounding footfalls ringing from the walls of the devastated hangar.

But as you flee from the gargantuan beast, it rips one of the limp mechs from its cradle and hurls it after you. The proximity alarm sounds in your helm-cockpit a second before the flung Samurai hits.

Your mech is knocked to the ground, and you could have been badly injured yourself – thrown around inside the cockpit – if it wasn't for the fact that you are restrained in your seat-harness.

(Deduct 5 *Integrity* points and 2 *Endurance* points.)

The robot's Combat AI informing you via panicked red flashing characters on the HUD that the kaiju is coming, you compel *Samurai 47* to get up as quickly as possible.

Turn to **117**.

Gradually the gas cloud clears, but the Kani-Oni remain. If the DNA Bomb has had any effect on them, it has only made them more aggressive. (Cross off the DNA Bomb from your Adventure Sheet.)

Snapping their pincers, they spring across the rocks on their ten legs, while you activate your own weapons to defend yourself from their attack.

First KANI-ONI				
SPEED	ARMOUR	MELEE	ARTILLERY	INTEGRITY
3	4	3	3	10

Second KANI-ONI				
SPEED	ARMOUR	MELEE	ARTILLERY	INTEGRITY
3	4	3	3	8

Third KANI-ONI				
SPEED	ARMOUR	MELEE	ARTILLERY	INTEGRITY
3	4	3	3	12

If you overcome your enemies, turn to **518**.

You pass the wrecked frontage of a toy shop. Amidst the sodden chibi plushies and melted action figures, you see a diorama showing charred remote control robots battling giant plastic monsters.

Turn to **420** to keep exploring the city.

Your mech rises into the sky above the jungle-clad island, the jump-jets built into its feet spewing smoke and flames. The satellite dish dwindles below you, as you punch in the coordinates for the ruined capital city of Japan.

The jump-jets are not designed for prolonged flight and soon the HUD is warning you that their continued use is putting a strain on the reactor core. (Add 1 to your mech's *Reactor* score.)

But that is not your only problem. The mech's scanners, and your own eyes, can tell that you are heading into a storm. You can see the wall of spiralling cloud quite clearly through the screen, as the previously blue sky turns the colour of granite, and you feel the mech being buffeted by the heightening winds. It is time to set *Ronin 47* down before the reactor enters the critical zone.

But before you can drop back into the ocean, the cyclone hits. Winds approaching 200 kilometres per hour batter the armoured war-suit with the force of hammers, throwing it about as if it were nothing more than a ragdoll, and you lose all control of the machine.

Caught by the typhoon, *Ronin 47* is carried back into the air, higher and higher, as rain and ice bombard its hull, like a relentless barrage of bullets. (Deduct 4 points from your mech's *Integrity* score.)

And then, as suddenly as you were seized by the storm, you find yourself in a pocket of still air and the mech drops one hundred metres down into the ocean. Back in the water, you resume your journey. But where have you landed exactly?

Roll one die (or pick a card). If the number rolled is odd (or the card is red), turn to **198**. If the number (rolled) is even (or the card is black), turn to **318**.

141

Nine hundred kilometres north of Tokugawa Island, a smudge of green appears on the horizon, and steadily grows to become a craggy mountain peak, poking up from the North Pacific, its flanks smothered with dense tropical jungle. Rising from the summit of the island is a colossal construction of metal and concrete, and a vast parabolic dish.

It is from this location that the Tengu Satellite Array is managed and directed, and it could be your route to tracking down Kira and the stolen Shogun-mech.

In no time, *Ronin 47* is striding out of the sea and up onto the island. All that stands between you and access to the Tengu Satellite Array is two thousand metres of jungle and one hundred metres of climbing over topography that could generously be described as 'rugged terrain.' And then there will be the facility's defences to neutralise as well.

If your mech is equipped with Enhanced Scanners, turn to **187**. If not, turn to **269**.

142

(Strike the Hunter-Killer Missile from your Adventure Sheet.)

It is a direct hit! The Tsuchigumo's arachnoid limbs and abdomen might be covered in thick chitin, but they are no match for the Hunter-Killer's explosive warhead. The kaiju loses two of its hideous multi-jointed legs completely, while a hole is blown in its side from which dribble strings of white, rubbery flesh.

Roll one die and add 6, giving a total between 7 and 12. This is how many points you may deduct from the Tsuchigumo's *Integrity* score, should you come to fight it; if this is the case you may also deduct 1 from its *Speed* score and 1 from its *Melee* score.

If you now want to engage the kaiju-spider in battle, turn to **205**. However, if you have a DNA Bomb and wish to detonate it now, turn to **6**.

143

The mech's scanners have detected life-signs nearby but they are having trouble pinpointing them. Whatever it is the sensors have picked up either seems to be somehow underneath the island or perhaps even inside it. There is something else here with you.

If you want, you could try deploying some Drones, to help you pinpoint the creature's position, as long as your mech is equipped with them (turn to **162**), or launch some Depth Charges and make a pre-emptive strike against the beast, if you have some (turn to **212**).

Alternatively, you could submerge *Ronin 47* and swim down in the hope of finding out where the life-signs are coming from (turn to **242**), or you could land on the island and hope that the beast doesn't follow you onto dry land (turn to **64**).

144

Something has been carried inside the base by the sudden rush of water. By the fitfully flickering lights of the flooded corridor, you get the impression of slimy flesh the colour of a corpse, eerie spots of bioluminescence, and too many teeth. And then the Abyssal Horror attacks. (In this battle, the pelagic predator has the initiative.)

ABYSSAL HORROR   COMBAT 7   ENDURANCE 8

If the battle lasts for more Combat Rounds than your current *Endurance* score, turn to **163**. If you manage to defeat the monster in fewer Combat Rounds, turn to **5**.

145

Throwing away your chance to escape, you take a deep breath and hurl yourself at the door at the end of the corridor. But it's no good; no matter what you do – even attacking the door with your katana – it refuses to open. And all the while, gas continues to be pumped into the confined space.

You fight to hold your breath as you throw yourself at the door by which you entered, but that won't open either. Soon you cannot help but open your mouth in order to expel the carbon dioxide from your lungs. With your subsequent breath, you inhale a great lungful of the toxic gas.

You lose consciousness immediately and do not wake up again.

Your adventure is over.

THE END

146

Targeting a point that you estimate to be the middle of the minefield, you subject the area to an artillery barrage, firing off rocket after rocket, until the ammunition hoppers are severely depleted. (Permanently deduct 1 *Artillery* point.)

But it has the desired effect, as one spherical mine after another detonates, filling the air over the sea with smoke and noise.

Take an Artillery test. If you pass the test, turn to **585**, but if you fail the test, turn to **125**.

147

As your robot form grapples with the worm, the digital representation of the virus suddenly disintegrates into strings of glowing green zeros and ones that rain down onto the obsidian plain, where they explode into brilliant sparks on making contact with the glassy surface.

And then, before your eyes, your gauntleted robot hands start to come apart in the same way…

You open your eyes.

Add 1 point to your *Melee* score, even if this takes it above its starting level, and then turn to **588**.

148

As you descend and the light penetrating the sea from above fades, the shadowy silhouette of a ship, four hundred metres long, appears on the HUD. It is lying on its starboard side at the edge of an abyssal cliff. And it's not alone down here.

With a twist of its enormous tail, something huge powers up from the abyss towards you and proximity alarms inside the mech's helm start to chime.

Turn to **120** and engage the beast in battle, cutting straight to the Close Combat phase.

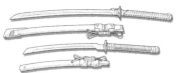

149

Outside the laboratory again, do you want to take the corridor now to your left, that you suspect leads to the second airlock (turn to **276**), or do you want to follow the passageway that is now in front of you (turn to **332**)?

150

Perturbed by the firework-burst of Flares, the Gumyocho returns to its roost, located in a cave high up on the central rocky crag of the island, leaving you to resume your journey. You certainly don't intend to remain anywhere near the monster's island.

But you feel exhausted after your ordeal, and when you come to another shoal of reefs – as you come ever closer to the southern shores of Japan, you make the sensible decision to stop and rest for what remains of the night.

Climbing out onto one of the largest of the reefs, you put the mech into standby mode.

If you have an active Spider repair droid and want to instruct it to make repairs to *Ronin 47*, turn to **299**. If not, or you do not want to deploy it at this time, turn to **354**.

151

That last collision sent the two mechs reeling. As the pilot of the Russian giant recovers himself and steadies the war-machine, you seize your chance.

Hailing on all frequencies, you say in English, your common tongue, "Ivan! Wait! Listen to me!"

If you have the code word *Trusted* recorded on your Adventure Sheet, turn to **127**. If not, turn to **103**.

152

The tech appears to have been designed with ease of use in mind; you will just need to connect it to your mech's cockpit controls to turn *Ronin 47* into a giant transmitter. However, you will also need to know the correct frequency to use for the emitter to actually have any effect on the kaiju.

Record the Signal Transmitter on your Adventure Sheet, along with the code word *Untested*, and then turn to **183**.

153

Servos straining, and with the reactor threatening to go into the red, finally the mech breaks free of the kaiju's clutches. But you are not out of danger yet.

Add 1 point to your war-machines' *Reactor* score and then turn to **376**.

154

The comm crackles with static and then a familiar voice comes over the comm. "Incoming!"

A missile streaks down out of the snow-riven sky and hits the heavy ordnance mech on the left, causing it to stumble as a ball of smoke and flame envelops its right shoulder.

Moments later, *Rising Sun* lands in a crouch beside you, the carbon-fibre muscle bundles in its legs absorbing the force of the impact.

"Come, my friend," Kanesada says. "There are deaths to be avenged. Do not falter now, for quickness is the essence of war."

As *Rising Sun* engages the already injured Oni, you prepare to engage the other one.

If you want to hit it with a Hunter-Killer Missile, if you have one, turn to **556**. If not, turn to **534.**

155

A ball of mucus collects at the creature's mouth and suddenly the horror spits it at you. Its aim is spot-on and the glob of vile gloop splashes against the hull of your mech, where it proceeds to eat through the ablative armour.

Before you can submerge *Ronin 47* in seawater, and wash off the corrosive slime, it has caused your mech significant damage that you doubt you are going to be able to repair unless you happen to stumble upon a fully-staffed and fully-operational Guardian hangar.

(Deduct 1 *Armour* point from your mech and 5 *Integrity* points.)

How do you want to respond to the Sazae-Oni's attack? Will you retaliate (turn to **175**), or do you want to depart as quickly as you can (turn to **2**)?

156

The fight is not going your way, and there is a very good chance that Director Asano's death, along with all the other deaths Kira caused the day he doomed Ako Base to its fate will go unavenged. But what can you do to reverse that situation?

If you have an operational and fully charged Spider repair droid on board, and want to set that on the Shogun, turn to **174**. If you want to overload *Ronin 47*'s reactor, even though you know what that will mean for you, turn to **200**. If you just want to keep battling on, turn to **136**. Alternatively, if *Ronin 47* is fitted with a Booster Rocket and you want to attempt to flee this fight, turn to **314**.

157

At your behest, a starburst of flares launches from the Samurai's shoulder batteries. (Cross off one use of the Flares from your Adventure Sheet.)

The Kappa screams, half-blinded by the sudden burst of intense light, and raises a scaly paw, as big as a tank, in front of its turtle-beaked face.

This is your chance! Urging the Samurai forwards, you attack the kaiju while it is caught off-guard, injuring the strange beast before it can put up any form of defence (and giving your mech the initiative in the battle to come).

KAPPA				
SPEED	ARMOUR	MELEE	ARTILLERY	INTEGRITY
2	4	3	2	20

If you are victorious against the Kappa, turn to **179**.

Powering up *Ronin 47*'s weapons, you prepare to engage in battle with those dishonourable individuals who sought to ambush you, rather than face you in a fair fight.

First WRECKER-MECH				
SPEED	ARMOUR	MELEE	ARTILLERY	INTEGRITY
2	4	4	2	20

Second WRECKER-MECH				
SPEED	ARMOUR	MELEE	ARTILLERY	INTEGRITY
2	4	3	2	25

If *Ronin 47* defeats both of the scavenger-mechs, turn to **131**.

You must engage both sentry-droids in battle. (Fight the Ogumo-mechs at the same time.)

First OGUMO-MECH				
SPEED	ARMOUR	MELEE	ARTILLERY	INTEGRITY
2	4	2	3	15

OGUMO-MECH				
SPEED	ARMOUR	MELEE	ARTILLERY	INTEGRITY
2	4	2	3	12

If *Ronin 47* destroys the automatons, turn to **111**.

You are surprised to come upon a makeshift monument to those who fell during K-Day, but there is no sign of who made it, and you wonder where they found the fresh flowers to lay at its base. Turn to **545**.

The Hunter-Killer is as effective underwater as it is above. It streaks from its shoulder launcher and hits the sub with catastrophic results.

Strike the Hunter-Killer Missile from your Adventure Sheet and turn to **45**.

You deploy the Drones, which assume a diamond formation as they rise over the island, and wait for a compound image, formed from their many camera-eyes, to take shape upon the screen in front of you.

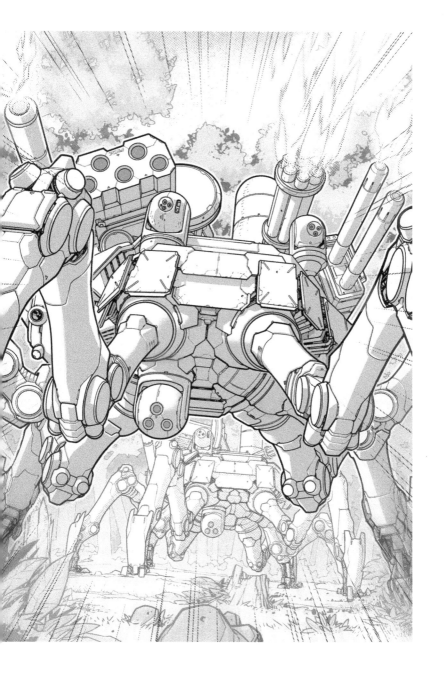

First you see the top of *Ronin 47*'s helm, as if you are looking down on it from above, and the craggy grey rock of the island rising out of the sea beside it. But as the Drones rise higher, you notice other rocky outcrops rising from the sea – a trail of them, in line with the central ridge of the island, to the south, and a larger outcropping to the north. And then you see what is staring you in the face and you gasp in shock. You can't believe you didn't see it sooner!

It is not an island at all. It is a dormant kaiju, resting just below the surface of the becalmed sea! And then it starts to move...

How do you want to react? Will you:

Launch a Hunter-Killer Missile (if you can)?	Turn to **191**.
Deploy Depth Charges (if you can)?	Turn to **212**.
Attack the beast before it can attack you?	Turn to **306**.
Attempt to flee?	Turn to **272**.

163

As you fight for survival, your oxygen supply is depleted far more quickly than you expected it to be. Either there wasn't as much air in the tanks as you had thought, or the aqualung has been damaged during your battle with the horror. But, whatever the truth of it, the upshot is that before you can make it safely back to *Ronin 47*, you die from hypoxia.

Your adventure is over.

THE END

164

You launch a salvo of flares directly at the approaching monster. (Cross off one use of the Flares from your Adventure Sheet.)

Its sensitive eyes blinded by the sudden starburst of intense red light, with one flick of its mighty tale, the Isonade turns and retreats into the pelagic gloom, while you resume your ascent.

Surfacing at last, you are relieved to see clear blue skies through the HUD; but there is no time to lose. Setting off northwards again in pursuit of the stolen Shogun, you put as much distance between you and the Isonade's territorial waters as you can, as quickly as you can.

Turn to **141**.

165

Pointing the device at the creatures, you pull the trigger. The effect is instantaneous; the hybrid monstrosities are possessed by a crippling palsy. While they are in this incapacitated state, you cut them both down with your blade. Turn to **235**.

166

Your muscles straining, you manage to lift the bar high enough to pull yourself free. Despite being in a lot of pain, you're glad that no bones have been broken.

Picking yourself up – and finding that your legs can still support your weight – you make for the exit.

Turn to **402**.

167

You pass the wrecked façade of a cinema complex. A banner flapping from its mooring on the front of the building proclaims the name of the last film screened there: *Pacific Rim 6 – Kaiju World*.

Turn to **420**.

168

As you set off once more, the mech's proximity alarms start to chime. Something is approaching from both left and right, but not just one thing. There are several somethings.

Ronin 47's Combat AI soon identifies the genus of kaiju that is approaching, at speed; they are Ikuchi, monstrously mutated eels. While individually not as large as many kaiju, only growing to ten metres in length, they hunt in packs. In addition, they visibly generate hugely powerful electrical discharges – which crackle across their writhing forms in blinding arcs of purple lightning –

thanks to an electrogenic tissue in their makeup. This means they are more than capable of taking on a mech like yours and winning!

How do you want to counter the threat-posed by the approaching Ikuchi? Will you:

Launch a Hunter-Killer Missile (if you can)?	Turn to **265**.
Deploy Depth Charges (if you can)?	Turn to **225**.
Launch Flares (if you can)?	Turn to **245**.
Engage the mutated eels in battle?	Turn to **292**.

169

With a flick of its massive tail, the Shachihoko makes its final attack run, its jaws distending as if the fish intends to swallow you and your mech whole.

SHACHIHOKO				
SPEED	ARMOUR	MELEE	ARTILLERY	INTEGRITY
4	2	5	1	30

If you manage to kill the abyss-dweller, turn to **305**.

170

A hail of metallic debris strikes your mech, much of it penetrating the robot's shielding and causing damage to the superstructure beneath.

Roll one die and add 2. Deduct this many *Integrity* points from your mech. (Alternatively, pick a card and deduct its face value from your mech's *Integrity* score, unless it is a 9 or above, in which case deduct 8 points from the Samurai's *Integrity* score; if it is less than 3 you must deduct 3 *Integrity* points.)

If your mech has lost 7-8 *Integrity* points, you must also deduct 1 point from its *Armour* score.

If *Ronin 47* is still operational, you set off across the now negated minefield, heading for Tokyo Bay.

Turn to **288**.

171

Ronin 47's scanners soon locate the *Gojira*. As you feared, it is three hundred metres down on the sea-floor and you can detect no signs of life on board. But then a ping on the oscilloscope readout on the screen in front of you reveals that there is something down there other than the sunken vessel, and it is most definitely alive.

If you want to take your mech to the bottom of the ocean to investigate the shipwreck, even at the risk of coming face to face with whatever it is the scanners have detected, turn to **218**. If you think that if the ship has already sunk there is nothing to be gained by boarding it now, turn to **195**.

172

Your attacker must be close, so how will you respond to this attempted assault?

Deploy a flight of Drones, if you can?	Turn to **197**.
Engage a Cloaking Device, if you have one?	Turn to **121**.
Perform a long-range sensor sweep, if *Ronin 47* has Enhanced Scanners?	Turn to **254**.
Keep moving, in the hope that your attacker loses your position again?	Turn to **582**.

173

So, the Traitor Kira has gone to ground at the top of Mount Fuji. The only question that remains is how to you want to approach his hideout?

If you have a Booster Rocket and want to use it now, turn to **584**. If not, *Ronin 47* will have to walk there – turn to **7**.

174

You give the Spider its instructions – via desperately shouted voice commands – and then turn your attention back to the Shogun as you continue your battle with the traitor Kira.

As you do so, the Spider manages to enter the Shogun – via a gap between its hull and one of its shoulder-mounted rocket arrays – and sets to work, attacking the prototype from within.

Deduct 1 point from both the Shogun's *Melee* score and its *Artillery* score, and then turn to **136**.

175

Which of your weapons do you want to use against the giant sea-snail? Do you want to:

Deploy Flares (if you can)?	Turn to **185**.
Launch a Hunter-Killer Missile (if you can)?	Turn to **226**.
Engage the Sazae-Oni in combat?	Turn to **243**.

176

For several agonising moments you can see nothing through the miasmic cloud, until it finally starts to dissipate on the breeze blowing between the broken buildings.

And then you see the Tsuchigumo once more, its chitinous carapace blackening like a bruise as its legs give way beneath it. It works its mandibles feebly for a moment and then is still.

Your DNA Bomb was a success! Cross it off your Adventure Sheet and then turn to **233**.

177

Upon entering the cockpit once more, before doing anything else, you check the mech's manifest and see that the DNA Bomb you created has indeed been delivered to the robot and is now safely stowed within the payload compartment in its chest.

Now turn to **417**.

178

You activate the jump jets and *Ronin 47* rises into the sky on a cone of smoke and flames, soon passing out of range of the Wreckers' artillery weapons.

As you rise higher, the enormity of the Western Pacific Garbage Patch becomes clear. How could the human race have been such poor custodians of a planet on which they are merely fleeting tenants?

Before long, hazard lights start to flash inside the cockpit, accompanied by a noisy alarm, as the reactor readings start to enter the red. (Add 1 your mech's *Reactor* score.)

Adjusting the mech's sensitive flight controls, you start to descend again, eventually touching down at the edge of the continental shelf south of Honshu Island.

Turn to **566**.

179

The monster's body crashes to the ground, setting the limp forms of the other Samurai swinging within their maintenance cradles, viscous green blood oozing from a hundred savage wounds.

Quitting the Guardian hangar, leaving your murdered comrades entombed within their dead mechs, you make it to the launch pad. The wrecks of Tatsu dropships and Kirin escape craft lie scattered about, now no more than burning piles of wreckage, while a host of kaiju are scaling the rocky wall of the extinct caldera, in which the landing pad has been built.

Samurai 47's AI counts twelve of the giant monsters, but the signs are that there are more on the way, a relentless tide of mutated mega-fauna.

Although not designed for flight, not like the Shogun, every Samurai is equipped with jump jets, which can provide lift – to get the mech out of a particularly sticky situation – but only briefly, and prolonged use puts great strain on the reactor core.

What do you want to do? Will you:

Activate *Samurai 47*'s jump jets?	Turn to **229**.
Flee from Ako Base on foot?	Turn to **255**.
Prepare to stand and fight the approaching kaiju?	Turn to **209**.

180

As *Ronin 47* continues on its way, it crushes the wrecks of cars and broken bicycles beneath its huge feet without even noticing. Turn to **435**.

You wake after what feels like several hours' sleep. Checking your chronometer, you realise you have spent one entire night here.

Later that day, you are collected again by the Wreckers and taken to the hangar to lead *Ronin 47* into battle once more. But who will your opponent be this time?

The crowd of gamblers cheers when *Ronin 47* enters the arena, but the roars of adulation for your opponent are even louder. It is the red menace, the Russian giant. *Ronin 47*'s sluggish AI translates the Cyrillic letters on its hull plating as *Volos*, while its database dredges up the fact that *'Volos'* was the name of a chthonic deity from Russia's mythic past.

As tall as an Oni-class mech, the Russian machine is not unlike a great bear in the way it hunches its shoulders, which are weighed down with heavy ordnance, and rocks from side to side on its pelvic pivot like some cage fighter eager for the bout to commence. It looks powerful enough to lift *Ronin 47* off the ground.

And then a booming voice rings out across the chamber and in English says, "It's the fight you've been waiting for – *Ronin 47*, piloted by Commander Oishi, versus Ivan 'The Bear' Bukovski and *Volos*!"

As a great cheer goes up from the bloodthirsty crowd, you are struck by inspiration. But before you can do anything about implementing your idea, and putting your hastily-formulated plan into action, *Volos* barrels towards you, spoiling for a fight. (Cut straight to the Close Combat phase of battle.)

VOLOS				
SPEED	ARMOUR	MELEE	ARTILLERY	INTEGRITY
2	4	4	-	28

After 5 Combat Rounds, if *Ronin 47* is still in the fight, or if you reduce *Volos*'s Integrity score to 20 points or fewer, turn to **151**.

182

As you are about to re-enter the ocean, something rises from the waters covering the continental shelf. Several somethings, in fact. They look like nothing less than gigantic jellyfish, but their arms are solid and rubbery.

You have become the unwitting target of a pack of hunting Umibozu. They emerge from the sea, each one fifteen metres tall, ready to tear *Ronin 47* apart in search of food. (You must fight all three Umibozu at the same time.)

First UMIBOZU				
SPEED	ARMOUR	MELEE	ARTILLERY	INTEGRITY
3	1	4	1	15

Second UMIBOZU				
SPEED	ARMOUR	MELEE	ARTILLERY	INTEGRITY
3	1	4	1	12

Third UMIBOZU				
SPEED	ARMOUR	MELEE	ARTILLERY	INTEGRITY
3	1	4	1	15

If the Umibozu make a successful strike against *Ronin 47*, mutated stinging cells in their elongated limbs hit the mech with a jolt of circuit-disrupting bio-electricity, meaning that you will have to reduce the mech's *Melee Rating* by 1 point during the next Combat Round. However, if the mech is fitted with EMP Shielding, you may ignore this additional damage.

If you defeat all three of the Umibozu, the corrupted jellyfish-kaiju dead, you leave the Vault's isolated island.

Turn to **141**.

183

Exiting the lab, keen to continue your mission and see what difference the device makes, should you encounter any more kaiju, you hurry back to Airlock 2 and *Ronin 47*. Turn to **276.**

184

The kaiju winds its monstrous, worm-like body around your Samurai, ensuring that you cannot get free of its slimy clutches.

As it heads deeper, tightening its muscular coils around your mech all the time, a hazard sign starts to flash red on the screen. You have passed the point of no return, with regard to standard mech tolerances, and there is a very real danger that the mech's hull will rupture under the intense pressure. But still your descent continues.

The only light at these abyssal depths is that given off by your mech and the bioluminescent creatures that call this freezing hell home.

But then the lights inside the cockpit start to flicker and interference sweeps in waves across the HUD, and you can hear horrible creaking sounds reverberating throughout the superstructure of the mech.

If your Samurai has an Upgraded Hull, turn to **61**. If not, turn to **214.**

185

The creature recoils before the intense burst of brilliant red flares, its eye-stalks and tentacles retracting into its boneless body, but your assault doesn't deter it for long.

Cross off one use of the Flares from your Adventure Sheet, and then turn to **155.**

186

You set down above the snowline of the dormant volcano, *Ronin 47* bending its knees as it absorbs the impact of its landing, which sends a cloud of white powder up into the air around it.

And then, as the powder settles again, you catch sight of your objective for the first time, close to the peak of Mount Fuji. It looks like an outcropping of black rock, but then you make out the stacked, sloping, butto-style roofs and realise that the vast structure is man-made. Facing you is a wall a hundred metres tall. But before you can even attempt to breach the walls of the fortress, you are going to have to deal with the red-hulled Oni-mechs that are trudging towards you across the snowfield, their artillery weapons primed.

If you have the code word *Allied* recorded on your Adventure Sheet, turn to **154**. If not, turn to **438**.

187

As *Ronin 47*'s sensors sweep the jungle around you, forever on the lookout for danger, they detect movement close to the parabolic antenna. Something is descending from the summit on an intercept course.

If you want to deploy a flight of Drones, to gather more information about this potential threat, and are able to do so, turn to **207**. If not, turn to **313**.

There is an audible *CLICK!* and the door at the far end of the corridor opens.

"Step this way," comes the voice again, and so you do as you are bidden.

Exiting the corridor, you enter a cavernous man-made metal-walled space. It is roughly circular, like the lift shaft, but at least twenty times bigger. Surrounding the walls are mech gantries and repair cradles, but none of them are occupied at present.

Hearing the hum of more robotic drones, you turn to see an old man exit a control booth and approach you, flanked by a pair of the levitating droids. He is wearing the uniform of an engineer.

"Hello!" he says, excitedly. "It's a long time since we last had any visitors." And then his face darkens abruptly. "Tell me, what news is there from Ako Base?"

You tell him about the attack and Deputy Director Kira's traitorous actions, and the engineer's expression becomes even more solemn.

"It is worse than I thought," he says. "As soon as we lost the signal from Ako Base, I knew something was wrong, I just never expected it would be so bad. I am Hara Mototoki, by the way."

You introduce yourself, telling Mototoki that you intend to avenge the deaths of Director Asano and the other Ako Base personnel with your mech *Ronin 47*.

"Then you have come to the right place!" he says, beaming. "We have all sorts of weapons and armour upgrades in the armoury. We'll just bring your Samurai through and then we can get started."

"I know there is only a skeleton staff here, but where is the rest of your team?" you ask Mototoki.

"Team?" he laughs. "You're looking at him! But don't worry, with a little help from the droids and yourself, we'll get your mech upgraded in no time."

Accompanied by the ever-present drones, Mototoki leads you from the mech-hangar through a door into the armoury. Arrayed on the walls and hanging from the ceiling are all manner of massive mech weapons and great pieces of ablative armour.

"So," he says, pulling up an inventory on a computer screen in a secondary control room off the armoury itself, "what's it to be?"

Listed below are the weapons, armour and other upgrades available. To find out more about any of them, turn to the relevant section number.

Artillery

| Hunter-Killer Missile | Turn to **460**. |

Melee

| Sunblade | Turn to **410**. |

Upgrades

Depth Charges	Turn to **310**.
Flares	Turn to **360**.
Booster Rocket	Turn to **490**.

Armour

| Upgraded Hull | Turn to **220**. |
| EMP Shielding | Turn to **260**. |

You may only select one upgrade to be added to your mech, but note that upgrades may take your mech's attributes above their starting scores.

When you are done researching the different upgrades that are available, turn to **24**.

189

You place your palm against the scanner to the right of the door and it opens, admitting you to a large laboratory that is full of what look like gigantic test tubes of bubbling liquid. In the centre of the room is a computer console. Accessing this you soon discover what the scientists were working on before they left – either of their own volition or having been forced out, you have no idea which.

The kaijuologists based here were searching for a way to reverse the effects of the K-Compound and, judging by the evidence you uncover in the files stored on the computer, they were close to finding a solution.

They had isolated four compounds which they hoped, when brought together in the correct combination, would cause any living material mutated by the K-Compound to unravel at a molecular level. However, the scientists discovered that they couldn't simply combine all four together, as the different elements would then work against each other, rendering the new compound inert and therefore ineffective.

If you want to attempt to complete the researchers' unfinished work, turn to **426**. If you would rather leave well enough alone, you can either see what lies beyond the door at the other end of the passageway (turn to **547**), or head back to *Ronin 47* (turn to **276**).

190

Targeting a point that could be considered roughly the middle of the minefield, you launch the heavy ordnance weapon. The missile hits one of the spherical mines and the two devices detonate simultaneously.

Cross the Hunter-Killer Missile off your Adventure Sheet and turn to **585.**

191

Targeting the 'island' beneath the waterline, you fire the missile. It enters the ocean, leaving a pool of oily iridescence on the surface, and detonates a split second later sending a great column of water into the air between you and your target.

(Cross off the Hunter-Killer Missile on your Adventure Sheet.)

Roll one die and multiply the number by 5. (Alternatively, pick a card and if it is a 7 or higher, assume that the number you have picked is a 6; then multiply this randomly-generated number by 5.)

Make a note that the resulting total is the amount of *Integrity* points' damage you have already caused the strange beast and then turn to **306**.

192

You turn tail and run as fast as you can, accompanied by the wailing of alarms, as the sub pulls away from Yokai Base while the airlock is still open.

A wall of freezing water rushes after you, and before you can make it back to *Ronin 47*, the torrent knocks you off your feet and carries you along with it. As the aqualung kicks in, supplying you with oxygen, you are glad you had the foresight to put on your helmet before entering Yokai Base.

Roll one die (or pick a card). If the number rolled is odd (or the card is red), turn to **144**. If the number (rolled) is even (or the card is black), turn to **5**.

193

As you pilot the mech northwards, just below the waves, the war-machine's scanners alert you to potential danger ahead. There's a storm brewing – a tropical cyclone is gaining in power and heading in your direction.

You want to avoid running into the typhoon if at all possible; the integrity of *Ronin 47*'s hull could be adversely affected by the force of such a storm. The Climate Catastrophe of the early 21st century has only made such storms even more unpredictable and dangerous.

Deprived of the option of continuing directly north, for Honshu Island and Tokyo, which way do you want to go in the hope of evading the typhoon?

Do you want to set a course for the northwest (turn to **198**), or northeast (turn to **318**)?

194

An oil tanker lies on its side, blocking an intersection. But *Ronin 47* simply steps over it and continues on its way. Turn to **115**.

195

Whatever the scientists on board the *Gojira* might have been able to do to help you in your quest for revenge against the traitor Kira, there is nothing they can do for you now that they're dead.

You have wasted enough time on this wild goose chase already. It is time to resume your journey north in pursuit of the stolen Shogun.

Turn to **141**.

196

It is no good – the lighting rig is simply too heavy for you to shift.

Moments later, your worst fears are confirmed, when the dome caves in, and tonnes of reinforced concrete comes crashing down on top of you.

Your adventure is over.

THE END

197

The flight of Drones takes to the air, rapidly rising high above the rubble and wreckage of what was once the magnificent capital city of Japan.

In the moments before a second fusillade of rockets takes them all out, the Drones relay the position of your attacker. There, hidden behind a still-standing skyscraper, is the colossal form of an Oni-mech. Taller and heavier than your Samurai-class machine, the Oni also outguns you. The only way you can hope to overcome it is in close combat. And so, you set off once more, but you now know its position. The Oni-mech is at grid reference C9.

Cross off one use of the Drones from your Adventure Sheet and then turn to **420**, to resume your exploration of the ruined metropolis.

The mech courses through the waves, just below the surface like a submarine, as you put kilometre after kilometre between your position and the steadily worsening typhoon.

Suddenly every alarm seems to sound inside the cockpit at once, as something hurtles up from the ocean depths. Your first impression of the image relayed via the HUD, is that it is a blunt-nosed monster sprouting a mass of tentacles. But then you realise that it is not one kaiju but two, locked in the deadly embrace of battle.

The blunt-headed monster is a Bake-kujira, a grossly mutated whale, its body covered in bony growths, while the tentacles belong to a gigantic squid-kaiju known as an Akkorokamui. The two colossal creatures are clearly engaged in a battle to the death, following which the winner will doubtless consume the loser.

The monsters surface, throwing up a great spume of water, twenty metres into the air, the flukes of the Bake-kujira's tail missing *Ronin 47* by a matter of mere centimetres and trapping the mech within the whirlpool generated by its sudden emergence from the sea.

So far as you can tell, either the kaiju have not noticed the presence of *Ronin 47*, or they are too caught up in their battle to care.

What do you want to do? Will you:

Try to evade the battling sea-monsters?	Turn to **307**.
Join the battle, fighting on the whale's side against the squid?	Turn to **428**.
Join the battle, but fighting on the squid's side against the whale?	Turn to **485**.
Launch a Hunter-Killer Missile into the fray (if you can)?	Turn to **507**.

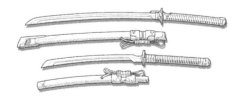

Dr Kitsune's 'pets' might not be large, but that doesn't make them any less dangerous! (In this battle you have the initiative, but you must fight the hybrids at the same time.)

	COMBAT	ENDURANCE
First YOKAI	7	7
Second YOKAI	8	6

If you kill the horrors, turn to **235**.

Your fingers flying over the control panel in front of you, you bypass all fail-safes and defensive security measures, before setting the reactor to overload.

When the query "Are you sure you want to execute this instruction?" appears on the screen, you hesitate for a moment, your hand hovering over the virtual keypad, before selecting "Execute," in doing so, initiating the Seppuku Protocol…

As a graphic on the HUD shows the temperature inside the core rising, you briefly consider ejecting, in the hope you might actually be able to save yourself. But then you think better of it.

Bathed in the bronze glow of the screens in front of you, your features assume a serene composure as you consider Sun Tzu's *The Art of War* once more: *"He who wishes to fight must first count the cost."*

You may have avenged the deaths of Director Asano and your companions, but it is at the cost of your own life.

Your adventure is over.

THE END

201

While you rest and recuperate, the Spider sets about making repairs to *Ronin 47*.

Restore the mech's *Melee*, *Artillery* and *Integrity* scores to their current maximum levels, if any of them have been reduced, and then turn to **181**.

202

Slowly the cloud of gas is dispersed by the sea-breeze, but the Kani-Oni still remain.

Cross off the DNA Bomb from your Adventure Sheet and turn to **493**.

203

Once you are inside the cockpit, you plug the transmitter unit into the control console and then run a diagnostic check, to make sure it has aligned with the mech's systems and is functioning correctly. However, you will still need to know the correct frequency to enter for the emitter to actually have an effect on any kaiju.

Now turn to **417**.

204

Before you can launch the missile, a pair of mechs collides with *Ronin 47*, and send it crashing onto its back on the half-submerged reef. (Deduct 10 *Integrity* points.) Only then do the proximity alarms start to sound.

Your ambushers are two Ninja-class mechs, their hulls painted a dull, matte black. They are slightly shorter than the standard Samurai model war-machine, and less well-armoured, but they are also more agile. Where *Ronin 47* is armed with a single melee weapon, the Ninjas are each armed with a pair of Electro-Wakizashi swords – mech-swords similar in design and function to the standard Electro-Katana, but with a shorter blade and packing slightly less of a punch.

You have no choice but to defend yourself against the Ninjas, but because *Ronin 47* is lying on its back, you must reduce the mech's

Melee score by 2 points for the first Combat Round, as you struggle to get it back on its feet. (Go straight to the Close Combat phase in this battle.)

First NINJA-MECH				
SPEED	ARMOUR	MELEE	ARTILLERY	INTEGRITY
5	2	5	2	20

Second NINJA-MECH				
SPEED	ARMOUR	MELEE	ARTILLERY	INTEGRITY
5	2	5	2	18

If you manage to defeat both Ninjas, turn to **19**.

205

The Samurai-class robots were built for this very purpose – to eliminate the threat posed by the monstrous kaiju – and so that is what you will do now, before the monster can wrap your mech in its corrosive webs.

TSUCHIGUMO				
SPEED	ARMOUR	MELEE	ARTILLERY	INTEGRITY
4	1	4	3	15

If *Ronin 47* is using a Flame-Thrower, you may roll one additional die when determining damage.

If you manage to kill the Tsuchigumo, turn to **233**.

206

As you trigger the weapon, a pulse of electromagnetic energy ripples out across the mountainside, sending a bow-wave of powdery snow before it.

The Oni-mechs immediately come to a complete stop – midstride in one case – their hulls wreathed in lightning, as their electrical systems fail.

(Cross the EMP Device off your Adventure Sheet; you will not be able to use it again.)

If *Ronin 47* is fitted with EMP Shielding, turn to **290**. If not, turn to **271**.

207

The hatches that give access to the Drone hangars in *Ronin 47*'s back open and the devices take to the air. You direct them towards the location of the approaching sensor anomaly and wait for the aerial view of the huge satellite dish and surrounding jungle to come to clarity on the screen in front of you.

And then you see them – after all, they are not hard to miss. Two large robotic stalkers – each looking like a cross between a crab and a tarantula, although with a ten-metre leg-span – are making their way towards you through the untamed forest.

Suddenly the Ogumo-mechs open up with the guns built into their armoured carapaces and the image on the cockpit screen abruptly goes dark, as the machines blast your Drones out of the sky.

(Cross off one use of the Drones from your Adventure Sheet.)

How do you want to respond? Will you:

Deploy Flares (if you can)?	Turn to **228**.
Launch a Hunter-Killer Missile (if you can)?	Turn to **248**.
Broadcast clearance codes identifying yourself as an ally and not an enemy?	Turn to **289**.
Bring *Ronin 47*'s weapons online and prepare for battle?	Turn to **313**.

208

You feel stiff after remaining cooped up in the cockpit of your mech for so long.

Deduct 1 *Agility* point and turn to **420**.

Kaiju pour over the lip of the caldera and down onto the launch pad, batting aside the burning hulks of dropships and crushing the bodies of the dead underfoot, in their eagerness to get at your mech.

Lighting your weapons, you hit the monsters with everything you've got, but it's not enough. You make a valiant last stand, taking down fully half the horrors that are assaulting the base – your mech losing one of its arms in the process – but in the end, although your death is an honourable one, it is still a fruitless sacrifice.

As your mech has its other arm ripped from its shoulder-socket in a spray of sparks, you initiate the Seppuku Protocol, overloading the Samurai's reactor, knowing that your death will at least mean something then.

Your adventure is over.

THE END

210

You pass a burnt-out supermarket. Herds of shopping trolleys remain gathered outside, some still containing the rotting remains of abandoned groceries. Turn to **435**.

211

You activate the Yurei Corporation-made 'ghostware' Cloaking Device, not knowing how long it will remain operational for before either its circuits burn out or the reactor core overloads.

As *Ronin 47* continues to fly towards Mount Fuji, the robotic gun-drones ignore it. A human pilot would be able to see that your mech is still there, but the flying weapons are blind to it now.

Do you want to open fire on the gun-drones (turn to **403**), or do you want to ignore them in turn and keep on towards your ultimate destination (turn to **186**)?

The Depth Charges tumble into the void and when they reach a depth of thirty metres, having not made contact with anything, they detonate.

The island that is not an island stirs at your rude awakening and begins to rise from the depths. Your ill-judged actions have awoken it.

Make a note that you have already caused the strange beast 5 *Integrity* points of damage and then turn to **315**.

213

The flight of Drones takes to the air, rapidly rising high above the rubble and wreckage of what was once the magnificent capital city of Japan.

In the moments before a second fusillade of rockets takes them all out, the Drones relay the position of your attacker. There, hidden behind a still-standing skyscraper, is the colossal form of an Oni-mech. Taller and heavier than your Samurai-class machine, the Oni also outguns you. The only way you can hope to overcome it is in close combat, and so you set off once more, but you now know its position. The Oni-mech is at grid reference I3.

Cross off one use of the Drones from your Adventure Sheet and then turn to **420**, to resume your exploration of the ruined metropolis.

214

The groaning sounds you can hear are those of metal under duress. The pressure down here must be in excess of 200 atmospheres!

Take an Armour test. If your mech passes the test, turn to **61**; if it fails the test, turn to **244**.

215

Finally, you round the corner of a building and there before you, squatting in the middle of the broken street is a colossal mech, bristling with all manner of rocket pods and missile launchers.

It is five metres taller than *Ronin 47* and probably weighs twice as much. Not only that, but its head has been sculpted to look like one of the red-skinned demons of legend, so as to help it intimidate any kaiju it may encounter.

But right now, its target isn't one of the giant mutants – it's you!

Will you:

Target the Oni-class mech with a Hunter-Killer Missile (if you have one)?	Turn to **251**.
Trigger an EMP Device (if you have one)?	Turn to **301**.
Engage the heavy ordnance mech in close combat?	Turn to **274**.

216

There's no time to go in search of the *Gojira* now, otherwise you will never catch up with Kira and the stolen Shogun. Your only choice is to keep heading north.

If you have the code word *Delayed* recorded on your Adventure Sheet, turn to **182**. If not turn to **141**.

217

Ronin 47 rises out of the sea, propelled by only its jump-jets, and seeming to levitate above the water as you guide it towards Tokyo Bay. By the time you reach the Miura peninsula, the reactor readings are in the red and you are forced to set down again, still outside the city, but at least you are clear of the sentient minefield.

Add 1 to your mech's *Reactor* point and turn to **288**.

As you descend, the light penetrating the sea from above fades and the shadowy silhouette of the *Gojira* comes into view. The ship must be four hundred metres long! It is currently lying on its starboard side at the edge of an abyssal cliff.

And then the reason for the oscilloscope return makes its presence felt, as something powers up from the black depths of the ocean towards you with one twist of its massive tail, and proximity alarms inside the helm-cockpit start to sound. But you are ready for it.

Turn to **120**.

219

Deciding that it is your best course of action, you launch a fusillade of depth charges into the water around you. Moments later, they detonate. (Cross off one use of the Depth Charges from your Adventure Sheet.)

The underwater explosions rip through the body of the monstrous fish, but whilst they cause it savage injures, they also provoke its savage fury, and it attacks *Ronin 47*.

SHACHIHOKO				
SPEED	ARMOUR	MELEE	ARTILLERY	INTEGRITY
4	2	5	1	15

If you manage to kill the abyss-dweller, turn to **305**.

220

Upgrading the hull of your mech will make it more able to withstand extremes of heat and pressure, but without affecting its speed. If you opt for the Upgraded Hull, *Ronin 47* gains 1 *Armour* point and 5 *Integrity* points. However, please note that the mech's *Armour* score may not exceed 5 points.

When you are ready, turn back to the section you just came from.

The klaxon sounds once more, signalling that the bout is over. As you and the American exit the arena, you see the Russian mech and the Chinese Guan Yu getting ready to enter it.

Who knows how long it will be before you have to fight in the arena again, or when you will be able to effect a breakout? For the time being, the sensible approach would be to keep biding your time, learning all you can about your captors and the gladiator ring, and only make your move when you know their every weakness. For as *The Art of War* states, *"Victorious warriors win first and then go to war, while defeated warriors go to war first and then seek to win."*

The guard escort takes you back to the cells, where you decide to get some rest, and maybe eat something. (Now would be a good time to consume some Rations or use a Medi-Pack, if you are able to.)

If there is still a fully-charged Spider droid on board *Ronin 47*, turn to **201**. If not, turn to **181**.

222

Your search is over! Turn to **215**.

223

Putting ashore on the Gumyocho's island – and finding a spot that is not strewn with the bird-kaiju's prodigious, stinking, acidic guano – you put the mech into standby mode.

If you have an active Spider repair droid and want to instruct it to make repairs to *Ronin 47*, turn to **256**. If not, or you do not want to deploy it at this time, turn to **4**.

224

Before you can take a step towards the looming Shogun, all manner of monsters starts to pour over the lip of the crater – turtle-like Kappa, arachnoid Tsuchigumo, and airborne Gumyocho among them. Still following your signal-lure, the kaiju have penetrated the fortress itself.

However, you cannot let the presence of the monsters stop you from carrying out your mission. As they continue to pour into the crater and swarm over Kira's mountaintop hideaway, you take the fight to the Shogun-class mech.

But what method of attack do you want to use?

Fire a salvo of Flares (if you can)?	Turn to **352**.
Launch a flight of Drones (if you can)?	Turn to **381**.
Target the Shogun with a Hunter-Killer Missile (if you have one)?	Turn to **408**.
Trigger an EMP Device (if you have one)?	Turn to **495**.
Engage your nemesis in close combat?	Turn to **446**.

225

The depth charges sink into the sea around the mech, as the eel-monsters continue to close in. When the devices detonate, moments later, the Ikuchi are almost on top of you, but they are outside the blast radius of the explosives, and so come to no harm.

Cross off one use of the Depth Charges from your Adventure Sheet and turn to **292**.

226

Targeting the creature's shell, you fire the missile. (Remove the Hunter-Killer Missile from your Adventure Sheet.)

The mollusc is far too slow to move out of the way and the projectile scores a direct hit. The warhead detonates, and the kaiju is blasted to bits that come back down to earth as a stinking rain of blackened chunks of rock-hard shell and half-cooked seafood.

The Sazae-Oni utterly destroyed, you turn your attention back to the stricken Daimyo-mech.

Turn to **286**.

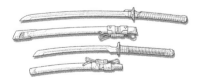

There is no time to celebrate your victory, as the gates of the fortress open and a tide of black-clad figures pours out. Many are riding snow-scooters or all-terrain vehicles, and they are accompanied by a squadron of automated airborne gun-drones.

Having seen you defeat his guard-mechs, Kira has sent his army of devoted followers to stop you. He must fear you and what you could be capable of!

But then the ground beneath *Ronin 47*'s feet begins to shake and the mech's sensors alert you to the tide of monstrously-mutated fauna that is surging up the slopes of the mountain towards your position. The kaiju are coming! The Signal Transmitter worked!

When they realise what is approaching, Kira's forces panic and run, but before they can make their escape, the kaiju catch up with them. Making the most of the distraction, with nothing now standing between you and your objective, you charge through the open gates of the fortress.

Turn to **18**.

You launch the flares directly into the forest in front of you, as the Ogumo-mechs reach your position. (Cross off one use of the Flares from your Adventure Sheet.)

The intense glare of the starburst overwhelms the simpler droids' sensors and they both come to an abrupt halt. Before they can reboot their visual acuity arrays, you leap into action and take out one of the automatons before turning your attention to the other one.

Before you can finish that mech too, it reactivates and brings its cannons to bear.

OGUMO-MECH				
SPEED	ARMOUR	MELEE	ARTILLERY	INTEGRITY
2	4	2	3	15

If you destroy the crab-like sentry droid, turn to **111**.

As the kaiju pour over the lip of the caldera and down onto the launch pad, your Samurai rises into the sky on a cone of smoke and flames, leaving the monsters far behind.

Soon Ako Base and Tokugawa Island are nothing more than a grey-black rock, dwindling amidst a vast expanse of cerulean ocean.

Hazard lights start to flash inside the cockpit, accompanied by a nagging alarm, as the reactor readings start to enter the red. (Add 1 point to your mech's *Reactor* score.)

Adjusting the mech's sensitive flight controls, such as they are, you start to make your descent, and soon pick out a small island roughly 500 clicks north of Tokugawa Island, and far out of reach of the kaiju attacking Ako Base. You have travelled a long way in only a short time and make landfall on a plateau at the top of the tiny island.

Turn to **337**.

You continue to hurry through the complex at a steady jog, until you enter a chrome-plated suiting-up room. And there, standing before an open door on the other side of the octagonal chamber, you see him – the traitor Kira!

The shock of suddenly running into your nemesis like this causes you to freeze at the threshold of the room. That hesitation is the chance Kira needs to flee through the doorway in front of him.

Snapping out of your stunned state – you can't let him escape you now! – you sprint after the man you have come all this way to kill.

Take an Endurance test. If you pass the test, turn to **466**. If you fail the test, turn to **312**.

The sun is setting as you find yourself approaching a shoal of coral reefs. It was to save these dying ecosystems that the K-Compound was originally developed but, thanks to the hubris of humankind, it proved too effective. The reef is still dead, the coral polyps that once inhabited it having mutated and left the bleached calcium deposits in search of prey, in the form of inconceivably large colony creatures now designated as Lusca.

You never went out on missions at night when Phoenix Squad was operating out of Ako Base, since many kaiju are more active at night, with monstrous creatures rising from the abyssal depths to feed. Creatures like the Lusca.

It might be a good idea to stop here for the night to rest – it's been a hectic day after all. However, you feel that Tokyo and Kira are within reach, and if you were to keep going you could reach Honshu Island by morning.

If you want to stop here to rest and maybe make what repairs you can to *Ronin 47*, turn to **267**. If you would prefer to press on across the sea as darkness falls, turn to **334**.

232

As you trigger the weapon, a pulse of electromagnetic energy ripples out across the mountainside, sending a bow-wave of powdery snow before it.

The Ninja-mechs immediately start to convulse as they are seized by a violent mechanical palsy, their superstructures wreathed in lightning, as their electrical systems shutdown.

(Cross the EMP Weapon off your Adventure Sheet; you will not be able to use it again.)

If *Ronin 47* is fitted with EMP Shielding, turn to **75**. If not, turn to **271**.

233

The arachnoid horror is dead!

Write the code word *Exterminated* on your Adventure Sheet, and if you have the code word *Allied* already written on your Adventure Sheet, turn to **257**; if not, turn to **582**.

234

Lightning fast, your fingers dance over the touch-sensitive screen. A split second later, the missile fires, hitting the mech that has just emerged from your left head on. The force of the rocket-strike lifts the robot off its feet and carries it out of range, before detonating and destroying the robotic war-suit utterly.

(Cross off the Hunter-Killer Missile on your Adventure Sheet.)

But one remains. It is slightly smaller than *Ronin 47* – shorter and less well-armoured – and its hull is a dull, matte black. It is apparent that the machine is more agile than a Samurai-mech, and it is armed with two close combat weapons. You recognise them as Electro-Wakizashi swords – similar in design and function to the Samurai's Electro-Katana, but not as long and packing slightly less of a punch. But there are two of them.

You have no choice but to defend yourself against your ambusher, which is clearly a Ninja-class mech. (Go straight to the Close Combat phase in this battle.)

NINJA-MECH				
SPEED	ARMOUR	MELEE	ARTILLERY	INTEGRITY
5	2	5	2	18

If you manage to defeat the Ninja, turn to **19**.

You set off at a sprint after Dr Kitsune, but before you can catch up with her, she makes it through Airlock 1 at the other end of the corridor. Without closing the inner door, she overrides the controls and opens the outer hatch, boarding the submersible.

It is then that you realise what she is planning to do. If her craft detaches while the inner airlock door is still open, the base will flood with seawater in mere moments!

If you want to try to reach Kitsune's submersible before it can depart, turn to **298**. If you want to turn tail and sprint back to the other airlock, and *Ronin 47*, as fast as you can, turn to **192**.

Entering the bunker, you make your way along a passageway large enough to accommodate mechs twice the height of *Ronin 47* to a circular chamber at its end. As you enter the chamber, warning klaxons start to sound, dirty yellow hazard beacons flash on and off, and the circular disc of the floor starts to descend. The whole chamber is one giant elevator.

The lift descends three hundred metres into the earth – the distance measured by a running counter on your HUD – before coming to a sudden stop.

You can see two doors in the curved wall at the bottom of the lift shaft. One is big enough to admit a mech, while the other is clearly only intended for human use. The shutters of the mech access remain down, while the smaller door slides open, as if of its own accord.

No one signals you, or attempts to communicate with you in any way, and when you try to open comms, you get back nothing but the hiss of untuned static.

Unable to activate the elevator either, it looks like you have no choice but to disembark from *Ronin 47* and proceed on foot without your mechanised companion.

Releasing your harness restraints, you pop the cockpit hatch and climb down from the mech, using the hand- and foot-holds built into its armoured plating. You also make sure you are armed, just in case.

Passing through the open door, you find yourself in a human-sized passageway, which is as claustrophobic as the cockpit of your mech. But while the mech's HUD at least helps create the illusion of space, by making the outside world appear inside the cockpit, here you are faced with nothing but bare metal walls and another door.

As you approach it, this second door slides open briefly to admit a pair of security drones. Red eye-lights pulse and mechadendrites twitch, while pincer-claws snap open and shut menacingly.

Do you want to make the first move and attack the drone-droids (turn to **122**), or will you remain perfectly still and wait for the security bots to make the first move (turn to **99**)?

Two matte-black mechs suddenly burst from the sea on either side of you, while *Ronin 47*'s proximity alarms remain stubbornly silent. Could they have developed a fault?

Where *Ronin 47* is armed with a single melee weapon, the Ninjas are each armed with a pair of Electro-Wakizashi swords – mech-swords similar in design and function to the standard Electro-Katana, but with a shorter blade and packing slightly less of a punch.

You have no choice but to defend yourself against these Ninja-class mechs but, thanks to your unerring ability to sniff out danger, no matter what or where it might be, you are ready for them. (Go straight to the Close Combat phase in this battle, and fight the mechs at the same time.)

First NINJA-MECH				
SPEED	ARMOUR	MELEE	ARTILLERY	INTEGRITY
5	2	5	2	20

Second NINJA-MECH				
SPEED	ARMOUR	MELEE	ARTILLERY	INTEGRITY
5	2	5	2	18

If you manage to defeat both Ninjas, turn to **19**.

You make it right the way across the minefield without setting off any of the steel spheres.

At the entrance to Tokyo Bay stand two looming gun-towers that are even taller than *Ronin 47*, designed to take down kaiju larger and more heavily-armoured than a Samurai-class mech. But it is a long time since they were last fired and they do not fire now, either.

Finally, you reach what were once the docks, on the outskirts of the ruins of Tokyo, and it is only then that the Cloaking Device gives up the ghost.

Strike the Cloaking Device from your Adventure Sheet and then turn to **370**.

Actuators whining, *Ronin 47* leaps forward, sprinting towards the breached vault.

Take a Speed test. If your mech passes the test, turn to **364**. However, if it fails the test, turn to **252**.

Thick smoke fills the corridor as the lights go out, and blood-red hazard lighting comes on at floor level. The evacuation klaxon starts to sound.

On your feet again, you grab the arm of an administrator who is coughing violently as she stumbles through the smoke. "What is going on?" you demand. She peers at you through unfocused eyes. Blood runs from a cut on her head. Breaking free of your grip, she staggers away from you, still coughing.

Another ground-shaking tremor ripples through the base and huge cracks appear in the concrete walls of the corridor.

Gathering your squad, you set off for Operations again and at a bulkhead door run into an officer who is directing injured and panicked personnel towards the emergency underground bunker.

"What's going on?" you shout over the wail of sirens.

"We're under attack!" he exclaims, as if barely able to believe what he is saying himself.

"Under attack?" you repeat in disbelief. "From whom?"

"Not who – what!" comes his reply. "Kaiju! In unprecedented numbers. More than we've ever seen before!"

"What happened to the early warning system? And what about the defence net?" Both of these measures were put in place precisely so that no kaiju could attack the base directly and certainly not without alerting those inside to the danger they were in.

"The defence net is down!" the officer declares, tears of shock running down his face. "So's the early warning alarm!"

But how can this be?

However, that is a question for another time, preferably when the base isn't under attack. Right now, Ako Base *is* under attack and there are people here who need your help.

You order the rest of Phoenix Squad back to the Samurai hangar, telling them to reactivate their mechs, ready to repel the attacking kaiju. But what about you? What will you do?

If you want to go with your squad, to add *Samurai 47*'s might to the fight, turn to **340**. However, if you want to force your way through to Operations, in case the people there, including Director Asano, need your help, turn to **42**.

241

You perform a long-range sensor scan and, in doing so, risk your enemy pinpointing your location with another rocket attack. There is a lot of interference – although whether that is being caused by the metal frameworks of the ruined buildings or whether it is fallout from whatever devices were detonated here during the desperate weeks after K-Day, you cannot tell – but *Ronin 47*'s Enhanced Scanners do manage to give you an approximate location for your foe.

You set off again, knowing that whatever is firing on you is located somewhere within grid squares I2, I3 and I4.

Turn to **420** to keep exploring Tokyo.

242

Submerging *Ronin 47*, you begin your descent of the almost sheer cliff face before you, as you head towards the seabed.

As the mech's hull-lights play over a fissure in the rugged rock, the 'fissure' suddenly opens, and you find yourself caught in the gaze of an enormous, yellow, reptilian eye.

This is no island! It is a colossal kaiju!

Do you want to attack the beast before it can attack you (turn to **306**), or will you attempt to flee (turn to **272**)?

243

The Sazae-Oni is truly hideous to look upon, but you won't have to for much longer.

SAZAE-ONI				
SPEED	ARMOUR	MELEE	ARTILLERY	INTEGRITY
1	4	2	4	15

If you slay the kaiju-mollusc, you turn your attention to the stricken Daimyo once more – turn to **286**.

244

Under the intense pressure, the hull of the mech starts to buckle and a dozen warning notifications flash up on the HUD between the waves of interference, even as a crack appears right across the middle of the screen, and sparking flashes illuminate the darkness as some electronic system fails.

Roll one die and add 3. Deduct this many *Integrity* points from your mech. (Alternatively, pick a card and deduct its face value from your mech's *Integrity* score, unless it is a 10 or a picture card, in which case deduct 9 points from the Samurai's *Integrity* score; if it is less than 4 you must deduct 4 *Integrity* points.)

If your *Samurai 47* has lost 5-7 *Integrity* points, you must also deduct 1 point from both its *Armour* score and *Melee* score, and add 1 point to the *Reactor* score.

Less than a minute has passed since the kaiju took hold of you and started to drag you towards the bottom of the sea. If you don't act fast, you will die down here, and the mech will become your coffin.

What desperate last-ditch attempt will you make to try to get free of the kaiju before it kills you? Will you:

Deploy Depth Charges (if you have them)?　　　　Turn to **356**.

Deploy Flares (if you have them)?　　　　Turn to **325**.

Try to break free again?　　　　Turn to **275**.

(Cross off one use of the Flares from your Adventure Sheet.)

The flares sink below the waves, blazing furiously as they descend into the stygian gloom. Two of the approaching hagfish-like horrors are startled by the sudden burst of light and literally turn tail and flee for the shelter of the reefs surrounding the island you have just left.

But two still remain and you must deal with them quickly, before their electrical discharges can damage the mech's vulnerable systems.

First IKUCHI

SPEED	ARMOUR	MELEE	ARTILLERY	INTEGRITY
4	1	3	1	10

Second IKUCHI

SPEED	ARMOUR	MELEE	ARTILLERY	INTEGRITY
4	1	3	1	10

If any of the Ikuchi make a successful strike against your mech, roll one die (or pick a card). If the number rolled is odd (or the card is red), determine the amount of damage your mech suffers in the usual way. However, if the number rolled is even (or the card is black), the mutated eel zaps *Ronin 47* with ten thousand volts of electricity, which causes 5 *Integrity* points of damage, regardless of your mech's *Armour* score, and you will have to reduce the mech's *Melee Rating* by 1 point during the next Combat Round, unless the mech is fitted with EMP Shielding, in which case you may ignore this additional damage.

If you kill the kaiju-eels, you set off again – turn to **193**.

The demonic robots open fire with their rocket batteries and missile launchers while you try to close the distance between *Ronin 47* and them as quickly as possible, so that your mech can engage them in close combat-combat. (You must fight the two Oni-mechs at the same time.)

First ONI-MECH				
SPEED	ARMOUR	MELEE	ARTILLERY	INTEGRITY
2	3	2	4	25

Second ONI-MECH				
SPEED	ARMOUR	MELEE	ARTILLERY	INTEGRITY
2	3	2	4	25

If you win the battle with the heavy artillery mechs, turn to **290**.

247

Ronin 47 rises from the sea on a column of oily smoke and incandescent flame.

The islands of Japan form a recognisable pattern below you, appearing on the HUD as they would in an atlas, but one that is relayed in real-time.

The Booster Rocket carries you over the Sagami-nada Sea and, as its fuel supply runs out, you control its descent, coming to land at last, among the shattered skyscrapers and blated ruins of Tokyo.

Cross the Booster Rocket off your Adventure Sheet and turn to **370**.

248

Targeting the approaching sentry mechs, you launch the Hunter-Killer. The missile shoots from its shoulder-mount into the forest. A moment later, it detonates with such force that *Ronin 47* is rocked by the shockwave and the jungle catches fire, a mushroom cloud of roiling smoke rising above the trees.

You may have taken a sledgehammer to crack a nut, but at least your approach was effective; the Ogumo-mechs have been utterly obliterated.

Cross the Hunter-Killer Missile off your Adventure Sheet and then turn to **111**.

The instant you activate the emergency eject, explosive seals around the collar where the mech's head connects to its body blow and the helm is jettisoned. A split second later, the pilot's cockpit is ejected, and a split second after that the core detonates.

Ronin 47 is consumed by a ball of superheated plasma, like a miniature sun, while the silver egg that is the cockpit compartment rockets heavenward, riding on the bow-wave of the reactor's detonation.

Your escape pod describes an arcing parabola across the sky before it starts to descend. As it does so, a parachute is deployed that only slightly slows your fall before the capsule lands in a snowdrift, a hundred metres above the snowline of the dormant volcano.

You can mourn the loss of *Ronin 47* later. For now, the most important thing is that you finish your mission.

You set off through the snow and it is not long before you catch sight of your objective, close to the peak of Mount Fuji. At first you mistake it for an outcropping of black rock, through the wind-blown snow, but then you are able to make out the stacked, sloping, butto-style roofs and you realise that the vast structure is man-made. Facing you is a wall a hundred metres tall, clearly designed to keep both mechs and monsters out. But what about something much smaller, like you?

It does not take you long to find a small grille near the base of the great wall. Unscrewing it, you squeeze through the narrow hole and into the ventilation system of Kira's mountaintop hideout. You wriggle through the narrow crawlspace until you reach another grille, but one that opens into the complex this time.

You freeze as a pair of black-clad soldiers run past. You overhear them say something about an explosion on the slopes of Mount Fuji, not far from the base, and once you are sure they are gone, you force the grille and emerge into a corridor aglow with red hazard lighting.

Turn to **510**.

250

The gas cloud does not remain for long, as it is gradually dispersed by the wind, but what it leaves at its passing is utter devastation.

The three Kani-Oni lie on the rocks, a soupy liquid pouring from every opening in their armour-hard carapaces as their very flesh unravels at a genetic level.

The DNA Bomb worked and far better than you could have hoped!

Strike the DNA Bomb from your Adventure Sheet and then turn to **518**.

251

At such close range, you cannot miss. The Hunter-Killer impacts against the hull of the Oni-mech, and for a moment the demonic war-machine is consumed by a ball of roiling flame and oily smoke.

(Cross the Hunter-Killer Missile off your Adventure Sheet.)

But when the smoke clears, you see that the mech still stands. However, the Hunter-Killer has taken out one of the robot's missile arrays.

Turn to **274** to fight the mech, but before you do so, deduct 1 point from its *Artillery* score and 10 points from its *Integrity* score.

252

Your mech is not quite quick enough, and, as it powers forward, the Wreckers move to block your way. Turn to **43**.

253

The gigantic shark suddenly breaks off from the fight and, as quickly as it appeared, vanishes back into the black depths of the pelagic abyss. Your dogged determination not to be beaten has driven it off.

You turn your attention to the wrecked ship and complete your descent to where it is resting at the edge of the crumbling precipice. Coming alongside the vessel, you can see that the keel of the former aircraft carrier has been torn open in several places, the great gouges in the metal looking like nothing less than huge claw marks. Whatever caused such damage, and sank the *Gojira*, it was something bigger than any other kaiju you've ever encountered, and it certainly can't have been the Isonade. You only hope that whatever it was, the *Gojira*'s doom isn't lurking nearby.

If you want to enter the shipwreck, possibly in the hope of finding out more about what befell it, turn to **277**. If you think you have discovered enough already, turn to **195**.

254

You perform a long-range sensor scan, thereby risking your enemy pinpointing your location with another rocket attack. There is a lot of interference – although whether that is being caused by the metal frameworks of the ruined buildings or whether it is fallout from whatever devices were detonated here during the desperate weeks after K-Day, you cannot tell – but *Ronin 47*'s Enhanced Scanners do manage to give you an approximate location for your foe.

You set off again, knowing that whatever is firing on you is located somewhere within grid squares B9, C9 or D9.

Turn to **420** to keep exploring Tokyo.

The kaiju are pouring into the caldera from the east and south, so you head north, your mech scaling the rocky walls with ease. Reaching the rim of the extinct volcano, *Samurai 47* dives off the top and, three seconds later, lands in the sea one hundred metres below.

But you're not safe even down here, under the waves, in the pelagic embrace of the sea. According to the oscilloscope sonar readings being relayed to you via the HUD, something is moving towards your position at speed. Moments later you see it for yourself, a pallid, serpentine form, spiralling out of the gloom towards you, the boneless limbs that surround its fanged maw splayed wide, ready to catch your mech in their deadly embrace.

It is the same species of kaiju Phoenix Squad battled at Hitode Atoll. Knowing that you cannot outrun the sea-monster, you prepare to fight.

ONI-HITODE				
SPEED	ARMOUR	MELEE	ARTILLERY	INTEGRITY
3	1	3	1	10

If you slay the beast, turn to **284**.

256

You instruct the Spider to maintain the reactor core and carry out any other general repairs to the war-suit. The robot sets to work, while you free yourself from your harness and hunker down in your seat in the hope of getting some rest. And you slowly drift off to sleep...

(Restore the mech's *Melee*, *Artillery* and *Integrity* scores to their current maximum levels, if any of them have been reduced, and deduct 1 point from its *Reactor* score. Also restore 3 *Endurance* points.)

Now turn to **4**.

The Tsuchigumo dead, Kanesada sprints from the bunker entrance across the shattered plaza and boards his Samurai once more before any other overgrown horrors turn up.

"*Rising Sun* detected energy signatures that looked like they could belong to another class of mech when we flew in from the south," your companion's voice comes over the comm. "I would recommend caution."

"But they could be a sign that Kira, or at least his forces, are in the city, which could in turn indicate the path to vengeance," you tell him.

"Then let us split up," Kanesada declares. "We have a better chance of finding them that way."

And so that is what you do.

Make a note that your starting grid square is E5 and then turn to **420.**

For several long seconds you can see nothing through the thick cloud of gas, and then it gradually dissipates, dispersed by the wind.

As it does so, the crab-kaiju are revealed once more. Two of them are lying on their backs, legs twitching feebly as their life ebbs from them, while the third is slumped on the rocks, unmoving, a watery slime dribbling from its mouthparts as its internal organs liquify.

Your DNA Bomb was a success!

Strike the DNA Bomb from your Adventure Sheet and then turn to **518**.

Still eight hundred kilometres from the southern shore of Honshu Island, you find yourself approaching a rugged island, seemingly devoid of plant life, covered with looming, rocky crags.

The mech's warning systems suddenly alert you to the fact that the reactor is in danger of overloading, which could cause it permanent damage.

The Samurai-class of mechs were not designed for prolonged usage, such as you have subjected yours to since the Ako incident. You are torn between resting for a while, so that the reactor might return to its optimal operational level and pursuing your vendetta to its ultimate conclusion.

So, do you want to spend a few hours on the island, giving the reactor core a chance to cool down (turn to **37**), or do you want to press on regardless (turn to **15**)?

260

EMP Shielding will protect your mech from electromagnetic pulses, which can be generated by certain hi-tech weapons but also things like the detonation of a nuclear warhead or a lightning strike.

Now turn back to the section you just came from.

261

You leap out of the way of the falling roof panels, which smash on the floor behind you. Turn to **240**.

The *USS Devastator* appears to enjoy getting the crowd hyped up, as if relishing their adulation. But as *The Art of War* teaches those who are willing to learn, *"If you know yourself but not the enemy, for every victory gained you will also suffer a defeat. If you know neither the enemy nor yourself, you will succumb in every battle."*

You heft *Ronin 47*'s own enormous melee weapon, signalling that you are ready, and then the fight begins. (Cut straight to the Close Combat phase of battle.)

USS DEVASTATOR				
SPEED	ARMOUR	MELEE	ARTILLERY	INTEGRITY
2	4	3	-	30

If you reduce the *Devastator's Integrity* score to 10 points or below, or after 10 Combat Rounds, whichever is sooner, turn to **221**.

As *Ronin 47* approaches the entrance to the Vault, the automated gun turrets activate and swivel to lock on to the advancing mech.

Remaining calm, you transmit the necessary protocols and pass codes that identify you as a friend rather than a foe.

The guns deactivate again and the doors to the underground bunker grind open.

Turn to **236**.

Even as you select the Hunter-Killer on the weapons interface screen, something bursts from the sea to either side of you, while the mech's proximity alarms remain worryingly silent.

Take an Agility test. If you pass the test, turn to **234**. If you fail the test, turn to **204**.

265

The mech's targeting systems lock onto to one of the Ikuchi and the Hunter-Killer blasts from its shoulder-mount. The missile torpedoes through the water and strikes the writhing eel, obliterating it utterly. (Strike the Hunter-Killer Missile from your Adventure Sheet; you cannot use it again.)

But three of the monsters still remain.

First IKUCHI				
SPEED	ARMOUR	MELEE	ARTILLERY	INTEGRITY
4	1	3	1	10

Second IKUCHI				
SPEED	ARMOUR	MELEE	ARTILLERY	INTEGRITY
4	1	3	1	8

Third IKUCHI				
SPEED	ARMOUR	MELEE	ARTILLERY	INTEGRITY
4	1	3	1	10

If any of the Ikuchi make a successful strike against your mech, roll one die (or pick a card). If the number rolled is odd (or the card is red), determine the amount of damage your mech suffers in the usual way. However, if the number rolled is even (or the card is black), the mutated eel zaps *Ronin 47* with ten thousand volts of electricity, which causes 5 *Integrity* points of damage, regardless of your mech's *Armour* score, and you will have to reduce the mech's *Melee Rating* by 1 point during the next Combat Round, unless the mech is fitted with EMP Shielding, in which case you may ignore this additional damage.

If you kill the kaiju-eels, you set off again – turn to **193**.

266

You enter a plaza park where the residents of Tokyo once exercised and socialised. The only sign now that any human ever set foot here are a few bones picked clean of flesh by scavengers.

Turn to **115**.

267

Climbing out onto one of the largest reefs, you put the mech into standby mode.

If you have an active Spider repair droid and want to instruct it to make repairs to *Ronin 47,* turn to **299**. If not, or you do not want to deploy it at this time, turn to **354**.

268

Glass and concrete crunch beneath *Ronin 47*'s heavy footfalls, as, no doubt, do the bones of the forgotten and unburied dead. Turn to **435**.

269

As your mech strides through the undergrowth, toppling entire trees that are in its path, the ground begins to rise steeply. You cross a stream and scramble up a bank of loose scree, and it is then the mech's scanners detect something approaching through the forest.

It is almost on top of you, so you are going to have to act fast. Will you:

Broadcast codes identifying yourself as an ally and not an enemy?	Turn to **289**.
Bring *Ronin 47*'s weapons online and prepare for battle?	Turn to **313**.

Striding back into the sea, until the continental shelf drops away beneath it and the robot is forced to assume its torpedo-like posture, *Ronin 47* resumes its submarine journey through the Pacific Ocean, heading north.

Roll one die (or pick a card). If the number rolled is odd (or the card is red), turn to **168**. If the number (rolled) is even (or the card is black), turn to **193**.

The EMP is just as effective against *Ronin 47*'s systems and Combat AI as it is against the other mechs. Unable to make it move, or even exit the giant robot now, there is nothing you can do as a veritable army of black-clad warriors pours down the side of the mountain, riding snowmobiles and light all-terrain vehicles.

Kira's private army topples the colossal mech and then sets to work with industrial cutting tools. Sooner rather than later, the troopers will cut their way into *Ronin 47,* and they won't lay their tools aside when they find you.

Your adventure ends here, on the slopes of Mount Fuji.

THE END

You have never encountered a kaiju as big as this one before! Trying not to panic, you increase power to the mech's thrusters with the intention of getting away from the gigantic, strange beast as fast as you can. Turn to **315**.

The Sagami-nada Sea is littered with intelligent mines, while the approach to Tokyo Bay is protected from kaiju attacks by sentry gun-towers. You doubt the latter are still functioning, since the city was last overrun years ago, but you cannot be so sure about the minefield.

Indeed, as you approach Honshu's southern coast, your scanners reveal that the sentient minefield is still in place, and at least some, if not all, of the AI-controlled floating bombs are operational.

How do you intend to negotiate the minefield and make it safely to shore? Will you:

Activate a Booster Rocket (if *Ronin 47* is fitted with one)?	Turn to **247**.
Fire up your mech's jump-jets (if you still can)?	Turn to **217**.
Launch a Hunter-Killer Missile (if you can)?	Turn to **190**.
Subject the minefield to an artillery barrage?	Turn to **146**.
Proceed with caution?	Turn to **107**.

274

Hoping that what *Ronin 47* lacks in artillery abilities, compared to the Oni-mech, will be more than compensated for by its greater speed, manoeuvrability, and capacity for close combat, you engage the demonic giant in battle.

ONI-MECH				
SPEED	ARMOUR	MELEE	ARTILLERY	INTEGRITY
2	3	2	4	25

If *Ronin 47* is still standing after 8 Combat Rounds, or if you reduce the Oni-mech's *Integrity* score to 15 points or fewer, whichever is sooner, turn to **375**.

275

It is as if you and *Samurai 47* are one. Straining your carbon fibre muscle bundles, you fight to be free of the kaiju's constricting hold.

Take a Combat test. If you pass the test, turn to **61**; if you fail the test, turn to **295**.

You are taken by surprise when you suddenly come face to face with someone you recognise. It is Dr Kitsune, Ako Base's Head of Kaiju Research!

As if that wasn't startling enough, her companions cause you to stumble to a halt in shock. One is following at her heels, like a faithful hound, only it looks nothing like any dog you've ever seen. It appears to be a cross between a salamander and a crocodile, while its grotesquely deformed head is part chameleon and part toad.

Even worse is the creature that is hovering in the air beside the doctor. Held aloft by fast-moving beetle wings, its body is that of a shrivelled monkey, but its head looks like an octopus, complete with dangling, rubbery, boneless limbs.

"Kitsune!" a voice suddenly crackles over the comm she is holding in one hand. Your pulse starts to race when you realise it is the traitor Kira you can hear speaking. "Do you have it?"

"I have it and am on my way back," Dr Kitsune replies. "I just have some loose ends I need to tie up here first."

If you ever had any doubts that Dr Kitsune was in league with the traitor Kira, they are dispelled now!

"I can't let you leave," you tell her, your grip tightening around the hilt of your katana.

"Is that so, Commander Oishi?" she challenges, a cruel smile twisting her lips. "Well, we'll just have to see what my pets have to say about that."

Kitsune gives a shrill whistle and the two hybrid monstrosities attack, while their mistress makes her escape.

If you have a Sonic Emitter and want to use it now, turn to **165**. If not, turn to **199**.

Because the aircraft carrier is lying on its side, the access port in the bottom of its keel – from where submersible vehicles could be easily deployed – is not only visible but accessible.

However, as you soon discover, while the flooded dock is big enough to accommodate your mech, *Ronin 47* is far too big to progress any further and enter the hold of the ship.

You are either going to have to exit the mech, in order to enter the sunken wreck (turn to **451**), try to force a way in (turn to **308**), or give up on this whole enterprise and abandon the *Gojira* here, on the seabed (turn to **8**).

278

Halfway across the minefield, believing that crossing the Sagami-nada minefield is an easier task than you had at first thought, you start to increase the mech's striding speed. But this has the effect of creating a greater wash, behind the mech as it advances, which sends waves rippling out across the sea in all directions.

It is almost inevitable that at some point these disturbed currents will send one of the mines into your path. When it does, it detonates with such force that it damages the Cloaking Device, which promptly shuts down.

(Deduct 8 *Integrity* points and 1 *Speed* point, and strike the Cloaking Device from your Adventure Sheet.)

If your mech is still operational, turn to **548**.

279

You have heard rumours that people still live here, amidst the ruins of their former home, but you see no one on the streets as you stride between the shattered apartment buildings.

Roll one die (or pick a card). If the number rolled is odd (or the card is red), turn to **420**. If the number (rolled) is even (or the card is black), turn to **115**.

280

A split-second after you activate the device, a pulse of electromagnetic energy sweeps through the gladiatorial arena, with *Ronin 47* at its epicentre.

Volos and the Wrecker-mechs become wreathed in ribbons of crackling corposant and contort as if in physical pain. Then, one by one, they shutdown, as their electrical systems are overwhelmed.

(Cross the EMP Device off your Adventure Sheet; you will not be able to use it again.)

If *Ronin 47* is fitted with EMP Shielding, turn to **441**. If not, turn to **478**.

281

You try to throw yourself out of the way, but your reactions are not quite fast enough – no doubt you are fatigued after your battle with the kaiju at Hitode Atoll.

Roll one die and add 1. Deduct this many *Endurance* points. (Alternatively, pick a card and deduct its face value from your *Endurance* score, unless it is 8 or above or a picture card, in which case deduct 7 points from your *Endurance* score.)

If you lose 4 *Endurance* points or more, also deduct 1 *Combat* point and 1 *Agility* point.

Now turn to **240**.

282

Despite the repairs you saw the American war-machine undergoing in the holding hangar, it is quite clear that the servos in its right leg are still malfunctioning. You can use that knowledge to your advantage in the battle to come. For as *The Art of War* states, *"If you know the enemy and know yourself, you need not fear the result of a hundred battles."*

For the duration of the battle to come, you may add a temporary 1 point bonus to your mech's *Speed* and *Melee* scores.

Turn to **262**.

283

You find yourself at an intersection, but which way will you go now – north, east, or west?

As you are pondering the best way to go, turn to **545**.

The bifurcated body of the kaiju sinks into the darkness, as you pilot your mech away from Tokugawa Island, intending to put as much distance as possible between you and Ako Base – and, more importantly, the kaiju attacking it.

Almost 500 kilometres later, the Samurai's sensors tell you that you are approaching a small island and you decide to make land there, so that you can more accurately assess your Samurai's status.

So it is that *Samurai 47* strides from the waves onto a pebbly beach before making the ascent to a flattened plateau close to the island's summit.

Turn to **337**.

Even as the head of the mech is jettisoned, in readiness for the cockpit compartment to be ejected, the core detonates, and *Ronin 47* vanishes in a ball of superheated plasma half a kilometre wide.

You and your faithful mech are utterly obliterated, down to your component atoms. Your adventure is over.

THE END

According to scans carried out by your mech's own AI, the reason the Daimyo fell was because one of the electro-waisaki blades wielded by the Ninjas penetrated the cockpit, killing the pilot. There is actually little wrong with the war-suit itself, although you suspect feedback from the pilot's death, via the pilot-mech interface, could have scrambled the mech's machine-mind. You certainly won't be swapping your loyal *Ronin 47* for the Daimyo war-suit.

However, the titanic war-machine has been kitted out with two experimental weapons, the likes of which you have only heard rumours about, having never actually seen them for yourself before.

The first is an impressive, shoulder-mounted gun that has been given the designation 'Raijin Cannon,' and that is clearly an energy projectile weapon of some kind. Your Combat AI's scans reveal the second device to be an Electromagnetic Pulse Device.

What is a Honjo mech doing with such weapons? Was the Daimyo-mech carrying out an experimental weapons test before it was ambushed? But what is most concerning is why were your allies developing weapons that are clearly intended for killing other mechs and not kaiju? What was Honjo Base planning?

Which piece of equipment do you want to try to salvage from the Daimyo-mech?

The Raijin Lightning Cannon?   Turn to **320**.

The EMP Device?   Turn to **347**.

287

As you explore the devastated city, you wonder when the final evacuation of Tokyo was ordered and how many made it out alive. Turn to **335**.

288

The entrance to Tokyo Bay is guarded by a pair of monolithic sentinels – great gun-towers that are taller than *Ronin 47* by a good ten metres and bristling with high calibre cannons and energy weapons. This is hardly surprising, since they were intended to repel kaiju that are taller and more heavily-armoured than a Samurai-class mech.

Despite your speculation – or maybe even your hope – that the decades-old guardians would no longer be operational, as you come within range, their drooping gun turrets rise and fix on you. Whatever you intend to do to get past Tokyo's ancient defences, you are going to have to act fast.

Will you:

Activate a Cloaking Device (if you can)?   Turn to **505**.

Broadcast a signal stating that *Ronin 47*
is not a viable target?   Turn to **129**.

Launch a Hunter-Killer Missile at one
of the towers (if you can)?   Turn to **329**.

Trigger an EMP Device (if you have one)?	Turn to **487**.
Deploy Flares (if you can)?	Turn to **396**.
Deploy Drones (if you can)?	Turn to **418**.
Fire up the mech's jump-jets (if you still can)?	Turn to **439**.
Fire up a Booster Rocket (if you can)?	Turn to **464**.

289

If you have the code word *Connected* recorded on your Adventure Sheet, turn to **450**. If not, turn to **336**.

290

If you have the code word *Triggered* recorded on your Adventure Sheet, turn to **227**. If not, turn to **406.**

291

The pavements and streets of Tokyo were once teeming with people and jammed with traffic. But now there is only you and *Ronin 47*, or so it would seem. Turn to **420**.

292

Four of the fiends are closing on you and so it's time to defend yourself from the monstrously mutated eels. (Fight the Ikuchi two at a time.)

First IKUCHI				
SPEED	ARMOUR	MELEE	ARTILLERY	INTEGRITY
4	1	3	1	10

Second IKUCHI				
SPEED	ARMOUR	MELEE	ARTILLERY	INTEGRITY
4	1	3	1	8

Third IKUCHI				
SPEED	ARMOUR	MELEE	ARTILLERY	INTEGRITY
4	1	3	1	10

Fourth IKUCHI				
SPEED	ARMOUR	MELEE	ARTILLERY	INTEGRITY
4	1	3	1	8

If any of the Ikuchi make a successful strike against your mech, roll one die (or pick a card). If the number rolled is odd (or the card is red), determine the amount of damage your mech suffers in the usual way. However, if the number rolled is even (or the card is black), the mutated eel zaps *Ronin 47* with ten thousand volts of electricity, which causes 5 *Integrity* points of damage, regardless of your mech's *Armour* score, and you will have to reduce the mech's *Melee Rating* by 1 point during the next Combat Round, unless the mech is fitted with EMP Shielding, in which case you may ignore this additional damage.

If you kill the kaiju-eels, you set off again – turn to **193**.

293

The Hunter-Killer impacts against the hull of one of the Ninjas and detonates. A split second later the mech itself implodes. (Cross off the Hunter-Killer Missile from your Adventure Sheet.)

With only one Ninja left standing, the odds are definitely in *Ronin 47*'s favour.

NINJA-MECH				
SPEED	ARMOUR	MELEE	ARTILLERY	INTEGRITY
5	2	5	2	13

If you defeat the mech, turn to **75**.

It is just as you are pulling up information on the HUD – a combination of information from the Combat AI's data-banks, the map downloaded from the Tengu Array, and the mech's own real-time scans – that, ever a student of Sun Tzu's *The Art of War*, a part of your mind realises that this spot would make the perfect place for an ambush.

It is then that you sense something, not via the mech's scanners, but some sixth sense that suddenly has you reaching for *Ronin 47*'s haptic weapon controls and firing up the colossal war-machine's weapons.

If you have a Hunter-Killer Missile and want to launch now, turn to **264**. If not, turn to **237**.

It is no good. If you could not break free of the monster before, with the Samurai's systems already starting to fail, you have no chance now.

As the devil-starfish heads ever deeper into the fathomless abyssal trench, the war-machine's superstructure is crushed like an oil drum under a mech's foot.

And as the integrity of the hull gives way, so your body is suddenly exposed to the impossible pressures of the abyss and is turned into a pulverised soup before you can drown.

Your adventure, like your life, is over.

THE END

It is eerily quiet as you navigate the ruins and shattered highways of Tokyo. Turn to **545**.

Soon all that is left of the entrance to the bunker is a smoking hole surrounded by chunks of red-hot, deformed metal.

Add 1 to the mech's *Reactor* score and then turn to **236**.

You are mere metres from the airlock when the sub begins to pull away and freezing seawater immediately starts to pour into the passageway. You are knocked off your feet and dragged along by the surging tide as it sweeps through the complex. As the aqualung kicks in, supplying you with oxygen, you are glad you had the foresight to put on your helmet before entering Yokai Base.

But then you become aware of something in the water with you. The flickering lights of the flooded corridor reveal a predatory shadow gliding through the water towards you. You get the impression of a form that is somehow like that of an amalgam of an octopus, a dragon, and a human being.

But you don't need to know what it is to kill it, only your katana. (In this battle you have the initiative.)

AKACHAN KUTOURUFU   COMBAT 8   ENDURANCE 9

If the battle lasts for more Combat Rounds than your current *Endurance* score, turn to **163**. If you manage to defeat the monster in fewer Combat Rounds, turn to **5**.

299

Via the central control panel, you programme the Spider to maintain the reactor core and carry out any other general repairs to the war-suit. The robot sets to work, while you try to make yourself comfortable in the pilot's seat in the hope of getting some rest. Slowly, you drift off to sleep...

(Restore the mech's *Melee*, *Artillery* and *Integrity* scores to their current maximum levels, if any of them have been reduced, and deduct 1 point from its *Reactor* score. Also restore 3 *Endurance* points, and tick off one use of the Spider droid.)

Now turn to **354**.

300

As a graphic on the HUD shows the temperature inside the core rising, you briefly consider ejecting, in the hope you might actually be able to save yourself, but then you think better of it.

Bathed in the bronze glow of the screens in front of you, your expression is serene as you consider Sun Tzu's *The Art of War* once more: *"He will win who knows when to fight and when not to fight."*

You have avenged the deaths of Director Asano and your companions, but in doing so you have sacrificed your own life. There can be no more worthy warrior's death.

Your adventure is over.

THE END

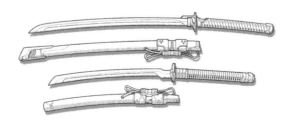

301

You activate the device, sending a pulse of electromagnetic energy rippling out across the ruined city, with *Ronin 47* at its epicentre.

(Cross the EMP Device off your Adventure Sheet; you will not be able to use it again.)

If *Ronin 47* is fitted with EMP Shielding, turn to **359**. If not, turn to **327**.

302

Your plan worked! The parasitic worms have been purged from the mech. As their bodies shrivel up, they unclog *Ronin 47*'s systems and mechanical joints, and within another thirty minutes you are on your way again. Turn to **273**.

303

Thankfully, you manage to roll the torpedo off your legs, freeing yourself, and only just in time.

As you swim back to *Ronin 47* and climb on board again, the crumbling cliff gives way at last, consigning the wreck of the *Gojira* to the pelagic abyss.

Turn to **8**.

304

You wait for several tense seconds, and then see two of the creature's long legs emerge from the cloud, soon followed by the rest of its arachnoid body. The DNA Bomb that you went to so much trouble to acquire has had no effect on the Tsuchigumo whatsoever, leaving you with no option but to defend yourself against its predatory attack. Turn to **205**.

305

If you have the code word *Weakened* recorded on your Adventure Sheet, turn to **361**. If not, turn to **475**.

In response to your attack, the kaiju comes to full alertness, and rises from the ocean, seawater cascading from the bony-ridges covering its grey-mottled hide, and that you mistook for rocky crags.

In Japanese mythology, Ryujin is the dragon god of the sea and storms. You feel as if you are facing it in the flesh. It stands before you now on its colossal hindlegs, the weight of its great reptilian head balanced by its broad tail.

Opening its jaws wide, it gives voice to a roar that seems to shake the very sky, as thick thunderheads, the colour of blacksmiths' anvils, roll in overhead, splitting the atmosphere with jagged bolts of lightning.

Three times as tall as *Ronin 47*, it is truly colossal – a Daikaiju, a giant of its kind! But you have committed yourself to battle now and can only hope your mech is powerful enough to make such a heroic stand against the gargantuan lizard-beast.

(Remember to deduct any *Integrity* points' damage you may have already caused the monster.)

DAIKAIJU				
SPEED	ARMOUR	MELEE	ARTILLERY	INTEGRITY
2	4	5	2	50

If you are still alive after 6 Combat Rounds, or if you manage to lower the monster's *Integrity* score to 20 points or below, whichever is sooner, turn to **486** at once.

Hoping that the two kaiju are too focused on fighting each other to worry about what a lone mech is doing out here in the ocean, you plot a course to avoid the battlezone.

How do you want to get away? Do you want to activate your mech's jump-jets (turn to **587**), fire up a Booster Rocket, if *Ronin 47* is equipped with one (turn to **330**), or simply 'swim' away (turn to **363**)?

308

How do you want to try to open up the ship so that you can explore it whilst still inside the protective Samurai war-suit?

If you want to use the mech's melee weapons, turn to **385**. If you want to bombard the vessel with your artillery weapons, turn to **322**.

309

The Ninjas must be equipped with some kind of 'ghostware' stealth tech, which is why *Ronin 47*'s systems were blind to their presence. But now that they have revealed themselves, you no longer need the automated weapons' systems to be able to target them when you can use the haptic controls to battle them in hand-to-hand combat.

First NINJA-MECH				
SPEED	ARMOUR	MELEE	ARTILLERY	INTEGRITY
5	2	5	2	15

Second NINJA-MECH				
SPEED	ARMOUR	MELEE	ARTILLERY	INTEGRITY
5	2	5	2	13

If you manage to defeat both of the Ninja-mechs, turn to **75**.

The Depth Charges that Mototoki has stored within the Vault are just the same as those stockpiled at Ako Base and serve exactly the same function – to be dropped into the water in the vicinity of a submerged kaiju, then detonating and subjecting the target to a powerful and destructive hydraulic shock. Selecting this upgrade will give you 3 uses of Depth Charges.

You may select this upgrade whether your mech is already equipped with Depth Charges or not.

Now turn back to the section you just came from.

Your Samurai's uplink down, and unable to communicate with anybody, you spend the return journey to Tokugawa Island and Ako Base alone with your thoughts, wondering over and over whether there was anything you could have done differently during your mission to Hitode Atoll so that Norikane did not end up meeting his death there.

****

An hour later, the landing bay of Ako Base opens like an orchid and *Tatsu 7* touches down inside before disgorging its payload. You and the other Samurai of Phoenix Squad make your way to Hangar 5, parking the mechs in their repair cradles before all disembarking. While the titanic battle-suits remain deactivated, Spider-class maintenance droids will effect repairs as specified by the mechs' computer-minds.

Taking your katana from its seat scabbard, you secure it to your belt before exiting the cockpit of your mech. As you climb down from *Samurai 47* you are met by Kanehide, who informs you rather curtly that Director Asano wishes to see Phoenix Squad immediately in the Central Operations control room.

Taking a deep breath, you lead the way, heading in the direction of the command hub of Ako Base. The Director has no doubt already heard of the loss of Norikane and *Samurai 39* and will be expecting a full debrief. The mechs are a precious resource and cannot be easily replaced. You will need to explain not just the loss of a fellow warrior but that of his battle-suit as well.

Leaving the Samurai hangar, you pass the great vaulted spaces where the Oni-class mechs – lumbering, heavily-armoured machines, packing some serious heavy artillery – and the Ninja-class robots – smaller, nimble war-suits, favoured for their close combat capabilities – are contained.

The final hangar you pass through is the largest within the facility and houses the newest war-machine that has yet to be tested in the field – the mighty, prototype Shogun-class mech. Combining the close combat capabilities of a Ninja with the heavy ordnance of an Oni, it is half as tall again as a Samurai and outclasses the older machines in every way. With its black paintjob, and standing thirty metres tall, surrounded by service gantries, it is a truly intimidating machine, the red glow in the eye-slit of its cockpit window only adding to its malevolent appearance.

****

You are following the bustling central spinal thoroughfare that will take you to base command when an earthquake strikes Ako Base. At least that's what it feels like.

You are thrown to the ground, along with the rest of the pilot-warriors under your command, as walls crack and electricity power conduits spark. Administrative staff cry out in shock and fear.

As you pick yourself up, an explosion rocks the corridor and, with a heavy groan, part of the ceiling comes down.

Take an Agility test. If you pass the test, turn to 261. If you fail the test, turn to **281**.

312

Kira has a head-start on you, and you are weary following your arduous journey to get here. Nonetheless, you set off after him regardless, following the echo of his fleeing footsteps down corridors, across passageway intersections, and along a grilled walkway suspended over what you realise is a fully automated production line, which is already working to replicate the stolen Shogun-mech many times over. You count at least ten of the titanic robot war-machines already in production.

This momentary distraction slows your progress, and a breathless Kira disappears through a door at the other end of the colossal factory space. Reaching the door yourself at last, you are relieved when it slides open, and you enter another corridor. But you are less pleased to discover what awaits you there.

Roll one die (or pick a card). If the number rolled is odd (or the card is red), turn to **346**. If the number rolled is even (or the card is black), turn to **415**.

313

If Deputy Director Kira's betrayal has taught you anything, it is to trust no one. Fearing the worst, but hoping you will soon be proved wrong, you prime the mech's weapons as the foliage ahead of you starts to shake and shiver. Something is closing on your position at speed.

Turn to **159**.

314

You fire the Booster Rocket but, as your mech slowly starts to lift off, the Shogun grabs hold of it in a titanic bearhug. The engine burns fuel rapidly, as it attempts to compensate and provide enough lift for the additional weight.

Ronin 47 clears the top of the gantry but then starts to lose height again. As it drops past the boarding platform, the Shogun lets go, grabbing hold of the superstructure of its landing pad to save itself. Unable to arrest your fall, now that the booster has used up all its fuel, and with not enough time for your mech's jump-jets to save you, *Ronin 47* splashes down in the seething fissure that is rapidly collapsing the crater floor, throwing up great spumes of molten rock before being swallowed by the hungry magma.

Your adventure is over.

THE END

It rises then from the ocean, an island no longer, seawater pouring off its scales and the bony plates covering its grey-mottled hide that you mistook for rocky crags.

In ancient Japanese mythology, Ryujin is the dragon god of the sea and storms. You feel as if you are standing before it now! It is supported by a pair of colossal hindlegs, the weight of its great reptilian head balanced by its broad tail.

Opening its jaws wide, it gives voice to a roar that seems to shake the very sky, as thick thunderheads, the colour of blacksmiths' anvils, roll in overhead, splitting the atmosphere with jagged bolts of lightning.

Roll one die (or pick a card). If the number rolled is odd (or the card is red), turn to **345**. If the number (rolled) is even (or the card is black), turn to **367**.

In the company of ten armed guards, you are led through a maze of narrow metal tunnels, past what you realise are other holding cells, as well as up and down staircases that double-back on themselves, until you and your armed escort enter a huge hangar that you realise must be on the other side of the arena-vault.

There you find half a dozen pilotless mechs, including your own, forlorn-looking, *Ronin 47.* By the sparking light of welding torches, you can see that the American mech is undergoing vital repairs, while the Korean robot hangs lifelessly from a jerry-rigged support cradle. But there are also three other machines.

You recognise a great, red robot as being a Russian Boyar-class heavy artillery machine, while there is also a four-armed Guan Yu-class mech of Chinese origin. It is sporting the latest in mimetic cloaking tech – that literally takes the form of a cloak comprised of polychromatic graphene scales – and is armed with a Guan-Dao Polearm, as befitting its famous namesake.

The last mech you can see appears to be another Samurai-class robot, but one with a red sun-disc motif painted on its white hull. It bears no number or other obvious classification marks.

"Get in!" the lead guard says, pointing at *Ronin 47's* open cockpit hatch.

As you scale the exterior of your mech, by means of the recessed rungs set into its hull, you consider taking out your escort as soon as you are inside. But then you spot the Wreckers' own spiky, beetle-like mechs lurking in the corners of the hangar. They would be on you in seconds.

You will just have to bide your time and have your revenge when the opportunity presents itself. You know what the Wreckers expect you to do. They expect you to fight, and fighting is something you are good at.

It feels reassuring to take your place inside *Ronin 47*'s cockpit once more, but that feeling soon passes as you attempt to interface with the mech's Combat AI. There is clearly something wrong, as if something is suppressing the CPU. On top of that, no matter what you try, you cannot bring the mech's artillery weapons online; only its melee weapons appear to be active.

The lighting within the cockpit is subdued and the HUD-projected image on the screen is awash with static interference.

The doors to the great arena grind open and you follow a track of lights in the floor into the gladiatorial chamber. Murmurs of excitement pass among the onlookers and then a great cheer rises from them as the American joins you.

The klaxon sounds for the battle to begin, and the *Devastator* assumes a familiar fighting stance, looking like a heavyweight boxer compared to your own mech's more refined form.

If you have the code word *Forewarned* recorded on your Adventure Sheet, turn to **282**. If not, turn to **262.**

317

A klaxon starts to wail inside the cockpit of the mech, which becomes bathed in a ruddy light. The reactor is overloading and has passed the point of no return. You have no hope of reversing the meltdown of the core, so the only thing you can do is try to escape before it is too late.

You make a grab for the emergency eject under your seat and pull hard on the handle, but have you done so quickly enough?

Take an Agility test. If you pass the test, turn to **249**. If you fail the test, turn to **285.**

318

The mech courses through the waves, just below the surface like a submarine, as you pilot it out of the path of the steadily worsening typhoon.

As the great bank of swirling cloud vanishes into the distance behind you, you come upon a series of half-submerged reefs, where the seabed is shallower, and bring *Ronin 47* to a stop to reassess the best way to go, now that the cyclone is no longer a threat to you.

Take a Combat test. If you pass the test, turn to **294**. If you fail the test, turn to **46**.

319

The rusted iron walls reverberate with the cheers of the prisoners and the desperate shouts of their captors, as the last of the Wrecker-mechs falls, the Russian giant *Volos* having made sure that the other two won't be bothering anyone ever again.

Now to find a way out of this place, wherever – and whatever – it is.

Focusing *Ronin 47*'s firepower on one wall, you are rewarded when daylight suddenly bursts into the chamber in the aftermath of your attack. Approaching the great rent you have made, you peer through it and find yourself gazing out across a collection of abandoned ships, actually within the Great Pacific Garbage Patch itself. You have been kept prisoner in the belly of an ancient supertanker!

Before you exit the hold, ready to resume your journey, you offer a final parting shot, taking out the wall to the holding cells that looks over the arena. You will let your fellow hostages take their revenge against the Wrecker pirates. You have your own quest for revenge to complete!

(Record the code word *Allied* on your Adventure Sheet.)

Tokyo lies 500 clicks roughly northwest of your current position, but how do you want to travel there?

If *Ronin 47* is equipped with a Booster Rocket, and you want to use it to reach Honshu Island, turn to **60**. If not, or you would prefer not to use the Booster Rocket at this time, you have no choice but to travel by sea – turn to **566**.

It is easy to detach the energy weapon from the Daimyo's shoulder mounting – partly because its shoulder mount was damaged during the giant mech's battle with the Ninjas – but *Ronin 47* will not be able to make use of it unless you can plug it into your mech's targeting systems and power supply. Such a thing would be a straightforward matter in a fully equipped Guardian hangar – with cranes, and lifting equipment, and robotic tools – but alone, hundreds of kilometres from the nearest refit facility, without a team of technicians and engineers to aid you, it will be a nigh impossible task.

If you have a fully-charged Spider repair droid stowed away on board *Ronin 47*, turn to **372**. If not, turn to **392**.

You cannot let the presence of the kaiju stop you from carrying out your mission, and so, as the monsters continue to pour into the crater and swarm over Kira's mountaintop hideaway, you take the fight to the Shogun-class mech.

But what method of attack do you want to use?

Fire a salvo of Flares (if you can)?	Turn to **352**.
Launch a flight of Drones (if you can)?	Turn to **381**.
Target the Shogun with a Hunter-Killer Missile (if you have one)?	Turn to **408**.
Trigger an EMP Device (if you have one)?	Turn to **495**.
Engage your nemesis in close combat?	Turn to **446**.

Exiting the flooded dock, dropping below the edge of the precipice, you open up with a fusillade of rockets. They spiral upwards through the water, trailing bubbles, before hitting the hull, a series of bulbous explosions blossoming in the water.

But the shockwaves produced by your bombardment weakens the cliff edge upon which the *Gojira* is lying. Sand and rock cascade into the abyssal void and then the shipwreck starts to move too. And you are right underneath it.

Take a Speed test. If you pass the test, turn to **365**. However, it you fail the test, turn to **342**.

Your reprieve lasts for only a second before everything goes black again. This time the lights do not come back on.

Your overloading of the mech's systems might have succeeded in ridding the robot of its infestation of parasites, but the power surge has also induced a total shutdown. Usually, it would be easy to remedy such a situation; someone, probably an engineer at Ako Base, would simply reboot it by throwing the switch in the mech's maintenance cradle. But with the power off, all hatches remain locked, and the war-machine's life support systems will be offline too.

Ronin 47 has become your tomb. All that awaits you is a slow death by suffocation, or a swift one by means of seppuku and a katana to the belly. The choice is yours but, whatever you choose, your adventure is over.

THE END

The longer you wander the streets of the city, the more uneasy you become.

Deduct 1 *Combat* point and turn to **420**.

Not knowing what else to do, you launch a salvo of flares into the abyss. (Cross off one use of the Flares from your Adventure Sheet.)

The worm-like creature that is wrapped around your mech suddenly releases its hold on *Samurai 47* and spirals away into the gloom, no doubt driven off by the sudden blinding light of the burning flares. But you are not out of danger yet.

Turn to **376**.

From somewhere comes the sound of gunshots, followed by a cry, and then silence. Life amidst the ruins of Tokyo is harsh, and often all too suddenly cut short.

Turn to **420**.

The EMP weapon is as devastatingly effective against *Ronin 47*'s systems and Combat AI as it is against the Oni-mech. Both giant robots are effectively dead in the water.

However, as you fight to reboot *Ronin 47*, a second Oni-class heavy ordnance mech trudges into view at the other end of the street. There is nothing you can do to defend yourself as the mech-killer opens up with everything it has, and *Ronin 47* is blown to kingdom come.

Your adventure, like your life, is over.

THE END

You manage to force the gates open a crack, but it is enough to get the mech's fingers into and then, carbon-fibres muscle bundles straining, *Ronin 47* forces the door to the underground bunker open. Turn to **236**.

The Hunter-Killer streaks from its shoulder-mounted launcher towards the left-hand tower.

If *Ronin 47* has Enhanced Targeting, turn to **358**. If not, roll one die (or pick a card); if the number rolled is odd (or the card is red), turn to **374**, but if the number rolled is even (or the card is black), turn to **358**.

With a subsonic roar, *Ronin 47* blasts into the sky, carrying you clear of the mega-kaiju smackdown.

As you climb higher, and the curvature of the Earth reveals more and more, you soon make out the islands of Japan in the distance.

However, while the Booster Rocket is far more effective than the mech's built-in jump-jets, it is still not designed to turn *Ronin 47* into a plane, and it doesn't have the range to carry you all the way to mainland Japan. On top of that, it is strictly one use only. (Strike the Booster Rocket from your Adventure Sheet; you may not use it again.)

As the rocket rapidly burns through its fuel supply, you realise you are going to have to find somewhere to land. Consulting a combination of the battle-computer's memory banks, the map downloaded from the Tengu Array, and the mech's own scanners, you isolate two suitable locations that are within range.

One – Yokai Base – lies to the west and is a top-secret scientific research facility. The other is a distress signal being broadcast from a point east of your current position. So which way do you want to go?

East?   Turn to **27**.

West?   Turn to **513**.

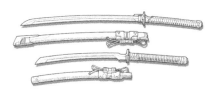

331

It is no good – you simply do not have the strength to extricate yourself.

Moments later, the crumbling cliff finally gives way, consigning the wreck of the *Gojira* to the pelagic abyss, with you still trapped on board.

Your adventure is over.

THE END

332

The wet footprints become less and less distinct until they peter out altogether at a T-junction. To both left and right the corridor ends at a door. Which way do you want to go?

Left?   Turn to **189**.

Right?   Turn to **547**.

333

You are at the intersection of a six-lane highway. But the only vehicles clogging the street now are the crushed and blackened cars that were abandoned the day Tokyo came under attack from the kaiju. Turn to **545**.

334

You press on into the night, skirting the reefs and heading in the direction of a rocky outcrop that lies en route to the Japanese islands.

However, Samurai-class mechs were not designed for prolonged missions, such as the one you have undertaken, and *Ronin 47*'s reactor is in danger of overloading as a result.

(Add 1 point to your mech's *Reactor* score.)

If your mech has Enhanced Scanners, turn to **581**. If not, turn to **555**.

You can't help noticing that the ruins in this district of the city appear to be covered by what looks like cobwebs, but cobwebs of gargantuan proportions.

If you have the code word *Exterminated* recorded on your Adventure Sheet, turn to **582**. If you have the code word *Bugged* written down, turn to **58**. If you have picked up neither code word, turn to **25**.

Ronin 47's uplink is still damaged and so you cannot transmit anything to anybody. Unable to broadcast the necessary codes and protocols that would identify you as an ally rather than an enemy, you are forced to bring your mech's weapons online as the Ogumo-mech's guns are already acquiring firing solutions.

Turn to **159**.

Popping the hatch, you are glad to exchange the sweaty, humid atmosphere inside the helm for the smell of fresh sea air.

This place – whatever it was once called before K-Day – might as well be half a world and fifty years away, for there is no sign of kaiju here, or the terrible betrayal that befell Ako Base.

Away, along a winding path, overgrown with weeds, and up a flight of steps, stands the weathered red gate that denotes a Shinto shrine. The paintwork is flaking but this peak was clearly once considered to be a sacred place.

You are about to climb down from the mech, to take a closer look, when you are startled as something with numerous jointed legs suddenly appears at the open hatch and peers in at you with its numerous, multi-faceted, red-glowing eyes.

It is a Spider – one of the automated repair droids that, guided by your mech's AI, would make good any damage *Samurai 47* had sustained in battle, for as long as it remained in its hangar cradle. It must have been repairing one of *Samurai 47*'s internal systems when you were forced to evacuate in a hurry, and so remained trapped onboard until you made landfall and put the mech into standby mode, just as you would have done in the Guardian hangar.

Via your cerebral link with the Samurai, you can instruct the Spider to carry out any repairs required by the war-suit. For one thing, the uplink is still not working, and it may be that the mech's reactor core could do with a little TLC.

What do you want to command the Spider droid to take care of first?

Repair the uplink?	Turn to **456**.
Maintain the reactor core?	Turn to **440**.
Carry out general repairs and basic mech maintenance?	Turn to **473**.

338

The burnt-out shells of cars, trucks, and public buses litter the street. Turn to **545**.

339

"Not so fast!" snaps one of the guards, striking you with a taser-rod as your body tenses, ready for action.

Roll one die and divide the result by 2, rounding fractions up, then add 1. Deduct this many *Endurance* points. (Alternatively, pick a card and if it is a 7 or higher, assume that the number you have picked is a 6; then divide this randomly-generated number by 2, rounding fractions up, and deduct this many *Endurance* points.)

If you are still alive, two of the guards pick you up between them and drag you out of the holding cell.

Turn to **316**.

If you hurry, you should be able to catch up with the rest of Phoenix Squad as they are strapping themselves into their Samurai-mechs.

Retracing your route from the Guardian hangar at a sprint, you first enter the hangar that is home to the Shogun-mech prototype and are surprised to see Deputy Director Kira of Ako Base and Dr Kitsune, Head of Kaiju Research, ahead of you. They are running towards the Shogun's maintenance bay, accompanied by a squad of armed guards.

But that is nothing compared to the shock that grips your heart when you see two of the armed men raise their weapons and gun down a pair of engineers who stand between them and the Shogun.

With Dr Kitsune following close behind, Kira starts to climb the support gantry, clearly intending to board the mech. You give a shout, commanding them to stop, and Dr Kitsune briefly turns her face in your direction before resuming her ascent.

You cannot believe that two of the most senior staff at Ako Base would demonstrate such callous cowardice, fleeing in the face of the kaiju attack, rather than join in the fight to defend the facility.

At a command from Kira, two of the black-clad soldiers turn to meet you as you run after the fleeing Deputy Director and his entourage. Whipping out your katana, you disarm them – the razor-sharp blade slicing through the barrels of both weapons in one fluid sweep – and they stagger back in surprise.

Before you can dispatch these traitors, they unsheathe their own blades and prepare to defend themselves in hand-to-hand combat. You must fight the traitorous soldiers at the same time, but at least you have the initiative in this battle. (You may not use Ranged Combat in this battle.)

	COMBAT	ENDURANCE
First SOLDIER	7	8
Second SOLDIER	7	7

If you win this fight, turn to **362**.

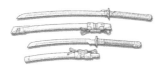

341

You reach an intersection where the tarmac of the road surface is fissured and broken. Through some of the larger cracks you can see exposed pipework and torn power conduits. Turn to **545**.

342

You activate the mech's manoeuvring thrusters, but it is too little, too late. The wreck slips from the crumbling cliff edge and collides with your mech. Trapped inside the dock area again, you cannot manoeuvre the mech quickly enough to break free of the sinking ship as it heads towards the dark depths.

And as you sink, so the forces acting on the hull of the mech increase dramatically. Under the intense pressure, it starts to buckle, and a dozen warning notifications flash up on the HUD, even as a crack appears across the screen and sparks flash as some electronic system or other fails.

Trapped in the belly of the stricken aircraft carrier, and with no way of getting out, as you sink ever deeper into the fathomless depths of an abyssal trench, *Ronin 47*'s superstructure is crushed as surely as an oil drum under a mech's foot.

As the integrity of the mech's hull gives way, so your body is suddenly exposed to the impossible pressures of the abyss, and you are turned into a bloody soup before you can drown.

Your adventure, like your life, is over.

THE END

343

At *Ronin 47*'s killing blow, the sinister black Shogun-mech poleaxes backwards over the edge of the collapsing crater into the seething magma. But you are not out of danger yet – Mount Fuji is clearly on the verge of a volcanic eruption.

Unless you want to consign yourself to a fiery fate, you have to get out of here now!

If *Ronin 47* has a Booster Rocket and you can still use it, turn to **368**. If not, you will have to rely on the giant robot's jump-jets to fly you out of trouble – turn to **394**. If the jump-jets are no longer operational, then your adventure is over.

344

(Strike the Hunter-Killer Missile from your Adventure Sheet.)

The rocket streaks from its shoulder mount and describes a spiralling course towards the overgrown avian.

The Gumyocho tries to swoop out of the way of the projectile, so rather than hit the creature in the middle of its breast, the missile strikes one of its wings instead. The subsequent explosion, blasts through bone and skin, and tears the pinion from the creature's body at the shoulder.

Screaming a death-cry with two voices, the colossal bird-kaiju crashes onto the rocks where the shore meets the sea. But it is not dead, until you put it out of its misery by careful application of *Ronin 47*'s lethal melee weapon.

Turn to **223**.

345

As the monster rises from the sea, one huge claw makes contact with *Ronin 47*, smashing the mech aside, just as a water buffalo would swat away a fly with its tail.

Deduct 5 *Integrity* points and, if the mech is still operational, turn to **458**.

346

Two black-clad Ninjas stand ready to defend their master. One is armed with a ninjato – a straight-bladed short sword – while the other is wielding a pair of sais. (The Shadow Warriors have the initiative in this battle, and you must fight them both at the same time.)

	COMBAT	ENDURANCE
First SHADOW WARRIOR	9	7
Second SHADOW WARRIOR	9	7

If you manage to defeat both your opponents, turn to **466**.

The EMP Device is fixed to the Daimyo's left arm, fitting over the wrist like a vambrace. It is easy to remove from the downed Daimyo and almost just as easy to attach to *Ronin 47*'s non-sword arm.

It is also clear that the weapon has been fired recently and, by your reckoning, it probably only has enough juice left for one more pulse.

(Record the EMP Device in the Upgrades box on your Adventure Sheet.)

If you are done stripping the Daimyo for parts, turn to **2**. If you want to try taking the Lightning Cannon as well, if you have not done so already, turn to **320**.

348

Bypassing the system's safety protocols, you generate a charge of electrostatic energy within the mech and then release it in an intense burst, effectively engineering a power surge.

For a moment the cockpit is plunged into darkness that is only alleviated by intermittent flashes of sparking, blue-white energy. And then, slowly, the lights glow back into life and the HUD boots up again.

Roll one die (or pick a card). If the number rolled is odd (or the card is red), turn to **302**. If the number (rolled) is even (or the card is black), turn to **323**.

349

Unfortunately, your mech is not powerful enough to penetrate the Vault.

What do you want to do now? Will you:

Try to wrench the doors open (if you haven't done so already)?	Turn to **398**.
Subject the gate to a barrage of artillery fire (if you haven't done so already)?	Turn to **378**.
Leave the island?	Turn to **216**.

350

It is eerily quiet as you navigate the ruins and shattered highways of Tokyo. Turn to **545**.

351

Before you can get out of the way, the torpedo tumbles from the steel brackets supporting it and falls on top of you, as if in slow motion. It pins you against the angled floor, crushing your legs and causing you to cry out in agony. (Deduct 4 *Endurance* points and 1 *Agility* point.)

Bracing your hands against the missile, and clenching your teeth against the pain, you push with all your might.

Take an Endurance test. If you pass the test, turn to **303**. If you fail the test, turn to **331**.

352

You launch the Flares at the Shogun but, as far as you can tell, they have absolutely no effect.

Before you can do anything else, the Shogun engages you in battle.

Cross off one use of the Flares and turn to **446**.

353

As you seize the Force-Shield, its forcefield flickers into life around it, giving off a crackling blue light. Thankfully, the device is in good working order!

While *Ronin 47* is using the Force-Shield you may add 2 points to the robot's *Armour* score but must deduct 1 point from its *Melee* score. You may discard the object at any time, losing both the stat bonus it provides and the penalty, but once discarded you may not use it again, as it is too cumbersome to take with you if you are not using it.

Hearing the Wrecker-mechs closing on you, you turn to face them. Turn to **43**.

The blaring klaxon of *Ronin 47*'s proximity alarm brings you to full alertness and has you scrambling to access the data feed from the mech's AI to find out what is happening.

You pull up images from the war-suit's ocular arrays on the screen in front of you. Appearing as glowing, multi-coloured blurs on the screen, thanks to the mech's infra-red cameras, you are horrified to see three monstrous crab-like creatures, each the size of a tank, scuttling towards you over the rocks, their powerful pincers snapping in expectation.

These Kani-Oni clearly intend to crack open the hard shell of the mech to find out what meaty surprise might lie inside.

How will you react to this threat? Will you:

Launch some Flares (if you can)?	Turn to **380**.
Launch a Hunter-Killer Missile (if you have one)?	Turn to **409**.
Activate a DNA Bomb (if you have one)?	Turn to **50**.
Fire up a Booster Rocket (if your mech is fitted with one)?	Turn to **434**.
Fire up *Ronin 47*'s jump-jets?	Turn to **465**.
Attack the Kani-Oni?	Turn to **493**.

355

The buildings here are intact, except for the fact that not a single one of them has any glass left in any of its windows. Return to **435**.

356

Not knowing what else to do, you launch a fusillade of depth charges into the water around you. A second later, they detonate. (Cross off one use of the Depth Charges from your Adventure Sheet.)

The underwater explosions rip through the body of the beast that has your mech in its coils, but *Samurai 47* is also caught within their blast radius.

(Deduct another 5 *Integrity* points from your mech.)

The kaiju releases its hold on the Samurai and spirals away into the gloom, no doubt not used to its prey fighting back. Then it suddenly turns and goes for you again, starfish arms reaching for you, its great, tooth-ringed maw yawning wide.

A prompt on the HUD informs you that this particular type of kaiju has the designation Oni-Hitode, or 'Devil-Starfish,' but you are ready for it.

ONI-HITODE				
SPEED	ARMOUR	MELEE	ARTILLERY	INTEGRITY
3	1	3	1	5

If you destroy the Oni-Hitode, turn to **407**.

357

Your prolonged fight and the strain put on *Ronin 47*'s power source are not good for the reactor. You need to land as quickly as you can. (Add 1 point to your mech's Reactor score.)

If this takes the *Reactor* score to 3 points, turn to **317** at once. If not, turn to **186**.

358

The missile hits the left-hand tower amidst its proliferation of gun-turrets. The resulting explosion cooks off the munitions arsenal and fuel cells buried within the structure, which blows the top off the tower. (Strike the Hunter-Killer Missile from your Adventure Sheet.)

When the smoke clears, you see that the sentinel is now no more than a column of shattered concrete and sheared-off iron struts, half as tall as it was to begin with.

But now the second tower has you in its sights and opens fire.

	KYOJIN GUN-TOWER			
SPEED	ARMOUR	MELEE	ARTILLERY	INTEGRITY
2	4	2	4	20

If you destroy the guardian gun before it can destroy you, turn to **543**.

359

Thanks to the shielding, *Ronin 47* is unaffected by the mech-killing blast. The Oni-mech incapacitated by your attack, you use a combination of your own mech's heavy artillery and melee weapons to tear the heavy ordnance robot apart. Turn to **449**.

360

The Flares stored within the armoury are identical to those that may already be fitted to your mech and have precisely the same effect – they can be used for distress signalling, illumination, or as defensive countermeasures. Selecting this upgrade will give you 3 uses of Flares.

When you are ready, turn back to the section you just came from.

361

Ronin 47 has been operating under duress at depths that it was not designed to withstand. Under the intense pressure, the hull of the mech finally starts to buckle and a dozen warning notifications flash up on the HUD between the waves of interference, even as a crack appears right across the middle of the cockpit screen, and sparking flashes illuminate the darkness as the robot's systems start to fail.

Roll one die and add 3. Deduct this many *Integrity* points from your mech. (Alternatively, pick a card and deduct its face value from your mech's *Integrity* score, unless it is a 10 or a picture card, in which case deduct 9 points from the Samurai's *Integrity* score; if it is less than 4 you must deduct 4 *Integrity* points.)

If your Samurai has lost 7-9 *Integrity* points, you must also deduct 1 point from both its *Armour* score and *Melee* score, and add 1 point to the *Reactor* score.

If *Ronin 47* is still operational, *Take an Integrity test*. If you pass the test, turn to **475**, but if you fail the test, turn to **433**.

362

The traitors are dead, but you are too late to stop Kira and Kitsune getting away.

With an inferno roar, the Shogun's rocket boosters fire and, rising on a column of smoke and flame, it blasts off through the now open dome.

There is only one option left open to you; you must board your own mech once more, join your fellow warriors in repelling the kaiju attack, and then go after the traitors.

However, before re-joining Phoenix Squad, do you want to search the bodies of the two men you just killed? If so, turn to **382**; if not, turn to **442**.

363

You plot an arcing path to take you around the battling monsters, hoping they will continue to ignore you.

Roll one die (or pick a card). If the number rolled is odd (or the card is red), turn to **384**. If the number rolled is even (or the card is black), turn to **404**.

364

Before the slower-moving Wrecker-mechs can intercept it, *Ronin 47* slips between them, and you do not stop until you reach the hole blasted in the armoury wall by the hastily-deployed missile.

Two weapons immediately catch your eye, and the Combat AI's pattern recognition subroutines identify them for you. One is a large Ho-musubi pattern Flame-Thrower, while the other is a colossal mace that looks like the sort of thing *Volos* would use to batter its enemies.

As you're about to grab one of them you notice that there is also a Force-Shield in the storage locker. Such a device, if it is fully operational, projects an energy field beyond the limits of the shield itself to protect the war-machine that is carrying it.

There's only time to take one of the items before the Wreckers are on top of you, so which is it to be?

The Flame-Thrower?	Turn to **399**.
The Mech-Mace?	Turn to **421**.
The Force-Shield?	Turn to **353**.

365

Activating the mech's manoeuvring thrusters, you pilot it out of the path of the plummeting vessel before it can hit you, but it's a close call, *Ronin 47*'s proximity alarms pinging in panic.

There is nothing you can do but watch as the iron corpse of the *Gojira* disappears into the gloom of the trench. Whatever secrets it might have held are lost forever.

Turn to **8**.

366

The street before you has been transformed into a huge crater by a violent explosion. But did it occur during K-Day or in its aftermath? Turn to **435**.

367

A colossal, clawed limb misses your mech by what seems like only centimetres, and gives you precious moments in which to decide your next course of action.

You doubt you could escape the gargantuan lizard in its home environment of the open sea, but you might be able to get away by air.

What do you want to do? Will you:

Ignite the mech's jump-jets, in order to
make your getaway?   Turn to **369**.

Fire up a Booster Rocket, if *Ronin 47*
has been fitted with one?   Turn to **419**.

Prepare to defend yourself against the colossus?   Turn to **458**.

368

Ronin 47 rises into the air atop a column of coruscating flame, as great limbs of lava leap from the cone of the volcano, as if intent on pulling it back down to earth. But your mech will not be beaten now and the seething cone of Mount Fuji starts to shrink beneath it, as the first incandescent lava-bombs hurtle into the sky, to land moments later amidst the wreckage of the collapsing factory-fortress.

Turn to **600**.

369

Ronin 47 rises into the sky on a cone of smoke and flames. But at the same time, the reptilian giant lashes out with its long tail and smacks the mech out of the air. You land back in the sea, hazard lights flashing inside the cockpit, while a graphic on the HUD warns you that the readings from the reactor have entered the red.

(Deduct 5 *Integrity* points and 1 *Armour* point, and add 1 point to your mech's *Reactor* score.)

If the mech is still operational, turn to **458**.

370

Tokyo was once a bustling, vibrant city, home to fourteen million people, but since the apocalyptic events of K-Day it is now little more than ruins. You have heard that a few people still live here, but you have also heard rumours of them turning to cannibalism in order to survive.

Nonetheless, it was here that the Tengu Array pinpointed energy readings that were many times greater in magnitude than would indicate mere cook-fires. You are convinced that there has been mech activity here, at least in the past 48 hours. But are they potential allies, enemies, or the traitor you have been hunting ever since Ako Base fell?

If you have the code word *Allied* recorded on your Adventure Sheet, turn to **14**. If not, make a note that your starting grid square is A1 and then turn to **420**.

371

Kicking your legs furiously, you manage to get out of the way before the torpedo falls onto you.

Making it to the other end of the chamber, you haul yourself through the open hatch and into the dock. From there, as the space turns slowly about you, you board the mech again via the airlock and resume your position in the pilot's seat.

Turn to **8**.

372

While you position the cannon against a free weapon attachment port, using the haptic controls in the cockpit, the Spider droid scuttles over the hull, connecting it to *Ronin 47*'s weapon control systems, targeting array, and reactor core power supply.

When all the necessary attachments have been made, you test-fire the gun and raise a whoop of joy as a bolt of what can only be described as coruscating lightning explodes from the artillery piece and obliterates a nearby sandbank.

(Add 1 point to your mech's *Artillery* score, even if this takes it to above its starting level.)

If you are done salvaging equipment from the Honjo mech, turn to **2**. If not, and you want to go after the EMP Device next, if you haven't done so already, turn to **347**.

Both its wizened, archaeopteryx-like heads shrieking at you, in a discordant dinosaurian duet, the Gumyocho presses home its attack. But you are ready for it.

GUMYOCHO				
SPEED	ARMOUR	MELEE	ARTILLERY	INTEGRITY
5	1	4	2	25

If you succeed in killing the Gumyocho, turn to **223**.

374

The Hunter-Killer is only halfway to the tower when the guns lock onto it and blast it out of the sky!

Cross the Hunter-Killer Missile off your Adventure Sheet and turn to **525**.

375

Hearing a great crash from the other end of the street, you are momentarily distracted by the arrival of a second colossal mech. There were two of the demon-robots hunting you through the ruins of Tokyo!

If you have the code word *Allied* recorded on your Adventure Sheet, turn to **412**. If not, turn to **471**.

A pair of these abyssal horrors suddenly strike from out of the darkness. They are even more lethally dangerous underwater than they would be at the surface.

A prompt on the HUD informs you that this particular type of kaiju has the designation Oni-Hitode, or 'Devil-Starfish.' (Fight the creatures one at a time.)

First ONI-HITODE				
SPEED	ARMOUR	MELEE	ARTILLERY	INTEGRITY
3	1	3	1	10

Second ONI-HITODE				
SPEED	ARMOUR	MELEE	ARTILLERY	INTEGRITY
3	1	3	1	8

If you manage to defeat both the kaiju, turn to **407**.

Bypassing the reactor's failsafe measures – having already sealed off the cockpit from the rest of the war-suit – you vent a portion of the liquid nitrogen into the mech's systems. This evaporates into a freezing gas that rushes through the mech's internal compartments, including its life-support systems, instantaneously freezing any organic matter it comes into contact with.

You only hope it is enough, but it comes at a price. From now on, it will be harder to maintain *Ronin 47*'s reactor core temperature.

(Add 1 point to the mech's current *Reactor* score and make a note that the *Reactor* score may no longer drop below 1 point.)

Turn to **302**.

Making your way back to the entrance to the valley, you lock your heavy ordnance weapons onto the sealed portal and open fire.

Take an Artillery test. If you pass the test, turn to **297**, but if you fail the test, turn to **349**.

A tremor passes through the street beneath *Ronin 47*'s feet. But it isn't an earthquake, or the precursor to a volcanic eruption; it is caused by a giant footfall. Turn to **215**.

(Cross off one use of the Flares from your Adventure Sheet.)

The Flares light up the night and the reef, revealing the oily mottled patterns of purple and green that cover the shells of the colossal crustaceans. The Kani-Oni freeze, observing you with their eye-stalks raised, but they do not shy away or retreat. Instead, they raise their snapping pincers in a threat display.

This is their territory, and they will not be intimidated by the likes of you!

What do you want to do now?

Launch a Hunter-Killer Missile (if you have one)?	Turn to **409**.
Activate a DNA Bomb (if you have one)?	Turn to **50**.
Fire up a Booster Rocket (if your mech is fitted with one)?	Turn to **434**.
Fire up *Ronin 47*'s jump-jets?	Turn to **465**.
Attack the Kani-Oni?	Turn to **493**.

The Drones home in on the Shogun, which automatically shoots them down with its guns, and *Ronin 47* is caught in the crossfire.

Roll 1 die and add 6 to the number rolled, and then deduct the total from your mech's *Integrity* score. (Alternatively, pick and card and if it is a 7 or above, it counts as a 6; add 6 to the number and deduct the total from your mech's *Integrity* score.)

If *Ronin 47* is still operational, turn to **446**.

382

A quick search of the soldier's bodies turns up two complete Medi-Packs.

Record the 2 Medi-Packs on your Adventure Sheet and then turn to **442**.

383

Roll one die (or pick a card). If the number rolled is odd (or the card is red), turn to **16**. If the number rolled is even (or the card is black), turn to **582**.

384

The ancestors must be smiling on you this day, for the kaiju do indeed ignore you and vanish beneath the waves once more as they continue their titanic contest to see which of them is the stronger.

Collating information from current surroundings, married with information retained within its memory core and that downloaded from the Tengu Satellite Array, *Ronin 47*'s Combat AI picks out two locations that may be of interest to you.

One – Yokai Base – lies to the northwest and is a top-secret scientific research facility. The other is a distress signal being broadcast from a point northeast of your current position.

Both routes will take you closer to Japan, but which way do you want to go?

Northeast?   Turn to **27**.

Northwest?   Turn to **513**.

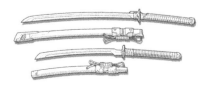

You attack the vessel with the mech's fists, hoping to tear your way inside.

Take a Melee test. If you pass the test, turn to **405**, but if you fail the test, turn to **128**.

A tremor passes through the street beneath *Ronin 47*'s feet. But it isn't an earthquake, or the precursor to a volcanic eruption; it is caused by a giant footfall.

Turn to **215**.

The fight over, the crowd gathered by the grille retreats to various corners of the steel dungeon, splitting up into small groups.

It's clear to you now what the Wreckers' scheme is; they capture mechs out on patrol, and their pilots, and then force them to fight each other, for the entertainment of the ne'er-do-wells who are drawn to this place, wherever this place might be.

You find a spot by yourself, to sit and think, and plot your escape.

Someone, wearing a ragged robe, their head hidden by a heavy cowl, approaches you and bows, before sitting down cross-legged beside you.

"The supreme art of war is?" the stranger says at last, speaking fluent Japanese.

"To subdue the enemy without fighting," you reply. "Is that how they caught you?"

"They used my own better nature against me. I was ambushed."

"In the Great Pacific Garbage Patch?" you ask.

"Just so. I am Kanesada of Okinawa Prefecture," the stranger says, pulling back his hood to reveal a hairless head and age-lined face. A livid red scar runs from the corner of his left eye down to his chin.

"Oishi of Ako Base," you offer in return. "There are still Guardians in Okinawa?"

"I was the last. And now I and my mech, *Rising Sun*, are trapped here."

"Where is here?" you ask.

"I do not know," Kanesada replies, "only that it cannot be far from the place where we were both taken."

"So, what do you know about this place?" you ask the old warrior.

He tells you that he has been here a week, and, in that time, he has discovered that no artillery weapons will work here. The Wreckers are employing some sort of dampener tech, which he believes must be located in the control room high above the arena.

Before he can reveal any more secrets, the door to the cell suddenly opens and a squad of armed guards enters. "You, come with me!" one of them snaps, pointing directly at you.

You look to your new friend as if to say, "This is our chance to get out of here." But, as if reading your mind, he shakes his head. "Go with them. Do what you have to do, and we will talk again later."

If you want to follow Kanesada's advice, turn to **316**. If you would prefer to seize this opportunity and make a break for it, turn to **339**.

388

Entering the frequency you discovered into the transmitter, you activate the device, in the hope that the signal will summon the kaiju to your current position and create a distraction, mindful of the ancient proverb, *"The enemy of my enemy is my friend."*

Record the code word *Triggered* on your Adventure Sheet and then turn to **246**.

Giving voice to another shrill cry that echoes from the cliffs of its rocky island roost, the Gumyocho emerges from the cloud with its talons raised and its fang-lined beaks open wide. (Go straight to the Close Combat phase of this battle.)

GUMYOCHO				
SPEED	ARMOUR	MELEE	ARTILLERY	INTEGRITY
5	1	5	2	20

If you manage to slay the two-headed aberration, turn to **223**.

390

You activate the experimental weapon, and an electromagnetic pulse bursts from the device set around *Ronin 47*'s wrist.

If your mech has been fitted with EMP Shielding, turn to **491**. If not, turn to **529**.

391

Keeping a close eye on your air supply gauge, you set off for the other end of the 400-metre long vessel.

A deep rumble suddenly passes through the ship, and it changes position around you. There can be only one explanation – the sea-cliff upon which the *Gojira* is resting is slowly giving way under the weight of 100,000 tonnes of steel.

Never mind whatever other secrets might be hidden on board, you have to get out of here as fast as you can, before the wreck sinks into the abyss with you trapped on board.

Heading in what you hope is the right direction for the dock, you enter a torpedo storage room. Exerting yourself, you swim for the other end of the room, and the dock that you can now see quite clearly through the open access hatch at the far end. However, as the ship tips towards port, one of the torpedoes rolls off its rack.

Take an Agility test. If you pass the test, turn to **371**. If you fail the test, turn to **351**.

Frustrating as the situation is, you have no way of attaching the Lightning Cannon to your mech and so are forced to leave it behind on the sandy atoll.

If you are done salvaging equipment from the Honjo mech, turn to **2**. If not, and you want to go after the EMP Device next, if you haven't done so already, turn to **347**.

"Come on then, new meat. Ivan will let you choose. Who do you think will win? The American or the Korean? And how many rations are you willing to risk on your choice?"

You may wager as many Rations as you want, as long as the amount does not exceed the total number of Rations you have left. Having decided how many portions of Rations you are willing to bet, you then need to decide which of the combatants will win the fight.

As the battle gets under way, you notice that the *Devastator's* rocket launcher and pulse cannon remain dormant.

Conduct the battle between the two mechs as you would a battle between *Ronin 47* and another giant robot created by the Guardian Programme. (Please note that the mechs' artillery weapons are inactive during this battle, so cut straight to the Close Combat phase.)

USS DEVASTATOR				
SPEED	ARMOUR	MELEE	ARTILLERY	INTEGRITY
2	4	3	-	30

SUHOSIN				
SPEED	ARMOUR	MELEE	ARTILLERY	INTEGRITY
4	2	4	-	25

As soon as one of the mechs has its *Integrity* score reduced to 15 points or fewer, the klaxon sounds again, and the fight is halted.

If the combatant you bet on winning did indeed win the bout, turn to **74**. If your choice of mech lost the battle, turn to **53**.

As great tentacles of lava leap from the seething caldera of the volcano, *Ronin 47* rises into the sky on a cone of smoke and flames, leaving imminent death and destruction behind.

But after all your beleaguered mech has been through, almost immediately hazard lights start to flash inside the cockpit,

accompanied by a nagging alarm, as the reactor readings start to enter the red.

Add 1 to your mech's *Reactor* score, and if this takes the mech's *Reactor* score to 3 points, turn to **300**. If not, turn to **600.**

395

(Cross off one use of the Flares from your Adventure Sheet.)

The intense red glow of the firework explosion of Flares causes the great bird to panic and recoil from your 'assault'. But for how long?

Roll one die (or pick a card). If the number rolled is odd (or the card is red), turn to **150**. If the number (rolled) is even (or the card is black), turn to **373**.

396

Ignoring the salvo of Flares, the sentinel gun-towers lock onto your position and finish processing their optimal firing solutions.

Cross off one use of the Flares from your Adventure Sheet and turn to **525**.

397

The DNA-killing concoction takes effect immediately. The monstrous bird's swooping descent becomes a plummeting death-dive and its body smashes onto the jagged rocks that form the shore-line of its island home. It doesn't move again and your mech's sensors confirm that the Gumyocho is indeed dead.

Turn to **223**.

398

Stepping up to the great doors, you have your mech force its fingertips into the narrow gap where the doors meet and attempt to pull them apart.

Take a Melee test. If you pass the test, turn to **328**, but if you fail the test, turn to **349**.

There isn't time to secure the Flame-Thrower to your mech – you would need an operational Spider to achieve such a thing anyway – so *Ronin 47* will just have to hold it as you would, if you were wielding a similar weapon.

While you are using the Flame-Thrower, you may deduct 1 point from your opponent's *Armour* score, but you must also reduce any *Integrity* damage you cause by 2 points. You may discard the weapon whenever you want.

And then the Wrecker-mechs are on top of you! Turn to **43**.

Gradually the gas cloud dissipates, but the Tsuchigumo is still there, perched among the ruins and its webs, as if poised to pounce. If the DNA Bomb has had any effect on the horror, it has only served to make the monster more aggressive.

Delete the DNA Bomb from your Adventure Sheet – you may not use it again – and turn to **205**.

The creaks and groans only become louder and more unsettling the deeper you descend, while red hazard indicators appear on the HUD.

Record the code word *Weakened* on your Adventure Sheet and then turn to **130**.

Leaving Operations at a run, you hear the ceiling come crashing down behind you, blocking your way back into the command centre. You race back to the Guardian hangar, arriving in time to see the Shogun blasting off through the now open dome, its rocket boosters carrying it into the sky on a column of smoke and flame.

You are too late! Deputy Director Kira – Kira the Betrayer! – has escaped, taking the prototype Shogun-mech with him, curse his soul!

There is only one option left open to you: you must board your own mech once more, join your fellow warriors in repelling the kaiju attack, and then set off in pursuit of the traitor.

Turn to **442**.

403

You open fire on the gun-drones and they return fire. (Conduct this battle only using *Artillery* scores to determine which side wins each Combat Round.)

GUN-DRONES				
SPEED	ARMOUR	MELEE	ARTILLERY	INTEGRITY
4	2	-	4	15

If *Ronin 47* wins the aerial dogfight with the traitor welcoming committee, turn to **357**.

404

Perhaps the kaiju's battle was about more than just food; perhaps it was about territory, and seeing as how you have invaded that territory, you become a target for both of them.

The sea-monsters break off from fighting each other and turn their attentions on you. You have no hope of getting away from them, so you turn and prepare to face their unified underwater charge.

AKKOROKAMUI				
SPEED	ARMOUR	MELEE	ARTILLERY	INTEGRITY
5	1	4	2	20

BAKE-KUJIRA				
SPEED	ARMOUR	MELEE	ARTILLERY	INTEGRITY
4	3	3	1	30

If the Bake-Kujira makes a successful strike against you, roll one die (or pick a card); if the number rolled is odd (or the card is red), the monster propels itself into *Ronin 47*, its battering-ram charge causing an additional 4 points of *Integrity* damage, and reducing the mech's *Armour* score by 1 point.

If the Akkorokamui wins a Combat Round against you, roll one die (or pick a card); if the number rolled is even (or the card is black), the giant squid grabs the mech in its tentacles and pulls it within range of its huge, beak-like mouth, where it delivers an additional 5 points of *Integrity* damage, and reducing the mech's *Armour* score by 1 point. The mech must also reduce its *Combat Rating* by 1 point until it wins a Combat Round against the cephalopod-kaiju, at which point it is able to break free of the monster's tentacles.

If you manage to eliminate both kaiju, turn to **557**.

405

Ronin 47's fingers penetrate the *Gojira*'s reinforced hull, but the vibrations set up by your savage attack have destabilised the vessel's position at the edge of the sea-cliff. Sand and rock cascade into the abyssal void, and the shipwreck starts to move too, as the cliff begins to collapse.

Realising that you have jeopardised your chance to pillage the wreck of whatever secrets it might contain, you move the mech out of the way as the research vessel slides over the edge of the precipice and slips away into the darkness of the trench.

Turn to **8**.

406

There is no time to celebrate your victory, as the gates of the fortress open and a tide of black-clad figures pours out. Many are riding snow-scooters or all-terrain vehicles, and they are accompanied by a squadron of automated airborne gun-drones.

Having seen you defeat his guard-mechs, Kira has sent his army of devoted followers to stop you. He must fear you and what you could be capable of!

How do you want to deal with this new threat?

Launch a Hunter-Killer Missile into

their midst (if you can)?   Turn to **427**.

Trigger an EMP Device (if you have one)?   Turn to **461**.

Engage the enemy?   Turn to **489**.

407

The worm-monsters dead, you head for the surface. But as you ascend, the proximity alarm starts to sound again, and you realise too late that something is closing on you from the surface. It is another Samurai!

It hits you before you can manoeuvre your own mech out of the way. (Deduct 4 *Integrity* points.)

The mech's running lights are dark and you catch a glimpse of the helm; its head has been bifurcated. The machine is already dead, as is its pilot. You read its designation before it disappears into the lightless gloom below: *Samurai 39*. It is Norikane's machine.

You swear to yourself then that Norikane's name will be recorded on the Honour Roll of the Fallen at Ako Base.

As you try to signal the other Samurai of Phoenix Squad, you hear nothing but dead air, and realise immediately that something is wrong.

Calling up a damage analysis on the screen in front of you, you see that *Samurai 47*'s uplink transmitter has been damaged by the collision with the other mech and is no longer operational.

****

You surface, moments later, in time to see the rest of Phoenix Squad take out the last of the abyssal hunters. Once you are sure the kaiju's assault has been repelled, you pop the cockpit hatch – the faceplate of your Samurai yawning open like a great mouth – so that you can signal to the other pilots in person that there is a problem.

Takanao opens her mech's helm too and you inform her of what has happened. Acting on your behalf, she checks-in with the surviving members of Phoenix Squad, before signalling to Lieutenant Tsunenari that you are ready for retrieval.

Less than twenty minutes later, the five remaining Samurai are back in the troop hold of the Tatsu.

Turn to **311**.

408

The missile streaks from where it is mounted on *Ronin 47*'s shoulder and strikes the Shogun, the force of the explosion sending the giant robot stumbling backwards.

Grabbing hold of the gantry and crushing the metal framework in its powerful grip, the Shogun regains its balance. You are awed by the fact that the Shogun still stands, although the Hunter-Killer missile has clearly caused it considerable damage.

(When you come to fight the Shogun-mech, deduct 1 point from its *Speed*, *Armour*, *Melee*, and *Artillery* scores, and 10 points from its *Integrity* score.)

For now, strike the Hunter-Killer Missile from your Adventure Sheet and turn to **446**.

409

There are three Kani-Oni, spread out across the rocks in front of you, so all you can do is aim at a spot between two of them and hope for the best.

(Strike the Hunter-Killer Missile from your Adventure Sheet.)

The missile streaks from its shoulder mount and hits its target, sending huge shards of rock, shattered chitinous limbs, and chunks of scorched crabmeat flying in all directions.

Only one Kani-Oni remains.

KANI-ONI				
SPEED	ARMOUR	MELEE	ARTILLERY	INTEGRITY
3	4	3	3	10

If you kill the crab-kaiju, turn to **518**.

410

The Sunblade is a close combat melee weapon. It contains its own power cell that superheats the sword, meaning that it is even more devastating against kaiju, slicing through their mutated flesh like it was sushi.

If you opt to arm *Ronin 47* with the Sunblade, it will do 1 additional die's worth of damage to other mechs and 3 additional dice's worth of damage against all kaiju.

Now turn back to the section you just came from.

411

Already unbalanced by their initial attack, *Ronin 47* stumbles under the Ninjas' twin assault and comes crashing down onto the half-submerged reef on its back. (Deduct 8 *Integrity* points.) Only then do the proximity alarms start to sound.

You have no choice but to defend yourself against the Ninja-class mechs, but because *Ronin 47* is lying on its back, you must reduce the mech's *Melee* score by 2 points for the duration of the first Combat Round, as you struggle to get it back on its feet. (In this battle, go straight to the Close Combat phase.)

First NINJA-MECH				
SPEED	ARMOUR	MELEE	ARTILLERY	INTEGRITY
5	2	5	2	20

Second NINJA-MECH				
SPEED	ARMOUR	MELEE	ARTILLERY	INTEGRITY
5	2	5	2	18

If you manage to defeat both Ninjas, turn to **19**.

412

Now it is the demonic robot's turn to be taken by surprise, as *Rising Sun* arrives at the street junction behind it, its ten-metre-long Electro-Katana laying a blow against its crimson adamantium alloy shell.

Kanesada has been stalking the new arrival through the streets of Tokyo while the Oni-mech was fully focused on finding you!

Rising Sun takes on the other Oni, while you finish the fight with your opponent.

Continue your battle with the Oni-mech, and if *Ronin 47* is victorious, turn to **452**.

413

Without their pilots, the mechs the Wreckers have captured are as good as useless to them, so it does not take long before a gang of guards enters the cell. While the majority make sure the rest of the prisoners keep their distance and don't attempt to escape, a pair of guards simply taser you and the Russian.

As you lie on the floor, spasming uncontrollably, you notice that one of the burliest guards has both your katana and your blaster hanging from a leather belt about his waist.

Roll one die and divide the result by 2, rounding fractions up, then add 1. Deduct this many *Endurance* points. (Alternatively, pick a card and if it is a 7 or higher, assume that the number you have picked is a 6; then divide this randomly-generated number by 2, rounding fractions up, and deduct this many *Endurance* points.)

If you are still alive, turn to **387**.

414

Hoping that the compounds you used to create the DNA Bomb will not harm non-K-Compound-mutated organic matter but sealing yourself inside your pilot's suit and helmet just in case, you activate the device while it is still inside the payload compartment.

At once, a toxic green gas is released from the metal cylinder that quickly finds its way into every nook and cranny of the war-suit, including the environmental controls and life support systems.

You follow its progress on the screen, as it spreads through the mech, via the graphic overlays on the screen in front of you. And as it does so, the blinking red dots indicating the parasitic life-forms wink out one by one.

Strike the DNA Bomb from your Adventure Sheet and turn to **302**.

415

A huge ogress of a woman blocks the way ahead, her blubbery body almost as wide as the corridor. She might be wearing the overalls of a factory worker, but she has the build of a Sumo wrestler. You have no choice but to try to put her out of action before she can crush you to death. (In this battle, you have the initiative.)

SUMO WRESTLER   COMBAT 8   ENDURANCE 10

If you defeat the Sumo Wrestler, turn to **466**.

416

The gas cloud clears, leaving behind only death. The gigantic arachnoid lies on its back at the bottom of a pile of rubble, its fifteen metre-long legs twitching, and a gelatinous black substance starts to ooze from between the chitinous plates, as the DNA-denaturing compounds cause its internal organs to liquify.

The DNA Bomb worked, and far better than you could have hoped. Strike it from your Adventure Sheet – it can only be used once – and then turn to **233**.

417

Back in the pilot's seat and strapped into your safety harness, you disengage *Ronin 47*'s docking clamps from the airlock coupling and guide the giant war-machine away from the sheer side of the trench.

On the HUD, you can see Dr Kitsune's submersible already powering through the war, heading for the surface. But before you can set off in pursuit, the vessel launches a cluster of torpedoes, that race through the water towards your mech.

There is not even time to bring the mech's artillery weapons online before the torpedoes hit.

Take an Armour test. If *Ronin 47* passes the test, turn to **514**; if the war-machine fails the test, turn to **455**.

418

As the Drones take to the air, the Kyojin gun-towers open fire, picking off each of the airborne devices with precision kill-shots.

Cross off one use of Drones from your Adventure Sheet and turn to **525**.

419

Ronin 47 rockets heavenward on a cone of smoke and flames, leaving the Daikaiju far behind. (Cross off the Booster Rocket from your Adventure Sheet.)

Unfortunately, the booster burns through its fuel supply at a startling rate and there is not enough to carry *Ronin 47* the rest of the way to Japan. You are forced to put down still some two hundred kilometres south of Honshu Island.

Turn to **566**.

You set out across the city, picking your way between the toppled skyscrapers and the burnt-out shells of tenement buildings.

Look at the city plan below. Shaded squares indicate ruined buildings *Ronin 47* cannot pass through. The white squares with three-digit numbers in them indicate the city streets and squares that the mech can cross.

	A	B	C	D	E	F	G	H	I
9		540	215	540			160	591	355
8		379		484		266	333		430
7	520	279	326	194	586	444	167		124
6	115		571				291		210
5	463		287	480	335		435	366	551
4	341	576	101		472		208		569
3	296		589	139	324	291	593		222
2	383		350			435	180	386	569
1		545	283	338	457	268			
↑	A	B	C	D	E	F	G	H	I

As you explore the city, each turn you may move up to the number of white squares equal to *Ronin 47*'s *Speed* score. Please note, you can move north, south, east and west, assuming there are no buildings in the way, but you cannot move diagonally to an adjacent square.

When you have made your move, turn to the number printed in the square you have just landed on. (If you land on grid square A1, simply make another movement turn. It would make sense to bookmark this page, as you will be back here before you are done.

421

The heavy Mech-Mace appears to be welded together from several pieces of metal, but it will do the job, nonetheless.

While you are using the Mech-Mace, you may increase any *Integrity* damage you cause by 2 points, but you must also reduce *Ronin 47*'s *Speed* score by 1 point. You may discard the weapon at any time, losing both the damage bonus it provides and the *Speed* penalty.

Hearing the Wrecker-mechs closing on you, you turn to face them in battle. Turn to **43**.

422

Disconcerting creaking sounds echo throughout the superstructure of the mech, as the ocean exerts unimaginable pressure against it.

Do you want to risk continuing your descent (turn to **401**), or do you think it would be wiser to return to the surface and set a course for Tokyo (turn to **231**)?

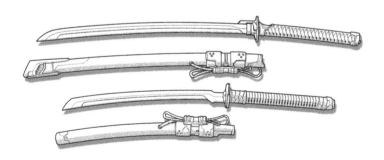

(Cross off one use of the Drones from your Adventure Sheet.)

The Drones take to the air, flying into the descending avian's path, crashing into its body and wings like a dozen independently deployed rockets.

They are not enough to stop the beast, but they have wounded and weakened it, so all you have to do is finish it off.

GUMYOCHO				
SPEED	ARMOUR	MELEE	ARTILLERY	INTEGRITY
4	1	4	2	20

If you kill the Gumyocho, turn to **223**.

424

You may have dealt with the guns, but the entrance to the Vault still remains sealed. You are going to have to force your way in.

Do you want to try to wrench the doors open (turn to **398**), or would you prefer to subject the gate to a barrage of artillery fire (turn to **378**)?

425

Unfortunately, the EMP works in exactly the way it is supposed to, in the case of *Ronin 47*. As your war-machine's systems fail, its actuators and servo-motors no longer powering its legs, the Samurai-class robot loses its balance and topples over.

Trapped inside the mech, there is nothing you can do as the Shogun's weapons blast it to smithereens.

Your adventure, like your life, is over.

THE END

The four components have each been given a name for ease of identification. They are Amabie, Byakko, Chochinbi, and Datsue-ba, and each one has a different value associated with it.

Compound	Value
Amabie	8
Byakko	16
Chochinbi	64
Datsue-ba	128

Using the computer console, you simply need to select three of the compounds to be combined. The automated machinery in the lab will then do the rest, mixing those three elements and placing the resulting concoction in a large metal canister, in effect creating a weapon that, when triggered, will denature the DNA of any kaiju. At least, that is the hope.

You can even instruct the computer to have the device delivered to Airlock 2, where *Ronin 47* is docked. And so, you set about your work.

Select three different compounds and add their individual values together. Then record the DNA Bomb on your Adventure Sheet, along with the total of the three values.

Write down the code word *Modified* on your Adventure Sheet and then turn to **183**.

The Hunter-Killer locks on to a half-track in the vanguard of the advancing forces. A split second later, where the armoured vehicle was only a moment before, there is now a rapidly expanding ball of oily smoke and flame while huge chunks of shrapnel take out yet more of Kira's forces. (Strike the Hunter-Killer Missile from your Adventure Sheet.)

Roll 1 die and add 6. When you come to engage Kira's army, you may deduct that many points from their combined *Integrity* score. Then divide the total by 6, rounding fractions up, and deduct that many points from their *Artillery* score.

Turn to **489**.

The monstrous squid has the whale trapped in the crushing embrace of its ten-metre long arms, but it still has two colossal tentacles free, with which it lashes out at *Ronin 47*, as you join the fray.

AKKOROKAMUI				
SPEED	ARMOUR	MELEE	ARTILLERY	INTEGRITY
5	1	3	2	20

If you kill the killer cephalopod, turn to **459**.

Your mech's sensors start to register all manner of returns and, staring at the screen before you in horror, you see a thick, rippling carpet of detritus lying on the surface of the sea that is so thick you cannot see any water at all.

In the late 20th century, the Great Pacific Garbage Patch spanned the waters from the West Coast of North America all the way to Southeast Asia, and was comprised of the Western Garbage Patch, located near the islands of Japan, and the Eastern Garbage Patch, located between the US states of Hawaii and California.

Since K-Day, the Pacific trash vortex has also collected the wrecks of drifting vessels whose crews were forced to abandon ship when they were attacked by the ever-increasing numbers of kaiju. Salvage crews are known to search these garbage-ridden seas for valuables, such as useful pieces of forgotten tech.

And then a new reading flashes up on the HUD – *Ronin 47* has detected human life-signs. As the giant robot scans the debris field, you catch sight of a figure lying prone on a piece of floating wreckage, unmoving and unprotected from the blazing sun. It appears to be a young woman and if it wasn't for the fact that you can read her vital signs on the screen in front of you, you could have easily believed that she was dead.

Do you want to disembark from *Ronin 47* to help the young woman (turn to **448**), or do you want to leave her to her fate (turn to **516**)?

Piles of rubble fill the street, forcing you to take it slow as you guide *Ronin 47* over and around them. Turn to **435**.

Your Drones are designed for reconnaissance and carry only the most rudimentary defensive armaments. They are certainly no match for the much larger flying gun-batteries. (Cross off one use of the Drones.)

However, they do obstruct the weapon-drones, and some even collide with them, knocking out their guns and in rare cases sending them both plummeting to their mutually assured destruction.

But then the remainder of the gun-drones are on top of you.

Roll 1 die; when you come to fight the gun-drones, you may deduct that many points from their combined *Integrity* score. Then divide the total by 3, rounding fractions up, and deduct that many points from their *Artillery* score.

Now turn to **403**.

It is time you were on your way. Nozomi leads you back to the entrance to her hideout, unbolts the steel hatch, and bids you both farewell. But as you are exiting the bunker, you freeze when you see what awaits you outside.

A vast shadow has fallen over the plaza, which draws your attention to the colossal creature that is even now examining the *Rising Sun*, probing Kanesada's mech with its monstrously elongated limbs. The kaiju's presence also answers the question, what made the colossal webs?

You know it is impossible for a spider to grow this large, but this is of course not actually an arachnid, but an eight-legged kaiju that just happens to look like a gigantic spider. But that doesn't make the encounter any less terrifying, particularly since *Ronin 47* is one hundred metres away on the other side of the plaza.

It would be suicide for Kanesada to attempt to reach his Samurai, but there might be a chance you can reach yours before the monster spots you.

Gathering yourself, you take a deep breath, body tensing, and then sprint from the shelter of the concrete bunker across the open square, heading for your parked war-machine.

Take an Endurance test. If you pass the test, turn to **453**. If you fail the test, turn to **477**.

433

It's no good, the war-machine's superstructure is compromised. As the mech implodes, so your body is suddenly exposed to the impossible pressures of the abyss, and flesh and bone are turned into a pulverised soup before you even have a chance to drown.

Your adventure, like your life, is over.

THE END

434

Firing up the booster, you rocket clear of the giant crab-monsters and into the night's sky. *Ronin 47* flies higher and higher and you direct it northwards towards Honshu.

With the coming of dawn, the lands of the rising sun come into view at long last. But what was once a nation of 130 million people is now a devastated wasteland, dotted with isolated pockets of humanity, its once great cities nothing more than monuments to humankind's overreaching hubris. For the kaiju now populate the land as well as proliferate within the sea.

The Booster Rocket's fuel spent, you are forced to land in the sea, but not many kilometres from Tokyo harbour.

Cross off the Booster Rocket from your Adventure Sheet and turn to **566**.

435

Warning lights within the cockpit start to flash red as you hear the roar of rockets coming from overhead. *Ronin 47* is the target of a missile barrage.

As the Combat AI tracks the incoming projectiles and calculates firing solutions, you activate your mech's own artillery weapons.

Take an Artillery test. If your mech passes the test, turn to **11**, but if you fail the test, turn to **36**.

436

Tokyo lies almost directly north of your current position, but still over one thousand kilometres away. However, roughly three hundred clicks from your current position to the northwest, your mech is picking up…

You do not realise that the Ninja-mech's reactor core is about to overload until it is too late to do anything about it.

Take an Armour test. If you pass the test, turn to **462**; if you fail the test, turn to **492**.

437

A port opens in your Samurai's abdomen, and with a series of hollow pops, half a dozen depth charges describe a broad arc through the air before hitting the water.

Roll one die (or pick a card). If the number rolled is odd (or the card is red), turn to **467**. If the number (rolled) is even (or the card is black), turn to **498**.

438

Oni-class mechs excel at long-range combat, so if you are to gain the advantage over them, you are going to have to act fast. Do you want to:

Launch a Hunter-Killer Missile at one of the mechs (if you can)?	Turn to **34**.
Trigger an EMP Device (if you have one)?	Turn to **206**.
Engage the enemy?	Turn to **246**.
Take off, in the hope of breaching the fortress that way?	Turn to **542**.

Alternatively, if you have a Signal Transmitter and want to activate it now, you will also need to know the correct frequency to set it to. If you do, multiple the frequency by 10, deduct the total from this section, and then turn to that new section.

If the section you turn to makes no sense, you do not have the right frequency and will have to try something else.

439

As *Ronin 47* takes off, the gun-turrets track its progress and, seconds later, take out the jump-jets with pinpoint accuracy, sending the 200-tonne mech crashing back into the sea.

Roll one die and add 3. Deduct this many *Integrity* points from your mech. (Alternatively, pick a card and deduct its face value from your mech's *Integrity* score, unless it is a 10 or a picture card, in which case deduct 9 points from the Samurai's *Integrity* score; if it is less than 4 you must deduct 4 *Integrity* points.)

In the battle to come, you much reduce your mech's *Combat Rating* by 2 points for the first Combat Round, as you struggle to regain control and target the towers. Now turn to **525**.

440

The droid chirrups in acknowledgement as the Samurai's computer-brain relays your instructions, and enters the mech's superstructure again, via a reactor cooling port in its back.

Deduct 1 point from the mech's *Reactor* score and turn to **496**.

441

The invisible pulse shuts down every mech in the place, apart from your own war-machine. The rusted iron walls reverberate with the desperate shouts of captors and captives, and before the Wrecker-mechs reboot, you use all the weapons at your disposal to smash a way out of wherever it is that have been held captive.

Focusing *Ronin 47*'s firepower on one wall, you are rewarded when daylight suddenly bursts into the chamber in the aftermath of your attack. Approaching the great rent, you peer through it and find yourself gazing out across a collection of abandoned ships, actually within the Great Pacific Garbage Patch itself. You have been in the belly of an ancient supertanker all along!

Before you exit the hold, ready to resume your journey, you offer a final parting shot, taking out the wall of the holding cell that looks over the arena. You will let your fellow prisoners take their revenge against the Wrecker pirates. You have your own quest for revenge to complete!

The hulking Russian bids you farewell with a cry of, "*Spatzibo, moy droog*. Thank you, my friend!"

Tokyo lies 500 clicks roughly northwest of your current position, but how do you want to travel there?

If *Ronin 47* is equipped with a Booster Rocket, and you want to use it to reach Honshu Island, turn to **60**. If not, or you would prefer not to use the Booster Rocket at this time, you have no choice but to travel by sea – turn to **566**.

Reaching the Guardian hangar, you find the rest of Phoenix Squad making their final checks before launching their mechs, as the other Samurai squads do the same. There are forty-seven Samurai-mechs stationed at Ako Base, which will be more than enough to halt the kaiju assault and save the besieged facility.

Swiftly climbing into the open cockpit of *Samurai 47*, you strap yourself into your seat-harness, close the helm, and bring the machine's motive and weapons systems online. A quick scan of the prompts that appear on the HUD in front of you informs you that in the time the mech has been on standby mode in its cradle, the Spider maintenance droids have managed to make some superficial repairs.

(Restore up to 10 *Integrity* points and 1 *Melee* point to your mech but note that you may not exceed the Samurai's starting scores.)

The lights in the hangar suddenly start to flicker and then go out. But if anything, the lighting in the hangar is even brighter than usual, as coruscating arcs of lightning suddenly wreath the mechs hanging within their maintenance cradles. The Spider droids haven't managed to repair your mech's uplink unit yet, so you cannot hear the screams of the other pilots, but from the contorted shapes their mechs are making, you can imagine the indescribable agony they must be in as they are electrocuted inside their war-suits.

It appears that your mech is the only one not affected.

Of course – the uplink! Something must have been uploaded to the base's computer systems – a virus of some kind – and that must be what has caused the other mechs to overload, killing the pilots trapped inside them. But because your uplink is down, you and your mech have been saved from such an ignominious end.

You assume that whatever piece of malicious software has done for every other mech in the Guardian hangar has also been uploaded to every Tatsu dropship and Kirin escape craft attempting to carry the Ako Base personnel to safety. Your assumption is proved to be correct when a scrambling shuttle suddenly comes through the side of the hangar, smashing a great hole in one armoured wall. And it is heading straight for you!

You are going to have to act fast to avoid being hit by the out-of-control aircraft. Do you want to:

Flee from the crashing Kirin?   Turn to **468**.

Try to catch it?   Turn to **504**.

443

Using the helm's automated cleaning systems to flush the worm's body from the cockpit, you seal the grille in place over the vent once more.

Re-calibrating the mech's scanners for living matter, you initiate a diagnostic scan. In thirty seconds, it is complete.

There on the screen in front of you is a two-dimensional elevation of *Ronin 47*. Overlaid on the image are numerous red dots, clustered around the right knee joint, but also at the base of the mech's titanium alloy spine, inside the storage compartment in its chest, and even in the ventilation system where it connects to the helm.

An image relayed from an internal camera reveals a writhing mass of the fluke worm horrors. It would appear they are everywhere!

The mech's AI has identified the worms as being of the classification Oseichu – K-Compound mutated parasites that are usually found in the digestive tracts of the shark-like Isonade or the mutated descendants of cetaceans, such as Bake-kujira.

You can only surmise that, when you retrieved the dormant Spider droid from the gut of the ghost whale, the parasites found their way on board *Ronin 47* via an exhaust port or some similar access point.

It would only have needed one of them to invade the mech; the Oseichu reproduce via fragmentation, segments shed by the parent growing into completely new organisms. Usually this occurs when there is a sufficient food supply, but experiments in labs at Ako Base revealed that omicron radiation can have the same effect on the parasites. In other words, they can feed on the very radiation generated by a Samurai-mech's reactor core.

And now *Ronin 47* is infested with them. You are going to have to somehow purge the parasites from your mech or you're going to be left dead in the water – but how?

If you have a DNA Bomb, and you want to trigger it while it is still inside the mech, turn to **414**. If you want to release a portion of the liquid nitrogen that is used to cool the reactor into the robot's superstructure to drive out the critters, turn to **377**. If you want to overload the war-machine's circuits in the hope of frying the worms with a burst of electrical energy, turn to **348**.

444

The sun beats down on the broken buildings, creating a kaleidoscope of light on the hull of your mech. Turn to **115**.

445

The effect of the DNA-killing concoction on the Gumyocho is as swift as it is fatal. The monstrous bird's swooping descent becomes a plummeting death-dive and its body smashes onto the jagged rocks that form the shore-line of its island home. Its wings twitch once, then twice, and a last ululating cry escapes the avian's twin throats. Then it breathes no more, your mech's sensors confirming that the Gumyocho is indeed dead. Turn to **223**.

"Appear weak when you are strong, and strong when you are weak," as Sun Tzu wrote in *The Art of War*. But whether *Ronin 47* appears weak or strong to the traitor Kira and the crew of the Shogun, you care not. You only care that he pays for the lives of all those who died the day he doomed Tokugawa Island to attack from the kaiju with his blood, and you shall not rest until the Shogun is destroyed and he is dead.

(Remember to deduct any damage *Ronin 47* may have already caused the bigger mech and then conduct the battle between the two titans as normal.)

SHOGUN-MECH				
SPEED	ARMOUR	MELEE	ARTILLERY	INTEGRITY
4	4	4	4	35

After 6 Combat Rounds, if you are still in the fight, turn to **554**.

Swooping down from the velvet-black sky, on wings that are an amalgamation of bat-like taut skin and iridescent feathers, comes a truly immense avian with the wingspan of a super stratocruiser.

You have heard stories of the Gumyocho but have never encountered one yourself. It was not only the sea creatures that fed on the mutated polyps that were in their turn changed by the K-Compound; the same went for the seabirds that ate the fish that had eaten the smaller invertebrates. And when those seabirds bred, over the years they spawned ever bigger offspring that began to display grotesque mutations of their own, such as those clearly visible in this monster's make-up.

In basic shape and form, the Gumyocho looks not unlike a stork or some other water-fowl. But where it differs, other than in its monstrous size, is in the chaotic colours of its sparse plumage and its semi-saurian heads, for the Gumyocho has two of them!

Maybe the monster bird has its own aberrant chicks to feed, or perhaps it mistook the flashing white form of your mech powering through the sea for a fish, or maybe it's just because you have strayed into its territory. Whatever the reason for the Gumyocho's aggressive behaviour, you have no choice but to defend yourself against the avian kaiju. But how?

Do you want to:

Deploy a flight of Drones (if you can)?	Turn to **423**.
Launch some Flares (if you can)?	Turn to **395**.
Launch a Hunter-Killer Missile (if *Ronin 47* is equipped with one)?	Turn to **344**.
Activate a DNA Bomb (if you have one)?	Turn to **597**.
Prepare to engage in combat with the Gumyocho?	Turn to **373**.

448

The sea is shallow enough for *Ronin 47* to stand on the seafloor and still have its torso above the surface, so you bring the great mech to a halt and pop the cockpit hatch.

You have the colossal robot hold onto the piece of wreckage, so that it doesn't drift away or tip over when you step onto it, and then climb down *Ronin 47*'s façade, using the rungs built into the mech's superstructure.

Cautiously, you approach the unconscious young woman. As you bend down to shake her by the shoulder, a pair of figures launch themselves out of the water and land on the floating wreckage, setting it rocking. They are both wearing underwater survival suits and are carrying curious weapons that look like a cross between a crossbow and a rocket launcher. One of them depresses the trigger on his weapon and a net flies from the barrel, unfolding as it shoots through the air.

Take an Agility test. If you pass the test, turn to **470**. If you fail the test, turn to **497**.

Despite having explored the ruined city, it seems you are still no closer to finding your nemesis. Where could he be?

If you think you know the location where Kira is hiding, convert the name of the place into numbers using the code A=1, B=2, C=3... Z=26, then add 44, and turn to the section that has the same number as the total.

If the paragraph makes no sense, then you have made a mistake or chosen the wrong location and, unable to go on, your adventure is over.

THE END

450

You transmit the necessary codes identifying your mech as being on the same side as the sentry droids, but they take no notice, their guns finding firing solutions before you can even activate *Ronin 47*'s weapons.

The cannons open fire, raking your robot war-machine with intense energy blasts.

Roll one die and add 3; deduct this many *Integrity* points from your mech. (Alternatively, pick a card and deduct its face value from your mech's *Integrity* score, unless it is a 10 or a picture card, in which case deduct 9 points from the Samurai's *Integrity* score; if it is less than 4 you must deduct 4 *Integrity* points.)

If *Ronin 47* has lost 6-9 *Integrity* points, you must also deduct 1 point from its *Armour* score.

If you are still alive after enduring this barrage, turn to **159**.

451

The Kevlar-weave bodyglove you wear should protect you from the freezing cold of the ocean while the helmet of your Samurai pilot's suit also has a limited air supply. It should be enough for a thirty-minute foray into the bowels of the *Gojira*, providing nothing goes wrong.

Donning your helmet and having checked that the in-built aqualung is fully functional, you disengage the seat-harness and make your way to the airlock built into the back of the mech, via a hatch behind your seat in the cockpit. You take your katana with you, of course, just in case. (Please note that you cannot use your blaster underwater.)

Moments later, you exit the airlock into the freezing depths of the ocean. Swimming to the dock in the bottom of the keel, you turn the wheel-handle of a door which then opens easily, admitting you to the flooded passageways and internal spaces of the ship.

Almost immediately, the body of a drowned sailor drifts past you, its flesh grey and bloated from the time it has spent in the water, the eyes glassy and lifeless. This apparition brings home to you how careful you are going to have to be whilst on board the *Gojira*, if you are to avoid the sailor's fate becoming yours.

You set your chronometer to countdown from thirty minutes. That is how long you have until you must be back inside *Ronin 47*, if you want to avoid ending up like the drowned wretch. The ship is huge, so which way do you want to head in your search for secrets.

Towards the bow?   Turn to **476**.

Towards the stern?   Turn to **530**.

452

"Oishi-san!" Kanesada hails you over the comm. "We have conquered our enemies."

"Another two traitors dead, but not the traitor I seek," you reply, thoughtfully.

"Do you know where the reprobate is hiding?" Kanesada asks.

You reply in the negative.

"Perhaps *they* know where he is skulking," he says, as his Samurai points at the downed Oni-mechs.

Perhaps Kanesada is right.

Using *Ronin 47*'s uplink and Combat AI, you hack into one of the Oni's computer systems. However, with its destruction in battle, some manner of 'Scorched Earth' protocol has been initiated and so you are only able to retrieve a limited amount of data before you have to logout again to preserve *Ronin 47*'s own processing power.

Among the information you do manage to download, however, is one half of a set of GPS coordinates: 35.3606° N. (Record this information on your Adventure Sheet.)

"I regret that you must go on without me, Oishi-san," Kanesada tells you. "*Rising Sun* must be repaired before it can fight again."

And so, thanking your companion, you prepare to continue your quest alone once more. However, before you do so, you pillage the Oni-mechs' ordnance weapons for additional rockets and missiles that *Ronin 47* can use. (Add 1 point to your mech's *Artillery* score, even if it takes it above its current maximum level.)

If you have now collected both halves of a set of GPS coordinates, ignore any numbers that appear after a decimal point and add the two numbers together, then turn to the section that is the same as the total. If the paragraph you turn to makes no sense, then you have made a mistake or do not actually have the information you need – turn to **449**.

453

Catching sight of you with no doubt more than one of its myriad eyes, the arachnoid kaiju extricates itself from the *Rising Sun* and starts to scuttle across the plaza in pursuit. But you are too quick, managing to reach *Ronin 47* and clamber up to the security of its cockpit before the eight-legged freak can catch up with you.

As you bring your mech's systems online, the AI's pattern recognition software informs you, via the HUD, that this particular kaiju has been classified as a Tsuchigumo, and you are going to have to act fast if *Ronin 47* is not to succumb to its massive fangs and acid-salivating jaws. So will you:

Launch a Hunter-Killer Missile at it (if you can)?   Turn to **142**.

Detonate a DNA Bomb (if you have one)?   Turn to **6**.

Activate *Ronin 47*'s other weapons and
attack the kaiju?   Turn to **205**.

As the gun turrets open fire, you fight back with both artillery and close combat weapons.

GUN-TURRETS				
SPEED	ARMOUR	MELEE	ARTILLERY	INTEGRITY
1	4	1	5	20

If you destroy the sentry guns before they can incapacitate your mech, turn to **424**.

455

The torpedoes hit the mech and detonate against its hull.

Roll one die and add 6. Deduct this many *Integrity* points from your mech. (Alternatively, pick a card and deduct its face value from your mech's *Integrity* score; picture cards are worth 11 and an Ace is worth 12. If the card is less than 7 you must deduct 7 *Integrity* points.)

If *Ronin 47* has lost 7-9 *Integrity* points, deduct 1 point from its *Armour* score. If it has lost 10-12 *Integrity* points, also deduct 1 point from its *Speed*, *Melee*, and Artillery scores.

If the mech is still operational, turn to **567**.

456

The droid scuttles up to the shoulder of the mech and, having clamped itself into position, starts to remove the cover of the uplink unit with an array of manipulator-digits and sets to work.

Record the code word *Connected* on your Adventure Sheet and then turn to **496**.

457

It is eerily quiet as you navigate the ruins and shattered highways of Tokyo. Turn to **545**.

Taking a firm grip of the controls, you prepare to defend yourself against the gargantuan beast.

Three times as tall as *Ronin 47*, it is truly colossal – a Daikaiju, a giant of its kind! But you have committed yourself to battle now and can only hope your mech is powerful enough to make such a heroic stand against the gargantuan lizard-beast.

(Remember to deduct any *Integrity* points' damage you may have already caused the monster.)

DAIKAIJU				
SPEED	ARMOUR	MELEE	ARTILLERY	INTEGRITY
2	4	5	2	50

If you are still alive after 6 Combat Rounds, or if you manage to lower the monster's *Integrity* score to 20 points or below, whichever is sooner, turn to **486** at once.

459

The squid-kaiju dead, the whale dives below the waves, chasing the chunks of cephalopod flesh as they disappear into the depths. It appears almost ghostly as it sinks out of range of your scanners.

Turn to **577**.

460

The Hunter-Killer Missile is a very particular piece of heavy ordnance. It may only be used once, but if deployed at the right time, it can have a devastating effect. It is also known as the Bunker-Buster for this very reason. Turn back to the section you just came from.

461

As you trigger the weapon, a pulse of electromagnetic energy ripples out across the mountainside, sending a bow-wave of powdery snow before it.

The vehicles come to an abrupt stop as the EMP fries their circuit boards. The soldiers' guns are useless too, each of them reliant on a microchip for their operation.

(Cross the EMP Device off your Adventure Sheet; you will not be able to use it again.)

If *Ronin 47* is fitted with EMP Shielding, turn to **558**. If not, turn to **536**.

462

The mech explodes, the force of the blast hurling *Ronin 47* backwards into the sea and peppering its hull plating with fragments of shrapnel. The pilot must have initiated the Seppuku Protocol.

(Deduct 20 *Integrity* points and 1 *Armour* point.)

If *Ronin 47* is still operational, turn to **595**. If not, then your adventure is over.

463

Downed electricity cables threaten to trip up *Ronin 47* as the giant robot negotiates the ruins. Turn to **545**.

464

As you take off, the gun-turrets simply track your progress and take out the Booster Rocket with pinpoint accuracy, sending *Ronin 47* plummeting back into the sea.

Roll one die and add 3. Deduct this many *Integrity* points from your mech. (Alternatively, pick a card and deduct its face value from your mech's *Integrity* score, unless it is a 10 or a picture card, in which case deduct 9 points from the Samurai's *Integrity* score; if it is less than 4 you must deduct 4 *Integrity* points.)

In the battle to come, you much reduce your mech's *Combat Rating* by 2 points for the first Combat Round, as you struggle to regain control and target the towers. Now turn to **525**.

As you fire up the jump-jets, a crab-monster makes a grab for *Ronin 47* with one of its huge pincers, the colossal claw clamping around one of the mech's legs and crushing it.

(Deduct 5 *Integrity* points and 1 *Speed* point, and note that you will not be able to use the mech's jump-jets again if you are given that option.)

You have no choice but to deactivate the mech's flight systems and return to the ground to face the monsters in battle. (In this battle, cut straight to the Close Combat phase.)

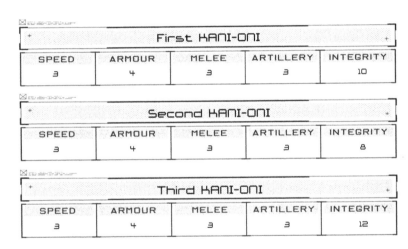

First KANI-ONI

SPEED	ARMOUR	MELEE	ARTILLERY	INTEGRITY
3	4	3	3	10

Second KANI-ONI

SPEED	ARMOUR	MELEE	ARTILLERY	INTEGRITY
3	4	3	3	8

Third KANI-ONI

SPEED	ARMOUR	MELEE	ARTILLERY	INTEGRITY
3	4	3	3	12

If you manage to kill all of the crab-kaiju, turn to **518**.

Maintaining a steady pace, you eventually catch up with the traitor when you burst through a door and suddenly find yourself outside. A cold wind is blowing across the top of the mountain, and you realise that you are standing at one end of a pier that juts out over the crater of Mount Fuji itself. At the other end of the walkway, supported by a tall, steel gantry that rises from the crater itself, is the stolen prototype Shogun-class mech.

Kira is already halfway to the Shogun. No doubt his crew are on board, readying the colossal mech for take-off.

Katana in hand, you leap down the steps from the door onto the walkway and set off after him at a run. Hearing you land on the pier, Kira spins round, and it is only then that you realise he is holding a blaster in one hand.

He doesn't give you a warning as to his intentions, but simply opens fire.

Take a Combat test. If you pass the test, turn to **549**. If you fail the test, turn to **482**.

The high explosive payload quickly sinks into the pelagic depths and disappears from view. A few seconds after that, they detonate with a suppressed *CRUMP*.

(Cross off one use of the Depth Charges from your Adventure Sheet.)

The shockwave of the explosion is picked up through your mech, although its stance remains firm.

A stream of bubbles rises to the surface to break at the centre of the blue hole. And then, suddenly, something is rushing up from the depths to challenge you, as a proximity alarm starts to sound inside the cockpit. Disturbed by the concussive charges, the kaiju the Tengu Satellite Array detected earlier charge to the surface to defend their territory.

A column of agglomerated cnidaria flesh bursts from the ocean in an explosion of seawater. It is as if some monstrous sea-worm has risen from the abyssal depths, but one of gargantuan proportions.

The column of flesh ends in a gaping maw, full of razor-sharp fangs, each one as long as your arm. The de facto head of the creature is ringed by vast starfish-like limbs that twitch and writhe independently of one another, as if possessed of a will of their own. More of these limbs emerge from the side of the creature's body, like tentacles, and the monster reaches for your Samurai with these pseudo-limbs.

A prompt on the HUD informs you that this particular kaiju has the designation Oni-Hitode, or 'Devil-Starfish,' and it is not alone. More of its kind have attacked *en masse*, forcing the entirety of Phoenix Squad to engage in battle.

At least as long as your mech is tall, the kaiju attacks.

ONI-HITODE				
SPEED	ARMOUR	MELEE	ARTILLERY	INTEGRITY
3	1	3	1	10

If you manage to defeat your kaiju attacker, turn to **560**.

468

Releasing the cradle's docking clamps, you free *Samurai 47* from its maintenance bay. The giant mech lands in a crouch on the hangar floor and, activating its motive drive, you run for it.

Take a Speed test. If you pass the test, turn to **488**. However, if you fail the test, turn to **524**.

469

The Flares burst from *Ronin 47* like a firework display. (Cross off one use of the Flares.)

The fusillade confuses the gun-drones' systems temporarily, either blinding their targeting arrays or causing them to de-select *Ronin 47* as a target and open fire on the blazing Flares instead.

You make the most of the distraction the Flares have created and open fire on the gun-drones before they can engage you. (Conduct this battle only using *Artillery* scores to determine which side wins each Combat Round.)

GUN-DRONES				
SPEED	ARMOUR	MELEE	ARTILLERY	INTEGRITY
4	2	-	2	15

If *Ronin 47* wins the aerial dogfight with the traitor welcoming committee, turn to **357**.

470

You dodge out of the way of the unfurling net and go for your attacker with your katana in your hand. It's a good thing you always take it with you when you exit *Ronin 47*, from force of habit if nothing else. (Your opponent has the initiative in this battle.)

FROGMAN   COMBAT 8   ENDURANCE 8

If you are still alive after 5 Combat Rounds, or you manage to lower your opponent's *Endurance* score to 4 points or fewer, whichever is sooner, you hear the hollow pop of the net-launcher in the other frogman's hands being fired – turn to **497** at once.

471

You must now engage the second mech in Long-Range Combat battle, whilst still trying to deal with its twin.

Second ONI-MECH				
SPEED	ARMOUR	MELEE	ARTILLERY	INTEGRITY
2	2	2	4	25

If *Ronin 47* bests both its enemies in battle, turn to **508**.

472

One hundred years ago, the population of Tokyo was almost fourteen million. You doubt even one thousandth of that number remains now.

Turn to **335**.

473

A dialogue commences between the mech and the droid, as the digital intelligence of one instructs the computer-brain of the other what repairs need to be made and where.

Restore your mech's *Melee*, *Artillery* and *Integrity* scores to their current maximum levels and then turn to **496**.

474

You fire up the Booster Rocket and the gigantic bird that has you in its clutches gives an ululating scream as its plumage catches fire. The bird lets go and dives into the sea, to put out the flames, before returning to its roost, in a cave atop the rocky outcrop. It knows better than to tussle with *Ronin 47* again.

With the coming of dawn, the lands of the rising sun come into view at long last. But what was once a nation of 130 million people is now a devastated wasteland, dotted with isolated pockets of humanity, its towering cities nothing more than monuments to

humankind's overreaching hubris. For the kaiju now populate the land as well as proliferate within the ocean.

The Booster Rocket's fuel spent, you are forced to land in the sea, but not many kilometres from Tokyo harbour.

Cross off the Booster Rocket from your Adventure Sheet and turn to **566**.

475

You make it back to the surface but there is no sign of Dr Kitsune's submersible, and it also appears to be out of range of your scanners

With no other option left open to you, you set off once more for Tokyo – turn to **231**.

476

Heading towards the bow, you come at last to the command deck of the ship. It is a huge space, flooded now of course, but nonetheless filled with computer interfaces and a wall of crackling display screens.

Most of the consoles are dead but some are still operational, despite being underwater. One screen is showing the oscilloscope recording of what would appear to be an animal call. It is made up of various frequencies, but the predominant vocalisation has a frequency of just 5 Hertz. (Make a note of this on your Adventure Sheet.)

Checking the chronometer, you see that you still have ten minutes of air remaining. It has taken you twenty minutes to find the command deck and access the *Gojira*'s databanks. The journey back to the dock should be much quicker.

You are about to leave when a chiming sound, strangely distorted by the water, starts to come from one of the consoles.

Do you want to swim across the command deck to the console to see why it is chiming (turn to **494**), or do you want to leave and return to *Ronin 47* before your oxygen runs out (turn to **515**)?

Catching sight of you with no doubt more than one of its myriad eyes, the arachnoid kaiju extricates itself from the *Rising Sun* and starts to scuttle across the plaza in pursuit.

Adrenaline gives the muscles in your legs a vital boost, but then the monstrous arachnoid spits a gobbet of web-like material straight at you.

Take an Agility test. If you pass the test, turn to **499**. If you fail the test, turn to **523**.

The EMP is just as effective against *Ronin 47*'s systems and Combat AI as it is against the other mechs. Unable to move or even exit the giant robot now, there is nothing you can do as the furious Wreckers work together to topple the colossal mech and then set to work cutting it open with fossil fuel-powered circular saws and oxyacetylene torches.

Sooner or later, they will force their way in, and they won't down their tools when they find you either. Your adventure is over.

THE END

You dodge out of the way just in time, and the hideous creature drops onto the floor of the cockpit with a splat. Oozing mucus, the grotesque thing rises up on its thick tail like a cobra about to strike.

The thing's 'head' is shaped like a flat, triangular paddle, and eyeless. It reminds you of a liver fluke, or a gut-dwelling, parasitic worm, but grown hundreds, if not thousands of times larger than is natural.

Grabbing your katana, you prepare to kill the parasite. (You have the initiative in this battle.)

OSEICHU   COMBAT 6   ENDURANCE 6

If you succeed in killing the creature, turn to **443**.

You start to wonder whether you are the hunter or the hunted. Turn to **335**.

You enter each of the three digits in turn and then punch the air again when text and numbers vanish to be replaced by a wireframe model of the Earth, surrounded by dozens of satellites in geostationary orbit.

Through an amalgamation of the information stored in *Ronin 47*'s data core and the real-time information relayed via the Tengu Array, you isolate the Shogun-mech's energy signature – which *Ronin 47* detected when Kira made his escape from Ako Base – and then track it to a location fourteen hundred kilometres almost directly north of your current position.

As the satellites home in on the spot, first a projection of the kaiju-devasted islands of Japan appears on the screen, and then the AI zooms in on Honshu Island, until finally you are looking at a detailed aerial image of Mount Fuji and the ruins of Tokyo.

Heat-scans reveal that there is activity among the ruins of Tokyo, while there is also an energy spike on Mount Fuji itself. Could it be about to erupt?

If it is, you need to act fast, before natural forces and tectonic activity rob you of your chance to be avenged against the traitor Kira and his followers.

Now that you know where Kira is, how do you want to proceed from here?

If you want to take to the sea again and pilot your mech towards Japan, turn to **270**. If you would rather engage *Ronin 47's* flight systems, turn to **96**.

The shot hits you in the shoulder, the force of it spinning you round, and you fall to your knees on the deck in shock. (Lose 4 *Endurance* points.)

Picking yourself up again, determined not to let the traitor get away, even if it is the last thing you ever do, you resume your stumbling run. But your nemesis has already reached the boarding platform at the end of the pier and punches a button on a control panel attached to the railing that encircles it.

The walkway immediately begins to retract, pulling away from the platform as it concertinas in on itself, back towards the pagoda factory-fortress.

It's now or never! Drawing on your last reserves of strength, you sprint towards the end of the retracting walkway, ready to fling yourself across the ever-widening void.

Take an Agility test. If you pass the test, turn to **573**. If you fail the test, turn to **522**.

483

Turning the mech around, you sprint for the sea once more as the gun turrets open fire.

Roll 1 die and add 6 to the number rolled, and then deduct the total from your mech's *Integrity* score. (Alternatively, pick a card and if it is a 7 or higher, it counts as a 6; then add 6 to the number and deduct the total from your mech's *Integrity* score.)

Reaching the coast again, you prepare to dive back into the sea.

Turn to **216**.

484

Warning markers start to appear on the HUD, alerting you to imminent danger. Turn to **215**.

485

The monstrous squid has the whale trapped in the crushing embrace of its long arms, and has clearly gained the advantage in its battle with the Bake-kujira. With you joining in on the mutated mollusc's side, the overgrown whale doesn't have a hope and it is dead in minutes.

Turn to **537**.

The god-like reptilian monster reels from your relentless assault and you see a chance to escape.

If you want to fire up the mech's jump-jets in order to get away, turn to **506**. If *Ronin 47* is equipped with a Booster Rocket and you want to use that to aid your flight from the monster, turn to **419**.

Alternatively, you can resume your battle with the Daikaiju. If you choose to do this, you have the initiative. If you are triumphant in this titanic clash, turn to **526**.

As the Kyojin gun-towers are still calculating firing solutions, you trigger the burst weapon. A pulse of electromagnetic energy ripples out across the Sagami-nada Sea, with you at its epicentre.

As the invisible EMP reaches the towers, their gun-turrets power down once more as the sentinels' computer minds are fried.

If *Ronin 47* is fitted with EMP Shielding, turn to **543**. If not, turn to **67**.

You sprint away from the crashing Kirin as it ploughs into the Samurai cradles. A moment later, an explosion rocks the hangar. Pieces of shrapnel the size of human beings come whickering through the air after you, several embedding themselves in the carapace of your mech.

Deduct 1 *Armour* point and 5 *Integrity* points, and then turn to **81**.

The forces ranged against you might be tiny, compared to your mech, like a colony of fire ants attacking a human being. But, just like the fire ants, they have a nasty bite.

TRAITOR ARMY				
SPEED	ARMOUR	MELEE	ARTILLERY	INTEGRITY
4	3	3	3	20

If you defeat the traitor's forces, turn to **558**.

490

The Booster Rocket is an improvement on the mech's built-in, short-range jump-jets, allowing for longer flight times, during which higher altitudes can be achieved. It also comes with its own fuel source and so will not put undue strain on *Ronin 47*'s reactor core. Turn back to the section you just came from.

491

Their electrical systems fried by the pulse, the gun-drones drop out of the sky, allowing you to continue the journey to your ultimate destination without further hindrance. Turn to **186**.

The mech explodes, the force of the blast hurling *Ronin 47* backwards into the sea. The pilot must have initiated the Seppuku Protocol.

As the Combat AI relays its damage assessment to the HUD, you realise that as well as peppering its hull plating with fragments of shrapnel, the exploding Ninja has also severely compromised both your mech's close combat capabilities and the actuators that control its robotic legs.

(Deduct 8 *Integrity* points, 1 *Armour* point, 1 *Melee* point, and 1 *Speed* point.)

If *Ronin 47* is still operational, turn to **595**. If not, then your adventure is over.

493

The Kani-Oni clack their pincers together, the sound they make as loud as gunshots, and spread out across the rocks in front of you as you activate *Ronin 47*'s weapons. (Fight the monsters one at a time.)

First KANI-ONI				
SPEED	ARMOUR	MELEE	ARTILLERY	INTEGRITY
3	4	3	3	10

Second KANI-ONI				
SPEED	ARMOUR	MELEE	ARTILLERY	INTEGRITY
3	4	3	3	8

Third KANI-ONI				
SPEED	ARMOUR	MELEE	ARTILLERY	INTEGRITY
3	4	3	3	12

If you manage to kill all of the crab-kaiju, turn to **518**.

Launching yourself off from the guard rail that circles one tier of the command deck, you swim over to the chiming terminal. On a screen built into the console you can see the target face of a sensor array. The *Gojira* lies at the centre, but the screen is showing the grainy green silhouette of something large circling the vessel in a slowly tightening spiral.

It looks to you like the Isonade – at least you hope it is, and not whatever sank the research vessel. Having to face the shark-kaiju in battle again would definitely be the lesser of two evils.

With whatever it is closing in on the stricken ship, it is time to leave while you still can.

Record the code word *Hunted* on your Adventure Sheet and turn to **515**.

A pulse of electromagnetic energy blasts outwards from the device, with *Ronin 47* at its epicentre. But the Shogun is not halted or even slowed by the pulse. In fact, it doesn't appear to be affected in any way whatsoever by the EMP.

Of course! As the first of a new generation of mechs, it is clearly shielded against such forms of attack. But can the same be said of *Ronin 47*?

If your mech is fitted with EMP Shielding, turn to **446**. If not, turn to **425**.

The shadows cast by the mech and the Shinto shrine lengthen as the sun sinks towards the western ocean.

A quick check of the Spider's status informs you that it will take at least eight hours to make its repairs. It looks like you're stuck here for the night.

The evening is warm and still, the only sounds the gentle susurrus of the waves lapping the shore below and the soft chirruping of the grasshoppers in the long grass.

Do you want to take a walk to the shrine (turn to **521**), or do you want to settle down and make camp for the night under the stars (turn to **541**)?

497

The net lands on top of you, but as you immediately start to pull it from you, a taser pulse of high voltage electricity passes through the metallic fibres and you lose consciousness.

Roll one die and add 1. Deduct this many *Endurance* points. (Alternatively, pick a card and deduct its face value from your *Endurance* score, unless it is 8 or above or a picture card, in which case deduct 7 points from your *Endurance* score.)

If you lose 4 *Endurance* points or more, also deduct 1 *Combat* point and 1 *Agility* point.

If you are still alive, turn to **112**.

498

The explosive payload lands close to the centre of the sea-hole and the depth charges quickly sink from view into the fathomless blue void.

(Cross off one use of the Depth Charges from your Adventure Sheet.)

A few seconds later, your mech detects the shockwave produced by the detonation of the charges, fifteen metres below.

A stream of bubbles rises to the surface to break at the centre of the blue hole. And then, suddenly, something is rushing up from the depths to challenge you, as a proximity alarm starts to sound inside the cockpit. Disturbed by the concussive charges, the kaiju the Tengu Satellite Array detected earlier charge to the surface to defend their territory.

A column of agglomerated cnidaria flesh bursts from the ocean in an explosion of seawater. It is as if some monstrous sea-worm has risen from the abyssal depths, but one of gargantuan proportions.

The column of flesh ends in a gaping maw, full of razor-sharp fangs, each one as long as your arm. The de facto head of the creature is ringed by vast starfish-like limbs that twitch and writhe independently of one another, as if possessed of a will of their own. More of these limbs emerge from the side of the creature's body, like tentacles, and the monster reaches for your Samurai with these pseudo-limbs.

However, you can see that large chunks are missing from the monster's body, and what remains are ragged holes where the cnidarian flesh has been cauterised – clearly injuries that have been caused by the exploding depth charges.

A prompt on the HUD informs you that this particular kaiju has the designation Oni-Hitode, or 'Devil-Starfish.' And it is not alone; more of its kind have attacked *en masse*, forcing the entirety of Phoenix Squad to engage in battle.

At least as long as your mech is tall, the kaiju attacks.

ONI-HITODE				
SPEED	ARMOUR	MELEE	ARTILLERY	INTEGRITY
3	1	2	1	6

If you manage to defeat your kaiju attacker, turn to **560**.

499

As the sticky ball hurtles towards you, you sidestep, and only just avoid being hit by it. The gobbet lands on the ground nearby and starts to hiss, as the saliva it is soaked with starts to eat into the metalled road surface. Turn to **552**.

500

"You are a deluded idiot, just like that old fool Asano!" Kira spits as his life ebbs from him. "I merely accepted the future we face is one where outdated ideals must be abandoned for progress to flourish; ideals you would give your life to hold onto in futility! I will watch from the depths of Hell just how long you can hold onto such sentimental nonsense before you inevitably join me!" And then he speaks no more.

Deputy Director Kira – the man who betrayed Director Asano, you, Phoenix Squad, and everyone else for whom Ako Base was home – is dead by your hand, your companions' untimely deaths avenged at long last. Not only that, but his army is routed.

But what happens to you now? You are a warrior without a master. Ronin.

But as you stand there, staring up at the titanic mech, bathed in a silvery light, you begin to formulate a plan.

For as Sun Tzu states in *The Art of War*, *"Opportunities multiply as they are seized."*

THE END

501

The sinuous horror lands on top of you. Uncoiling, it immediately latches onto the exposed flesh of your hand with its lamprey-like mouth and starts to feed on your blood. (Lose 2 *Endurance* points.)

Revolted, grabbing your katana, you plunge the blade into the grotesque thing. It responds by releasing its grip and dropping onto the floor. But, despite being eyeless, it is far from helpless. It rises up on its thick tail and sways menacingly before you like a snake as it attempts to latch onto your hand again. The thing's 'head' is shaped like a flat, triangular paddle, while its tail is a length of peristaltic muscle. It reminds you of a liver fluke, or a gut-dwelling, parasitic worm, but grown hundreds – if not thousands – of times larger than is natural. (In this battle, the parasitic Oseichu has the initiative.)

OSEICHU   COMBAT 6   ENDURANCE 4

If you kill the parasitic horror, turn to **443**.

502

Whatever it is that has you in its grasp gives a croaking cry as the mech's weapon makes contact with one of its taloned feet, and *Ronin 47* drops back into the sea, sending a small tsunami heading towards the island. Turn to **447**.

503

You fire off a salvo of flares into the abyss, hoping to blind the colossal anglerfish beast. (Cross off one use of the Flares from your Adventure Sheet.)

Roll one die (or pick a card). If the number rolled is odd (or the card is red), turn to **63**. If the number (rolled) is even (or the card is black), turn to **169**.

504

Bracing yourself within your seat, you raise your hands and arms in front of you – as if you are about to catch the crashing craft yourself – and, in response, via the haptic controls and neurocortical interface, *Samurai 47* mimics your movements precisely.

Seizing the hull of the Kirin's prow, you hope your mech's carbon-fibre muscle-bundles can take the strain.

Take an Integrity test. If you pass the test, turn to **546**. However, if you fail the test, turn to **524**.

505

You activate the Yurei Corporation-made 'ghostware' Cloaking Device, not knowing how long it will remain operational for before either its circuits burn out or the reactor core suffers burnout.

As you pilot *Ronin 47* towards the entrance to Tokyo Bay, the sentinels' guns power down once more, believing there to be no threat present now. The ghostware worked – *Ronin 47* has become invisible to the computer-minds of the Kyojin guns!

The Cloaking Device doesn't give up the ghost and deactivate until you are approaching the docks that once served the city of Tokyo.

Strike the Cloaking Device from your Adventure Sheet and then turn to **370**.

Ronin 47 rises into the sky on a cone of smoke and flames, leaving the Daikaiju far behind.

You direct the mech north, towards Honshu, not keen to conclude your flight too quickly, in case the Daikaiju has an equally colossal mate lurking somewhere nearby. But the jump-jets were not designed for prolonged flight and soon the HUD is warning you that your reliance on them is taking a toll on the reactor core. (Add 1 point to your mech's *Reactor* score.)

You have no choice but to land again as soon as possible.

Turn to **429**.

The missile's guidance systems lock on to one of the colossal kaiju and it fires from its shoulder-mounted launcher.

A split second later it impacts – after all, it could hardly miss so large a target – and detonates. Chunks of mutated whale-meat rain down around you as the Bake-kujira gives up the ghost in its battle with the Akkorokamui.

(Strike the Hunter-Killer Missile from your Adventure Sheet.)

While the whale-kaiju may be dead, the colossal squid-kaiju is still very much alive! Turn to **537**.

And so, the last of the Oni-mechs falls, taking one of the few remaining near-intact buildings with it, vanishing for a moment amidst a cloud of crumbling concrete, shattered glass, and dust.

However, it seems you are still no closer to tracking down your nemesis. But perhaps the Oni-mechs know where he is hiding...

Using *Ronin 47*'s uplink and Combat AI, you hack into one of the Oni's computer systems. However, with its destruction in battle, some manner of 'Scorched Earth' protocol has been initiated and so you are only able to retrieve a limited amount of data before you have to logout again, to preserve *Ronin 47*'s own processing power.

Among the information you do manage to download, however, is one half of a set of GPS coordinates: 35.3606° N. (Record this information on your Adventure Sheet.)

You also take the opportunity to raid the Oni-mechs' ordnance weapons for additional rockets and missiles that *Ronin 47* can use. (Add 1 point to your mech's *Artillery* score, even if it takes it above its current maximum level.)

If you have now collected both halves of a set of GPS coordinates, ignore any numbers that appear after a decimal point and add the two numbers together, then turn to the section that is the same as the total. If the paragraph you turn to makes no sense, then you have made a mistake or do not actually have the information you need – turn to **449**.

If you have not collected a complete set of GPS coordinates, also turn to **449**.

509

The Gumyocho emerges from the cloud as if it was nothing. Uttering another shrill, saurian cry, which seems to echo from the planet's distant, primeval past, it swoops down to attack. (Go straight to the Close Combat phase of this battle.)

GUMYOCHO				
SPEED	ARMOUR	MELEE	ARTILLERY	INTEGRITY
5	1	4	2	25

If you manage to slay the two-headed aberration, turn to **223**.

Keeping to the shadows, you make your way stealthily through the fortress complex. Your nerves are on edge, your heart racing. Every time you open a door or round a corner, you expect to run into a guard or someone from Kira's retinue. But it would appear that the distraction you created outside the walls of the fortress has drawn every member of personnel to the martialling yard of the complex.

You do not know where you are going but just keep heading deeper into the fortress. Considering what a coward Kira must be, you are confident he will be hiding as far away from any potential danger as possible.

As you approach yet another nondescript, stainless steel door, the portal slides open, and you enter what is clearly a large laboratory. All manner of pipes and rubber hoses snake across the grilled metal floor and connect to a series of large cylindrical tanks. Each one is three metres tall and filled with a sludgy, discoloured liquid. You can't tell if there is anything else inside the tanks or not, thanks to the opacity of the fluid.

And then the sound of boot heels clicking on the metal floor draws your attention to the figure emerging from the shadows at the back of the lab. You gasp! With her severe distinctive bobbed haircut and her white lab coat, you would know the woman anywhere. It is Dr Kitsune, the traitor Kira's partner-in-crime!

"Commander Oishi," she says, a cruel smile twisting her lips. "I'm surprised you've made it this far – you're certainly persistent, I'll give you that – but you have reached the end of your journey," she declares, punching a button on a control panel attached to one of the soup-filled cylinders.

The liquid immediately begins to drain from the tank, and you start when a fist punches the toughened glass from inside. The hand that forms the fist is the blue-grey of sharkskin. As the water-level drops, the horror contained within is revealed to you in all its terrible glory.

It appears to be a grotesque amalgam of fish and reptile, a combination of species – not unlike many subspecies of kaiju – only this one is many times smaller. But what is most horrible of all is that the monstrosity also displays human characteristics. Indeed, its hideous hybrid appearance brings to mind the Kaijin – the 'Sea Man' of legend.

It would appear that Dr Kitsune has been experimenting with the same irresponsible science that led to the creation of the K-Compound to create human-kaiju hybrids, no doubt with the intention of turning them into an elite fighting force for her paramour, the traitor Kira.

It is only as the last of the fluid seeps away that you realise you have been struck dumb and frozen to the spot by the revolting revelation. But what happens next shakes you out of your trance-like stupor.

The hybrid creature punches the glass again and this time a crack zigzags its way from the top of the tube to the bottom. At the next punch, the cylinder shatters and the monster steps free of its prison, standing upright on its hindlegs, a thick tail lashing behind it.

"Kill!" Dr Kitsune shrieks, pointing at you.

The hybrid opens its reptilian maw and gives voice to a bloodcurdling, primeval roar, and then turns on its creator. Grabbing the startled woman by the throat, it lifts her off the ground with one powerful webbed hand, cutting off her cry of surprise. It clenches its fist, and you hear the *SNICK!* as her neck is broken.

Casting the dead doctor's body aside, the creature roars again and starts to move towards you at speed.

If you are in possession of a Sonic Emitter and want to use it now turn to **89**. If not, turn to **30**.

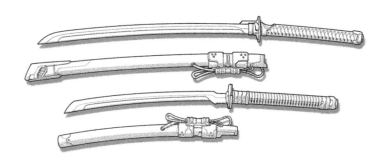

511

Exiting the cockpit of your own mech, katana in hand, you jump down onto the chest-plate of the Ninja lying prone on its back, as it is lapped by the waves.

Using your katana to deactivate the locks on the cockpit hatch of the Ninja, you force it open only to find that its occupant is ready for you.

The pilot leaps out of the downed mech, his own blade in hand. Swathed from head to toe in the black uniform of those loyal to the traitor Kira, he has the appearance of a true shadow warrior.

Take a Combat test. If you pass the test, turn to **533**. If you fail the test, turn to **553**.

512

Taking the metal cylinder from the mech's chest cavity, you hurl it towards the centre of the crater, where the kaiju are converging.

You watch with bated breath as the canister lands in the midst of the monsters and disappears from view. You do not hear the click of the 'bomb' opening but you know it has activated successfully when you see a toxic green cloud emanating from the heart of the crater, billowing into the air, enveloping the kaiju one by one.

You watch through the cockpit screen, wondering if you chose the correct combination of compounds to ensure that the bomb is effective against such a variety of mutated species.

Halve the number you have associated with the DNA Bomb and then turn to the section which is the same as the total to see what effect the gas has.

If you do not have a number associated with the DNA Bomb, turn to **44**.

513

Reaching the coordinates you have for Yokai Base, you are slightly confused to find yourself in the open ocean. There is no sign of the complex above the waves, and your scanners do not detect anything beneath the surface either. You can only imagine that the secret science facility is located within an abyssal trench far below the surface.

If you want to submerge *Ronin 47* in search of Yokai Base, turn to **562**. If you would rather give up your hunt for the hidden facility and continue on your way towards Japan, turn to **231**.

514

The torpedoes impact against the mech's hull and detonate, but your war-suit only suffers minimal impact damage. (Deduct 5 *Integrity* points.)

If *Ronin 47* is still operational, turn to **567**.

515

Leaving the command deck, you take what you hope will be a more direct route back to the dock and your waiting mech.

As you swim along another corridor, trying to ignore the floating bodies in your path, one of them suddenly starts to move. Horrified, you bring yourself to a stop and unsheathe your katana.

The corpse twitches again, its limbs flapping loosely in the currents created by the movements, as its belly distends.

Suddenly something bursts from the belly of the drowned man – it is a huge eel! Jaws open wide, the monstrous anguilliform fish attacks. (In this battle, the Giant Eel has the initiative.)

GIANT EEL   COMBAT 6   ENDURANCE 7

If you manage to kill the fish, turn to **572**.

516

Even though the thought of abandoning the woman to her fate ties your stomach in knots, you nonetheless steer the mech towards the northern edge of the Garbage Patch.

It is then that two mountains of metal rise out of the ocean to either side of you. Seawater streaming off them, they look like colossal, black metal sea urchins or crabs, but it is quite clear that they are some kind of mech, lashed together from the parts of other dead war-machines.

One has a bulbous cannon mounted on one shoulder, the barrel of the weapon glowing a brilliant plasma-blue as it powers up.

If *Ronin 47* is fitted with EMP shielding, turn to **559**; if not, turn to **538**.

517

As *Ronin 47* approaches the entrance to the Vault, the automated gun turrets activate. You desperately try to transmit the necessary protocols and passwords that would identify you as a non-hostile, but with the mech's uplink still damaged, you can't transmit anything.

The cockpit acquires a ruddy hue as the words 'TARGET LOCK' appear on the HUD in front of you.

Unable to prove to the Vault's computer systems that you are an ally rather than an enemy, you have only two choices open to you. You can try to flee, while you still can (turn to **483**), or prepare to take on the automated gun turrets (turn to **454**).

518

The threat eliminated, for the time being at least, you deactivate *Ronin 47* once more and wait for the morning to come.

When it does, at long last, you set off for Honshu Island once more as the rising sun paints the sea the colour of burnished gold.

Turn to **566**.

The standard scanner array fitted to all mechs coming out of the Ako facility only has a limited range. However, the Enhanced Scanners *Samurai 47* is fitted with, enable it to detect what is happening more than two hundred metres below the surface. And what your war-suit detects is six large entities, rising from the abyssal depths of the submarine sinkhole. The kaiju are coming.

How do you want to respond to this threat? Will you:

Deploy Depth Charges into the blue hole
(if you have them)? Turn to **498**.

Enter the blue hole yourself? Turn to **82**.

Order Phoenix Squad to maintain a defensive
position around the atoll and prepare for contact? Turn to **539**.

520

Twisting road signs point to avenues that are now buried under hundreds of tonnes of rock, and therefore inaccessible. Turn to **115**.

521

Reaching the top of the island, you just stand there, in the shadow of the great arch, as you contemplate all that has befallen you this fateful day; the destruction of Ako Base at the claws of the kaiju, and the deaths of the rest of Phoenix Squad – your fellow Samurai. Your friends.

Drawing your katana from its sheath, you kneel at the foot of the Shinto shrine. You swear upon your blade, glimmering in the blood-red light of the setting sun, that you will avenge the deaths of everyone who died so needlessly this day.

Alone with your thoughts, and exhausted by your adventures, you soon fall into a deep asleep.

Add 1 point to your *Endurance* score, then turn to **561**.

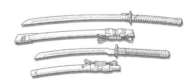

It is a valiant effort, but the yawning gap is already too wide for you to successfully traverse. Missing the edge of the boarding platform, you plummet into the crater of the dormant volcano.

Whether you survive the fall or not is immaterial, for as soon as the Shogun fires its rocket engines, everything inside the crater will be consumed in a cataclysmic firestorm.

You were so near and yet so far, and now your adventure is over.

THE END

The gobbet of sticky matter hits you, coating the right-hand side of your bodyglove, and immediately starts to dissolve the armoured Kevlar weave. The stuff is acidic!

It soon eats its way through the fabric and the sensation of the acid burning your skin causes you to cry out in agony. Despite the pain, you pull the web-like material from your protective suit with a glove, which you then have to discard, and your eyes widen as they fix on the raw flesh now visible through the hole in your sleeve.

(Deduct 3 *Endurance* points and 1 *Combat* point.)

If you are still alive, turn to **552**.

It is no good – your mech's systems fail you just when you need them the most. *Samurai 47* is flattened by the crashing Kirin, and a split-second later the aircraft explodes, with your war-machine right at the epicentre of the explosion.

Roll one die and add 6. (Alternatively, pick a card; Jacks are worth 10, Queens and Kings are worth 11, and an Ace is worth 12.) Now deduct your Samurai's *Armour* score from the total, then multiple this number by 5. Deduct the final total from your mech's *Integrity* score.

If your mech is still operational, turn to **81**. If not, you will forfeit your life as well when the Samurai's reactor core goes critical...

Locked onto your position now, the sentinel gun-towers open fire with everything they've got. (Fight them both at the same time.)

First KYOJIN GUN-TOWER				
SPEED	ARMOUR	MELEE	ARTILLERY	INTEGRITY
2	4	2	4	20

Second KYOJIN GUN-TOWER				
SPEED	ARMOUR	MELEE	ARTILLERY	INTEGRITY
2	4	2	4	20

If you destroy the automated guardian guns before they can obliterate you, turn to **543**.

526

The colossus falls at last, leaving you free to continue your journey. But before you depart, with the mech's robotic fist, you tear one of the immense teeth from the monster's jaw to keep as a trophy. Turn to **429**.

527

There is a lot of interference, although whether that is being caused by the metal frameworks of the ruined buildings or is the result of the fallout from whatever devices were detonated here during the desperate weeks of fighting after K-Day, you have no idea.

But, thanks to *Ronin 47*'s Enhanced Scanners, you are able to pick out two clear returns. Despite it not being possible to pinpoint their exact positions, you can tell that one is located to the northwest and the other to the southeast.

Now turn to **582**.

As the armoury's automated systems set about making the required alterations to your war-machine, Engineer Mototoki turns to you and says, "Do you want to select a second upgrade? If you're planning on going up against the Shogun you are going to want to be as well prepared as possible. I hear that the prototype benefits from all the latest tech developments, including an enhanced neurological interface and EMP shielding."

Aware that time is pressing, but knowing that it's going to take a while for the work on your mech to be completed, do you want to opt for an additional upgrade (turn to **544**), or will you just be content with the one you have already selected (turn to **73**)?

Ronin 47's systems and Combat AI are as susceptible to the EMP weapon's effects as the drones. As the flying gun-batteries drop out of the sky, *Ronin 47* follows them.

With all its systems incapacitated by the blast, you cannot even activate the emergency eject. *Ronin 47* will hit the ground before its computer core has time to reboot and from this height, you will not be walking away from such a landing.

Your adventure is over.

THE END

Making for the stern, you eventually come to a steel antechamber, and in front of you a wall constructed of glass panels. The central one is actually a door, with a keypad attached.

The much larger room beyond the reinforced glass is lit by an icy blue glow that reminds you of the bioluminescence given off by many deep-ocean dwellers. You can see banks of computer consoles, dissecting tables, high-powered microscopes, and aquarium tanks that still appear to be occupied by all manner of corals, molluscs, gastropods, and arthropods.

You try the door, but it is locked. Considering what was probably going on in the lab beyond, you doubt you would be able to break through the glass using your katana. Clearly you are going to need to type a code into the keypad if you want to enter the lab, but what could that code possibly be?

You take a closer look at the lock. It is a conventional ten-digit keypad beneath a glowing panel, on which the following image is projected:

17	24	01	08	15
23	_	07	_	16
04	06	13	20	22
10	_	19	_	03
11	18	25	02	09

There are four numbers missing from the grid. Perhaps if you could work out what they are and enter them into the keypad you might unlock the door.

If you know what the missing numbers are, add them together and then turn to the section with the same number as the total. If you cannot work out what numbers need to be entered, you will have to search elsewhere – turn to **550**.

531

Unsurprisingly, the bigger Shogun is stronger than your Samurai class robot.

If *Ronin 47* is equipped with Gyroscopic Stabilisers, turn to **110**. If not, turn to **70**.

532

As *Ronin 47* reaches the edge of the continental shelf and begins to stride from the Sagami-nada Sea, the great war-machine suddenly loses all motive function in its right leg. Fault icons start popping up on the HUD, as the illumination in the cockpit switches to the ruddy glow of hazard lighting. At the same time, you become aware of a foul stench entering the cockpit through a vent above your seat. It smells like gone-off shellfish.

Punching the release button on your harness, you climb out of your seat to investigate. As you examine the vent, you are startled when the grille is suddenly pushed out and something browny-grey, sinuous, and slimy – and roughly as long as your arm – slips out of the hole.

Take an Agility test. If you pass the test, turn to **479**. If you fail the test, turn to **501**.

533

Rapidly shifting your grip on your sword, you deflect the warrior's first bold strike and spin his blade out of the way, ready to engage in hand-to-hand combat with your ambusher. (In this battle, you have the initiative.)

SHADOW WARRIOR   COMBAT 10   ENDURANCE 8

If you reduce the Shadow Warrior's *Endurance* score to 2 points or fewer, turn to **574** at once.

534

You charge towards the other Oni, determined that the demonic robot will not stop you from breaching the walls of the traitor Kira's fortress and avenging the deaths of all those slaughtered during the Ako Incident.

First ONI-MECH				
SPEED	ARMOUR	MELEE	ARTILLERY	INTEGRITY
2	3	2	4	25

If you defeat the mech, turn to **570**.

Despite struggling to free the war-suit from the talons of whatever it is that has *Ronin 47* in its grasp, the giant robot is only released when the creature carrying it suddenly lets go.

You try to fire up the jump-jets but there is not time before the mech hits an outcropping of jagged rocks on the edge of the island.

(Deduct 8 *Integrity* points, 1 *Armour* point, 1 *Melee* point, and 1 *Artillery* point from your mech, as well as 3 *Endurance* points, as you are jolted about inside your pilot's harness.)

If you are still alive, and *Ronin 47* is still operational, turn to **447**.

536

The EMP is just as effective against *Ronin 47*'s systems and Combat AI as it is against other machines. Unable to make it move, or even exit the giant robot now, there is nothing you can do as Kira's private army topples the colossal mech and then sets to work with industrial cutting tools. Sooner or later, the troopers will cut their way into *Ronin 47*, and they won't lay their tools aside when they find you.

Your adventure ends here, on the slopes of Mount Fuji.

THE END

537

Rather than drag the whale's carcass to the bottom of the ocean to devour its prize, the Akkorokamui turns on you. Having seen how lethal *Ronin 47* can be in battle, it sees the mech as a threat that must also be eliminated.

AKKOROKAMUI				
SPEED	ARMOUR	MELEE	ARTILLERY	INTEGRITY
5	1	4	2	20

If the Akkorokamui wins a Combat Round against you, roll one die (or pick a card); if the number rolled is even (or the card is black), the giant squid grabs the mech in its tentacles and pulls it in range of its huge, beak-like mouth, where it delivers an additional 5 points of *Integrity* damage, and reducing the mech's *Armour* score by 1 point. The mech must also reduce its *Combat Rating* by 1 point until it wins a Combat Round against the cephalopod-kaiju, at which point it is able to break free of the monster's tentacles.

If you slay the colossal cephalopod, turn to **557**.

538

Ronin 47 is directly in the path of the cannon when it fires. The fuselage becomes wreathed in barely-contained lightning for a moment, as the mech's systems are overwhelmed by the energy burst.

Inside the cockpit, the lights go out and the screen shuts down, leaving you in total darkness. But you are already unconscious, having still been connected to the battle AI through the pilot-interface when the EM pulse hit.

Roll one die and add 1. Deduct this many *Endurance* points. (Alternatively, pick a card and deduct its face value from your *Endurance* score, unless it is 8 or above or a picture card, in which case deduct 7 points from your *Endurance* score.)

If you lose 4 *Endurance* points or more, also deduct 1 *Combat* point and 1 *Agility* point.

If you are still alive, turn to **112**.

539

You watch the proximity counter counting down on the screen as the kaiju rise to the surface until a tangle of the monsters bursts from the blue hole.

It looks like a hunting party of predatory abyssal worms has risen from the depths. Each one is a colossal column of flesh, which ends in a gaping maw, full of razor-sharp teeth, each one as long as your arm. This pseudo-head is ringed by vast starfish-like limbs which twitch and writhe independently of each other, as if each is possessed of a will of its own. More of these limbs emerge from the side of the creature's body, like tentacles.

A prompt appears on the HUD, as one of the creatures reaches for your mech with those horribly rippling limbs, informing you that this particular kaiju has been given the designation Oni-Hitode.

At least as long as your Mech is tall, the gargantuan devil-starfish attacks.

ONI-HITODE				
SPEED	ARMOUR	MELEE	ARTILLERY	INTEGRITY
3	1	3	1	10

If you manage to defeat the kaiju, turn to **560**.

540

Your search is over! Turn to **215**.

541

Exhausted emotionally as well as physically, you lay your head down on the cool turf and soon fall asleep.

But in your dreams, you relive everything that has befallen you during the day. You see the rest of the Samurai of Phoenix Squad contorted within their repair cradles, only now you can hear the agonised screams of your fellow pilots as they suffer fatal electrical burns as the systems of their war-suits overload and fail, as a result of the virus that has been uploaded to their computer brains.

If it hadn't been for the fact that *Samurai 47*'s uplink was damaged during the battle at Hitode Atoll, you would be dead too.

And then, in your dream, you see yourself in the form of *Samurai 47*, rising from the flames of the burning base, like a phoenix rising from its funeral pyre, to live again.

Restore up to 3 *Endurance* points and then turn to **561**.

542

As you engage *Ronin 47*'s jump-jets, intending to perform a great leap that will take you over the wall and into the fortress, the Oni-mechs focus their fire on your war-suit's propulsion systems.

Roll one die and add 3; deduct this many *Integrity* points from your mech. (Alternatively, pick a card and deduct its face value from your mech's *Integrity* score, unless it is a 10, or a picture card, in which case deduct 9 points from the Samurai's *Integrity* score; if it is less than 4 you must deduct 4 *Integrity* points.)

If your mech has lost 7-9 *Integrity* points, you must also deduct 1 point from its *Armour* score.

Add 1 point to your mech's *Reactor* score and, if *Ronin 47* has not been destroyed yet, turn to **565**.

543

Having conquered the Kyojin gun-towers, *Ronin 47* wades through the shallow waters of Tokyo Bay until it reaches the docks on the outskirts of the city. Turn to **370.**

544

Choose a second upgrade for your mech, but you need to be aware of the following restrictions. Firstly, you can only choose one upgrade from each category. Secondly, be aware that *Ronin 47* can only use one melee weapon at a time; if it is already armed with an Electro-Katana and you select the Sunblade, you have to leave the Electro-Katana behind. Thirdly, you may choose the Depth Charges or the Flares even if *Ronin 47* is already equipped with them.

Artillery

      Hunter-Killer Missile   Turn to **460**.

Melee

      Sunblade   Turn to **410**.

Upgrades

Depth Charges	Turn to **310**
Flares	Turn to **360**
Booster Rocket	Turn to **490**

Armour

Upgraded Hull	Turn to **220**
EMP Shielding	Turn to **260**

When you have finished making your second choice, Mototok enters it into the touch-screen console in front of him, throwing in casually, "And how about a third?"

If you want to choose one more upgrade for your mech, make your choice and then turn to **90**. If not, turn to **73**.

545

Roll one die (or pick a card). If the number rolled is odd (or the card is red), turn to **16**. If the number rolled is even (or the card is black), turn to **582**.

546

The Samurai braces itself and is pushed backwards by the momentum of the out-of-control craft, but its metal toes lock tight, gouging great channels in the floor of the hangar, as slowly the Kirin's engines cut-out and you are able to deposit it, rather unceremoniously, on the ground.

You scan the craft for life-signs but there are none; the passenger and crew are all dead, no doubt electrocuted in their seats during evac, like the Samurai pilots trapped inside the other mechs.

Turn to **81**.

547

The portal slides opens as you tap the door control, and you step over the threshold into a room packed with electronic equipment. Accessing the computer terminal in the lab, you soon discover that the engineers working here were attempting to perfect a transmitter that could broadcast frequencies to attract kaiju, with the intention of using it to lure the titans away from anywhere they might threaten remaining pockets of civilisation.

It soon becomes clear that it was this technology that Kira used to bring about the destruction of Ako Base, turning a device that was intended to help humankind into a weapon of terrifying power. However, it looks like the engineers were working on an improved version of the transmitter when they were forced to abandon the Yokai facility.

The device is no bigger than a black box flight recorder. If you want to take it with you, turn to **152**. If you would rather not put your faith in untested technology and want to leave the transmitter where it is, you can either see what lies beyond the door at the other end of the passageway (turn to **189**), or make your way back to *Ronin 47* (turn to **276**).

548

As *Ronin 47* strides through the sea, still waist-deep in the water, the sentient mines close on its position, driven by whirring propellers. You have no choice but to defend yourself, targeting the mines with your heavy ordnance weapons before they can come within range of the war-machine and explode, causing catastrophic damage. (Please note that you may not use your melee weapons during this encounter and must resolve the battle in the Long-Range Combat phase.)

SENTIENT MINEFIELD				
SPEED	ARMOUR	MELEE	ARTILLERY	INTEGRITY
2	2	-	2	30

If you manage to defeat the AI-controlled Mines, meaning that you have made it safely to the other side of the Sagami-nada Sea with your mech intact, turn to **288**.

549

With a flurry of dextrous blocks and parries, you deflect the energy bolts with the mirrored flat of your blade. One of them rebounds from your katana and hits the blaster, knocking it out of Kira's hand.

Resigning himself to his fate, realising that he has no other choice, Kira unsheathes his own blade and comes for you, determined to finish you one way or another. (In this battle, you have the initiative.)

KIRA   COMBAT 10   ENDURANCE 12

If you defeat your nemesis, turn to **500**.

550

Trailing bubbles from your aqualung, you start to retrace your route through the wreck.

You are startled when you detect movement ahead of you in the water. Something with elongated, chitinous limbs, is plucking at the corpse of a drowned scientist and dining on the briny flesh. As you move closer, the crustacean feels the need to defend its prize catch. You have no choice but to fight the Giant Spider Crab. (In this battle, you have the initiative.)

GIANT SPIDER CRAB   COMBAT 7   ENDURANCE 6

If you kill the decapod, turn to **572**.

551

Downed electricity cables threaten to trip up *Ronin 47* as the giant robot negotiates the ruins. Turn to **215**.

552

With the monstrous arachnoid rapidly closing the distance between you, you nonetheless manage to reach your mech and scramble up the outside of the robot to the security of its cockpit, shutting yourself in before the eight-legged freak can catch you.

As you strap in, you bring your mech's systems online and the AI's pattern recognition software informs you, via the HUD, that

this particular kaiju has been classified as a Tsuchigumo. You are going to have to act fast if *Ronin 47* is not to succumb to the monster's massive fangs and acid-salivating jaws. So will you:

Launch a Hunter-Killer Missile at it (if you can)?　　Turn to **142**.

Detonate a DNA Bomb (if you have one)?　　Turn to **6**.

Activate *Ronin 47*'s weapons and attack the kaiju?　　Turn to **205**.

553

The warrior's skills would appear to be superior to yours, or perhaps it is just that you were expecting him to have been stunned from the defeat of his mech. But whatever the truth of it, he catches you unawares and gets in underneath your guard, slicing the razor-sharp edge of his blade across your thigh. (Lose 2 *Endurance* points.)

And then you are fighting for your life once more. (In this battle, your enemy has the initiative.)

SHADOW WARRIOR　　　　　COMBAT 10　　ENDURANCE 8

If you reduce the Shadow Warrior's *Endurance* score to 2 points or fewer, turn to **574** at once.

554

This is truly a clash of titans, but who is winning the battle?

Suddenly an earthquake rocks the peak, and a great fissure appears in the bottom of the crater, from which rises scalding hot steam and within which you can see the orange glow of molten lava. It would appear that Kira's activities here – tapping the volcano for geothermal energy to power his mech-factory – have destabilised the magma chamber and Mount Fuji is about to erupt!

If you and *Ronin 47* have won more Combat Rounds so far, turn to **578**. If Kira and the Shogun have won more Combat Rounds up to this point, turn to **156**. If you have won the same number of Combat Rounds as the Shogun-mech, turn to **136**.

You are used to threats coming from below, in the ocean depths, but not from above. Which means you are taken utterly by surprise when the proximity alarms start to sound once more, and *Ronin 47* is suddenly dragged into the sky.

It soon becomes clear that something unimaginably huge has seized hold of the mech with its colossal talons. You have to get free, or who knows what fate might befall you?

If your mech is equipped with a Booster Rocket, and you want to fire it up now, turn to **474.**

If not, *Take a Melee test*. If you pass the test, turn to **502**, but if you fail the test, turn to **535.**

The missile hits the Oni's hull and detonates. (Cross off the Hunter-Killer Missile from your Adventure Sheet.)

When the smoke clears, you see that the Hunter-Killer has done some serious damage, blowing a great hole in the robot's torso and taking out one of its rocket-battery arms altogether.

Now all that remains is for you to put the demon-engine out of its misery.

ONI-MECH				
SPEED	ARMOUR	MELEE	ARTILLERY	INTEGRITY
2	3	2	2	15

If you defeat the mech, turn to **570.**

With both kaiju dead, you take a moment to recover and compose yourself after your epic battle.

Your moment of mindful mediation is disturbed by an insistent chiming from the Combat AI. Opening your eyes again, you see the bodies of the dead sea-monsters floating on the surface of the ocean, as they are rocked by the restless waves. Overlaid on this image is a red marker icon. The mech's scanners have detected something man-made that appears to be lodged somewhere inside the Bake-kujira.

If you want to use *Ronin 47*'s melee weapons to cut open the dead cetacean to look for the object, whatever it may be, turn to **598**. If you would prefer not to go rummaging in the guts of the leviathan, turn to **577**.

558

With nothing now standing between you and your objective, you stride past Kira's defeated forces and through the open gates of the fortress, the systems that operate them having also been damaged during your assault.

Do you want to exit your mech and continue on foot (turn to **510**), or do you want to continue to pilot *Ronin 47* into Kira's mountaintop lair (turn to **18**)?

559

The electromagnetic blast emitted by the weapon has no effect on *Ronin 47*, thanks to the EMP Shielding it is fitted with.

But it is not the only weapon with which the hybrid Wrecker mechs are armed. One carries a great club, in both hands, while the other has an iron wrecking ball hanging from the end of its right arm.

If you want to stand and face the Wreckers, turn to **158**. If you would rather attempt to flee, turn to **579**.

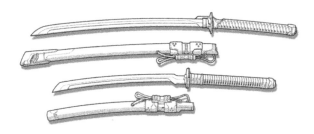

At the killing strike delivered by your Samurai, the integrity of the K-Compound fails and the colony creatures that make up the colossal devil-starfish come apart, falling into the sea like cnidaria rain.

However, not all of Phoenix Squad have fared so well against the kaiju of Hitode Atoll. While four of your team have successfully destroyed their attackers, one has suffered a catastrophic reactor core breach.

As the grasping tentacles of the Oni-Hitode start to penetrate Norikane's cockpit, *Samurai 39*'s reactor detonates with the force of a nuclear warhead. The Samurai is blown apart in an explosion that kills not only its wretched pilot but also vaporises the monster that was ultimately responsible for its destruction.

In that moment – even as your own mech is bombarded by pieces of shrapnel – you swear that Norikane's name will be recorded on the Honour Roll of the Fallen at Ako Base.

Take an Armour test. If your mech passes the test, turn to **596**. However, it your mech fails the test, turn to **580**.

You wake to the feeling of warmth on one side of your face and the coolness of moisture on the other, as the rising sun rouses you gently with its restorative rays.

You come to quickly, with a renewed sense of purpose and a plan. You will rise like a phoenix from the flames to avenge the deaths of your fellow warriors and all those who perished within Ako Base yesterday by slaying every kaiju you encounter. But before you set off on your hunt, you have another quarry to run to ground first – the traitor Kira.

Your master, Director Asano, is dead, which means that you are now a masterless samurai.

Taking a welding torch from the mech's tool kit, you burn two kanji characters onto the hull of your mech – *rou*, meaning 'wandering', and *nin*, meaning 'person' – for you are now ronin.

Climbing back into the cockpit of the renamed *Ronin 47*, you realise that you are too far away for your mech's scanners to track the stolen Shogun-mech, but you are sure that it was heading north, when it left Tokugawa Island.

If you are going to have to go toe-to-toe with the Shogun, you are going to need all the help you can get. Checking the map database contained within the mech's memory banks, you confirm your location 500 clicks north of Tokugawa Island.

Three hundred kilometres northwest of your current position lies the Vault, a secret Ako armoury operated by a skeleton staff. Hopefully the team based there are still loyal to Director Asano and, if so, might be persuaded to help you in your mission of vengeance.

You also know that the research vessel *Gojira* patrols the Pacific Rim. The prime directive of the scientific team aboard the converted aircraft carrier is to search for a way to reverse the mutagenic effects of the K-Compound and thereby destroy the kaiju that are steadily overrunning the planet.

Checking your mech's status, you see that the Spider droid has made the repairs you requested. However, you also see that the Samurai's jump-jets are offline. The Spider's energy reserves have been completely exhausted. Usually, having completed its task, the Spider would retire to its own recharge bay within the Guardian hangar, but seeing as it is unable to do that now, it is as good as dead.

Wherever you intend to go now, you will have to travel by sea, piloting *Ronin 47* as if it were a submersible, skimming along like a torpedo underneath the waves.

In which direction do you want to travel?

Northwest towards the Vault?   Turn to **583**.

Northeast in the hope of intercepting the *Gojira*?   Turn to **114**.

562

As your mech sinks towards the bottom of the ocean, the sunlight penetrating the water from above soon fades and you find yourself in the deep darkness of the Midnight Zone. *Ronin 47*'s running lights struggle to penetrate the gloom and you start to imagine all sorts of horrors waiting for you down there in the dark.

There is still no sign of the facility. Is it possible that it was been destroyed just like Ako Base?

If *Ronin 47* has an Upgraded Hull, turn to **130**. If not, turn to **422**.

563

Metallic debris pangs off the mech's armour, your war-suit suffering only minimal impact damage. (Deduct 5 *Integrity* points.)

If *Ronin 47* is still operational, you set off across the now disarmed minefield, heading for Tokyo Bay.

Turn to **288**.

564

The Hunter-Killer can only target one of the many gun-drones that are swarming towards you. However, it easily finds its objective and detonates, the shockwave from the explosion knocking several more out of the sky. (Strike the Hunter-Killer Missile from your Adventure Sheet.)

Roll 2 dice; when you come to engage the gun-drones, you may deduct this many points from their combined *Integrity* score. Then divide the total by 4, rounding fractions up, and deduct that many points from their Artillery score.

And then *Ronin 47* comes within range of the drones' guns. Turn to **403**.

565

Ronin 47 comes crashing back down to the ground, some way from the fortress walls but still outside the complex. You are going to have to try something else.

Do you want to:

Launch a Hunter-Killer Missile at one of the mechs (if you can)?	Turn to **34**.
Trigger an EMP Device (if you have one)?	Turn to **206**.
Engage the enemy?	Turn to **246**.

566

At last, the southern shore of Honshu Island and the region once known as the Kanagawa Prefecture come into view on the horizon. And beyond that, shrouded in early morning mist and barely visible on the screen in front of you, is the snow-capped peak of Mount Fuji.

If you have the code word *Invaded* recorded on your Adventure Sheet, turn to **532**. If not, turn to **273**.

567

You commence your pursuit, only for it to stall once again as something huge materialises from the gloom, the bioluminescent lure dangling in front of its gaping maw presaging its arrival.

As the smaller sub makes its escape, the Shachihoko – an abyss-dwelling anglerfish-kaiju of titanic proportions – makes a beeline for *Ronin 47*.

What do you want to do? Will you:

Launch Depth Charges (if you can)?	Turn to **219**.
Launch some Flares (if you can)?	Turn to **503**.
Launch a Hunter-Killer missile (if you can)?	Turn to **26**.
Prepare to fight for your life?	Turn to **169**.

Without access to the array, you have no hope of locating the traitor, Kira. And if you cannot find Kira, then you cannot avenge Director Asano and everyone else who died in the kaiju assault on Ako Base.

Exiting the building in despair, you kneel down on the ground in the shadow of the colossus. Taking your katana in hand once more, you select the wakizashi setting – the blade partially retracting into the hilt in response – and do the only honourable thing you can do; you commit seppuku, as a final atonement for failing to honour the memories of your beloved comrades, using the blade that still bears the blood of your enemies to disembowel yourself.

Your adventure is over.

THE END

569

Your search is over! Turn to **215**.

570

As your opponent falls, so does the other Oni, *Rising Sun* taking the robot's demonic head from its shoulders with a sweep of its Electro-Katana.

But there is no time to celebrate your victory, as the gates of the fortress open and a host of black-clad figures pour out. Many are riding snowmobiles and light all-terrain vehicles, and they are accompanied by a squadron of aerial gun-drones.

Having seen you defeat his guard-mechs, Kira has sent his army of devoted followers to stop you. He must be getting desperate!

'Go!' Kanesada shouts, as *Rising Sun* points at the open gate to the fortress with a huge, armour-plated arm. "I'll hold them off. You do what needs to be done!"

Leaving Kanesada to face Kira's army alone, you direct *Ronin 47* towards the open portal, even as the gates start to close, hoping to throw your mech through the gap before they can close completely. However, some of the soldiers direct their fire at *Ronin 47* as the giant robot runs past them.

Take a Speed test. If you pass the test, roll 1 die, multiply the result by 2 and deduct this many *Integrity* points. However, it you fail the test, roll 1 die and multiply the result by 4 before deducting the total from *Ronin 47*'s Integrity score.

If *Ronin 47* is still operational, turn to **18**. If not, you will have to abandon your mech and continue on foot – turn to **510.**

571

The skies above are clear and blue, while the streets you are exploring are grey and dark.

Turn to **115.**

572

Where do you want to go now?

If you want to explore the other part of the ship, turn to **391**. If you think you have gleaned all that you can from the *Gojira* and want to return to *Ronin 47*, turn to **592**.

573

Adrenaline and desperation giving your muscles a much needed power boost, you fling yourself into the void... and land safely on the other side.

But your continued survival is not a certainty. Kira turns from the hatch that leads to the cockpit of the Shogun, a long bladed katana of his own gripped tightly in both hands. (In this battle, Kira has the initiative.)

KIRA   COMBAT 10   ENDURANCE 12

If you are victorious in the battle with the traitor of Ako Base, turn to **500.**

Knocking the pilot's blade out of his grasp and kicking his feet out from under him, you pin him down on the hull of the Ninja-mech. The tip of your katana mere millimetres from his throat, you demand that he answers your questions.

Clearly intimidated by your furious focus, under interrogation he soon gives up some useful information, by giving you one half of a set of GPS coordinates: 138.7274° E. (Record this information on your Adventure Sheet.)

However, he then tries to bargain with you, offering the other half of the set of coordinates in return for his life. As you ponder his offer for a moment, he suddenly goes for you, hoping to cut you down while you are distracted.

He thought wrong, your blade putting an end to him at last. At least one half of a set of GPS coordinates is better than none.

Before you continue on your way, you salvage a Cloaking Device from one of the Ninja-mechs and find it relatively easy to install it in your own mech.

Also record the Cloaking Device on your Adventure Sheet and then turn to **595**.

"It will be a few hours before the work is complete," Mototoki says. "In the meantime, why don't we see to your needs?"

The engineer leads you through the complex to the personnel quarters, where he lives alone, and takes you to the medical bay. There he finds 2 Medi-Packs (record these on your Adventure Sheet), and even rustles you up some ramen noodle soup. You hadn't realised how hungry you were, and the freshly cooked food tastes so much better than the ration packs you've been surviving on. (Restore up to 4 *Endurance* points.)

Once your belly is full, and your wounds have been seen to, Mototoki takes you back to the lift shaft, where the upgraded *Ronin 47* is waiting for you, with everything in place.

You thank Engineer Mototoki, who activates the mech elevator, as you strap yourself into the cockpit of your war-suit.

Not long after, you emerge from the bunker entrance into daylight once more.

Deduct 1 point from your mech's *Reactor* score and turn to **216**.

576

You find yourself outside the entrance to a subway station. But the trains aren't running now, and the tunnels have doubtless been colonised by the scavengers who now inhabit the city – rats, cockroaches, and desperate, degenerate humans. Turn to **545**.

577

Japan and your target lie to the north, but there is more than one way to get there.

Collating information from real-time scans of its current surroundings – cross-referenced against information retained within its memory core and that which you downloaded from the Tengu Satellite Array – as *Ronin 47*'s Combat AI plots an optimal course to Tokyo, it picks out two locations that may be of interest to you.

One – Yokai Base – lies to the northwest and is a top-secret scientific research facility. The other is at present only demarcated by a distress signal being broadcast from a point northeast of your current location.

Both routes will take you closer to Japan, but which way do you want to go?

Northeast?   Turn to **27**.

Northwest?   Turn to **513**.

578

The Shogun suddenly rallies and seizing hold of *Ronin 47*, attempts to push it into the fissure.

Take a Melee test. If you pass the test, turn to **110**; if you fail the test, turn to **531**.

579

There is nothing to be gained in wasting precious time teaching these dishonourable thieves a lesson, and so you activate *Ronin 47*'s flight systems.

If your mech has been fitted with a Booster Rocket and you want to use it now, to escape the Wreckers, turn to **599**. If not, you will have to rely on the giant robot's jump jets to fly you out of trouble – turn to **178**.

580

Chunks of wreckage from *Samurai 39* batter your war-machine, causing considerable damage.

Roll one die and add 3. Deduct this many *Integrity* points from your mech. (Alternatively, pick a card and deduct its face value from your mech's *Integrity* score, unless it is a 10 or a picture card, in which case deduct 9 points from the Samurai's *Integrity* score; if it is less than 4 you must deduct 4 *Integrity* points.)

If *Samurai 47* has lost 7-9 *Integrity* points, you must also deduct 1 point from both its *Armour* and *Melee* scores.

Turn to **596**.

581

You are used to attacks coming from below, in the ocean depths, but not from above. However, according to *Ronin 47*'s scanners, that is exactly what is happening now. Turn to **447**.

582

You continue on your way through the devastated metropolis. Turn to **420** to keep exploring the city.

583

Several hours later, you reach a rocky island, which stands alone in the middle of the ocean. Taking the mech ashore, you can see few signs of life, for there is very little vegetation on this lonely outcrop, and no sign of human habitation at all. But that is because the humans who have made their home here don't live on the surface. The Vault, as its name would suggest, is hidden underground.

You head inland and soon come to a rocky valley, at the end of which lies the entrance to the facility – a heavily-reinforced pair of doors with a matching pair of heavy-duty sentry gun turrets to either side, not unlike the sort of weaponry you would expect to see being touted by an Oni-mech.

If you have the code word *Connected* recorded on your Adventure Sheet, turn to **263**. If not, turn to **517**.

584

Your mech rises into the sky on a column of oily smoke and incandescent flame, the ruins of what remains of Japan's capital city rapidly dwindling below you. The snow-capped mountain dominates the skyline to the southwest, and so you direct *Ronin 47* towards it, the robot homing in on the coordinates programmed into its navigation system.

It is not long before you are passing over the green lower slopes of the stratovolcano, and it is then that *Ronin 47* alerts you to the fact that someone has sent out a welcoming committee. A flight of gun-drones is approaching from the southwest and there can be no doubt that you are their target.

How will you respond? Will you:

Fire a Hunter-Killer Missile at the gun-drones, if you can?	Turn to **564**.
Activate an EMP Device, if you can?	Turn to **390**.
Activate a Cloaking Device, if you can?	Turn to **211**.
Launch some Flares, if you can?	Turn to **469**.
Launch your own flight of Drones, if you can?	Turn to **431**.
Engage the gun-drones in combat?	Turn to **403**.

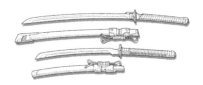

585

The blast radius triggers more of the mines, which also explode, triggering those nearby in turn, until a catastrophic chain reaction ripples out across the Sagami-nada Sea.

Although you are out of range of the sentient mines' sensors, *Ronin 47* is not out of range of the storm of shrapnel that sweeps in your direction.

Take an Armour test. If your mech passes the test, turn to **563**; if you fail the test, turn to **170**.

586

The longer you wander the streets of the city, the more uneasy you become.

Deduct 1 *Combat* point and turn to **420**.

587

Ronin 47 rises into the sky on a cone of smoke and flames. But the jump-jets were not designed for prolonged flight and soon the HUD is warning you that your reliance on them is taking a toll on the reactor core. You have no choice but to land again as soon as possible. (Add 1 to your mech's *Reactor* score.)

Roll one die (or pick a card). If the number rolled is odd (or the card is red), turn to **27**. If the number rolled is even (or the card is black), turn to **513**.

The HUD suddenly goes black, and for a moment you wonder if *Ronin 47* has succumbed to the malicious malware after all.

A split second later, the screen blinks back into life, and you can see the Shogun standing before you, beside its gantry in the cone of Mount Fuji's caldera.

Having failed to deactivate *Ronin 47*'s systems using the same Assassin Virus that took down Ako Base, Kira will have to face you in battle now. Or will he?

You suddenly notice a repeating waveform being projected at the top right-hand corner of the screen. The mech's database quickly finds a match for the signal; it has detected it before. And then you gasp in horror as the match is made. It is the same signal Kira broadcast using Ako Base's own instruments to attract the kaiju to ensure the island-complex's destruction.

While *Ronin 47* has been preoccupied with purging the virus from its computer core, Kira has not been idle. But he must be desperate if he would dare bring the kaiju here and risk the destruction of his own fortress-factory, just to eliminate the threat posed by you.

Before you can take a step towards the looming Shogun, all manner of monsters starts to pour over the lip of the crater – turtle-like Kappa, arachnoid Tsuchigumo, and airborne Gumyocho among them.

If *Ronin 47* is carrying a DNA Bomb and you want to detonate it now, turn to **512**. If not, turn to **44**.

As you explore the ruins of Tokyo, you wonder – and not for the first time – how humankind could have been so foolish as to let climate change go unchecked for so long. If the nations of the world had done something about it sooner, you wouldn't be in this situation now and the population of the planet would be counted in billions rather than millions. Turn to **545**.

590

Roll one die (or pick a card). If the number rolled is odd (or the card is red), turn to **231**. If the number (rolled) is even (or the card is black), turn to **429**.

591

The burnt-out shells of cars, trucks, and public buses litter the street. Turn to **545**.

592

You make it back to the dock and the waiting mech with five minutes of air still remaining. Entering via the airlock in the back of the war-suit, you take your place once more in the pilot's seat. Turn to **8**.

593

You have heard rumours that the inhabitants of the city that remained after K-Day have become degenerate savages, not averse to a spot of cannibalism, if the opportunity arises.

Roll one die (or pick a card). If the number rolled is odd (or the card is red), turn to **420**. If the number (rolled) is even (or the card is black), turn to **435**.

594

Returning to *Ronin 47*, you succeed in connecting the Combat AI to the satellite dish's systems and piggyback on the signal to access the array itself.

You punch the air in delight when the message 'CONNECTION COMPLETE' appears on the cockpit screen, but immediately feel deflated when the words 'ENTER ACCESS CODE' appear beneath it, followed by the following sequence of numbers:

| 0 | 1 | 0 | 4 | 0 | 9 | 1 | 6 | 2 | 5 | 3 | 6 | 4 | 9 | 6 | _ | _ | _ |

Three slots remain blank. If you can work out what the missing digits are, turn to the matching reference.

If you cannot work out what the missing numbers should be, or the reference you turn to makes no sense, meaning you have got the answer wrong, turn to **568**.

595

Collating information from its current surroundings, married with data retained within its memory core and that downloaded from the Tengu Satellite Array, you see that you are almost 800 kilometres due south of what is left of the city of Tokyo. However, approximately 150 clicks to the northwest, *Ronin 47* has picked up a distress signal.

Do you want to head due north towards Honshu Island and Tokyo (turn to **259**), or do you want to try to pinpoint the source of the distress signal (turn to **27**)?

596

A piece of shrapnel embeds itself in the shoulder of your Samurai, precisely where the uplink transmitter is located.

No longer able to transmit to or receive messages from your squad, you have no choice but to pop the hatch on your cockpit – the faceplate of your Samurai yawning open like a great mouth – so that you can signal to the other pilots in person that there is a problem.

Takanao opens her mech's helm too and you inform her of what has happened. Acting on your behalf, she checks-in with the surviving members of Phoenix Squad, before signalling to Lieutenant Tsunenari that you are ready for retrieval.

In less than twenty minutes, the five remaining Samurai are back in the troop hold of the Tatsu.

Turn to **311**.

597

Taking the metal cylinder from where it is hidden in the mech's chest cavity, you hurl it at the huge bird. As it tumbles end over end through the air, thick gas starts to escape from vents at both ends of the canister. The cloud expands rapidly, enveloping the Gumyocho in a toxic green miasma.

There is nothing you can do but wait with bated breath, wondering what effect the compounds you combined to make the DNA Bomb will have on the airborne horror.

Deduct the number you have associated with the DNA Bomb from this section and then turn to that new section to see what effect the gas has on the Gumyocho.

If you do not have a number associated with the DNA Bomb, turn to **373**.

598

As the carcass of the Bake-kujira remains on the surface of the sea, it is a straightforward if messy matter for you to gut the beast in search of the object the Combat AI detected.

As you suspected, it is in the belly of the beast, and you are glad the mech is hermetically sealed so you do not have to endure the toxic stench emanating from the kaiju's digestive tract.

Covered in slime and its outer casing pitted by acidic corrosion from the fluids in the Bake-kujira's stomach, it turns out that the object is a dormant Spider repair droid.

(Record the Spider in the Upgrades box on your Adventure Sheet. The maintenance droid has enough charge to carry out 4 sets of repairs. Each time it repairs the mech, roll one die and multiply the result by 5; this is the number of *Integrity* points restored to the mech by the repair droid's work. Alternatively, pick a card and if it is a 7 or higher, it counts as a 6; then multiply the result by 5 and restore this many *Integrity* points.)

Delighted with your find, you set off once more.

Record the code word *Invaded* on your Adventure Sheet as well, and then turn to **577**.

599

Ronin 47 rises from the sea on a column of coruscating flame, the exhaust fumes swallowing the Wrecker-mechs. It does not suit their tactics to waste vital energy trying to pursue you, and so they let you go.

Looking down at the planet below you, the visible landmasses form into the recognisable pattern of the islands of Japan, as if seen in an atlas projection, only one that is relayed in real-time.

The Booster Rocket carries you over the Sagami-nada Sea and, as its fuel supply rapidly runs out, you land among the shattered skyscrapers and devastated ruins of Tokyo.

Cross the Booster Rocket off your Adventure Sheet and turn to **370**.

600

Looking down at the planet below, you see Mount Fuji disappear beneath a spreading cloud of smoke and ash. Everything Kira wrought here – and that must have taken him months, if not years, to build in secret – is wiped from the face of the Earth in only a matter of minutes, as Mount Fuji erupts for the first time in over four hundred years.

Deputy Director Kira, the man who betrayed Director Asano, Phoenix Squad, and everyone else for whom Ako Base was their home, is dead by your hand, your companions' untimely deaths avenged at long last. Not only that, but his fortress-factory is destroyed, and his army routed.

But what happens to you now? You are still a warrior without a master. Ronin.

Gazing down at Honshu Island, bounded by the sapphire blue waters of the Pacific Ocean and the Sea of Japan, as *Ronin 47* is bathed in golden sunlight, you realise that you could go anywhere and do anything, now that your vow has been fulfilled.

For as Sun Tzu states in *The Art of War*, *"Opportunities multiply as they are seized."*

Whether you choose to hunt down every last kaiju on the planet, attempt to unite the surviving members of the human race, or retire to some isolated island to see out the rest of your days, the choice is yours.

THE END

ACKNOWLEDGEMENTS

There are a number of people without whom *RONIN 47* would not be what it is, and I would like to take this opportunity to thank them here.

Firstly, my grateful thanks go to the illustrator, Neil Googe, who produced the astonishing, action-packed artwork for the book, including a truly astounding cover, and Len O'Grady, who coloured Neil's art for the collector's hardback. In a similar vein, I would like to thank Chris Weston, Tazio Bettin, and Simon Fraser, who all produced pin-up pieces for the hardback edition of the book.

Thank go to Emma Barnes of Snowbooks as well, for her indefatigable patience and support, and Anna Torborg for doing such a fantastic job with the layout once again. And, as ever, I must also thank Kevin Abbotts, who created the bookmark and the hyperlinked eBook version of the adventure.

Thanks are also due to Lin Liren, who advised me on certain cultural aspects of the book, and my team of play-testers – Anton Killin, Emma Owen, and Victor Cheng in particular.

And lastly, a heartfelt thank you to everyone who pledged their support to this post-apocalyptic adventure through Kickstarter and Indiegogo, and whose support helped ensure that this fantasy became a reality.

RONIN 47 BACKERS

Gaijin

Bryan Howarth • Jayson Deare • Ismael Prieto Gallach

Ninja

David Wolf • Robert Biskin • Joonseok Oh •
Iván Rodríguez-Perales • Guy Reisman • Sam Richards •
Peter "Poit" van den Hooren • Ty Kendall • Przemek Piotrowski
• Jorge Peluso • Alysha Lancaster • Laszlo Makay •
Lasume • Jonathan Poston • Ruz • Terranaunt • J Kyle Kelsey •
James Meredith • • Adrien Maudet • Dominik Pintera •
Nina Silver Ch. • Ken Klein • Krauser • Tommy Chu • sl1605

Samurai

Alisher • Mark Lee Voss • Justin-Lee Morrison • Luke Sheridan
• Thea Shortman • Michael Reilly • Olivier Leclair •
Kevin Harvey • Federico "Quiet" Catalano • Andrew Betts •
Javier Fernandez-Sanguino (Alarion) • Robertson Sondoh Jr •
L. Luciel Miller • Tim Wild • Onihatsugo • Colin Deady •
Jennifer Brooks • Ieuan Scott • Tom Cottrell • Todd Rokely •
Michael Feldhusen • Alistair McLean • David Ameer Tavakoli •
Martin Keown • NIF • Nicodemus • Johnny Barrett •
Beau Chambers • Kjeld Froberg • Ondřej Zástěra • Ebest •
toolkidd • Andrew Smith • Tom Geraghty • A Kerr •
Michael Travis • Ignacio Blasco • Christopher Semler •
Mark Stoneham • Paul Taylor • Richie Stevens •
James Cleverley • Michael Hartland • Sean F. Smith •
Rebecca Kronenfeld • Kamarul Azmi Kamaruzaman •
Gál Sára Zsófia • David Standley • Pang Peow Yeong & family
• Stephen Healey • Andrew Hartley • Pitcairn Geeks & Gamers
• Paragrafka • Stephen Griffin • Tim Shannon • Chris Ryal •
PJ Montgomery • Brice WITTMANN • Er Niño de La Joaquina
• Luke Passingham • Adrián Soltész • Dirk Smith • Kotka •

Shaun Taylor-Coldwell • Sean Franks • Chris Jefferson •
Lee A. Chrimes • Hamad Alnajjar • DrLight • Mel Hall •
Peter "Wraithkal" Christiansen • Paul Kirk • Jules Fattorini •
Brian "Smidge" Twomey • Christopher Bloise • Ian Ross •
John Burkle • Harris Larson • electricwater • Owen Potter
• Matthew Richards • Adam Sparshott • Michael Hartley •
Alessandro Perna • James Kail • David Willems •
Paul 'fuzzy' Thirkettle • P. Devgan • Stephan Forkel •
Levi Prinzing • Peter Halls • The Great Firebreather! •
Marcia Sousa • John Conlan • Stu Baynham •
Andrew & Sydney Nichols • Andrew Mauney •
林立人 Lin Liren "Retaker of Names" • Dave Bowen •
Richard Catherall • Phillip Vaughan • Kayce Vanluik •
JediBotanist • R.Manley • Peter Mons • Olivier Vigneresse •
Matt Leitzen • Paul A Murphy aka Sunex Amures •
David Gotteri • Chris Halliday • Neil Parkin • Peter Cutting •
Miguel Diaz Rodriguez • Mark Lain • Owen Boushel •
Rob Burke • Dr Nic Velissaris •夏谷実• Phil Brumby • skorpio
• Stuart Lloyd • Aaron Torres • Stephen "Kuma" Redmond
• Matthias Rumpf • Henrik Spalk • Hans Peter Bak • Pietje •
Philip R Jurado • Luis • Frazer Barnard •
Zacharias Chun-pong Leung • Michael Stevens •
Stephen Mooney • Andrew Alvis • Demian Katz •
Sarinee Achavanuntakul • Niki Lybæk • Alistair Greer •
Zero the Butcher • Campbell Pentney • the white wolf •
Bryant Stevenson • Drakkar Darkholme • CAGeorgeFamily
• Connor W Dillingham • Evan Frawley • Johnny J Flores •
Simone "OldMariner" Carlini • Mark B Elliott • Josh Mattern •
Simon King • Christian Lindke • Jason Wooldridge •
Jason Chan • Ross MacTaggart • G. Hartman • Dana Francis •
KaS • Preston Poland • Jackson Griffiths • Steven Lord •
Marcus Corrin • Danny A Russell • Bret Van Dillon • Helen G •
Clay Gardner • Paul Gaston • Darren Davis • Leigh Harman •
Nii Ankrah-Wilson • Alejandro Alvarado •
Ronald Schachtner II • Joshua Dreller • Camilla Achler •
• Duncan Bailey • Adam Williams • Matthew Smith •
CJ.Endlessnite • Julian Sparrow • Pablo Maria Martinez Merino
• Luis Lauranzon • John Dennis • Gregory Allensworth

Daimyo

Kevin Abbotts • Chris Trapp • Ian Greenfield • Simon J. Painter • Matt Sheriff • Laurent JALICOUS aka Warlock-man • Louise Lee • Charles Revello • Mario Villanueva • Robert Wilde • Marc Thorpe • Kurosh Shadmand • Vin de Silva • Ang NamLeng • Michael Lee • Matthew Stephenson • Marcin Segit • Anders Svensson • Victor Cheng • Magnus Johansson • Michaël Lavoie • Ant O'Reilly • Andrew Wright • Rebecca Scott • [Redacted] • Rob Crewe • Ken Nagasako • Allan Matthews • Jill Wong @TheMotleyGeek • Phillip Bailey • Graham Hart • furrida • Robin Horton • René Batsford • Franck Teixido • Stefan Atanasov • Andy Bow • Daimyō Greg the Ûrban' • Sauro Lepri • David Poppel • Jonathan Caines • ***Paul Jones*** • Godwin-Matthew Teoh • Argentium Thri'ile • Chris Jackson • Mark Myers • Antonio Jorge García Lentisco • Pat Breen • Dominic Marcotte • Dennis Chang • Teodor Nikov • Matt Taylor • Vargarde, Mighty Werewolf • Psigh Dimitrios • Alexander Ballingall • Jon Trautman • Seth Martin • Edward Duggan • Leroy Brown • Poulpiche • Matthew Hernandez • Darren Uren • Marcelino "Ninja Dude" Collado IV • Nathan (N8Dogg5k) Barlow • Pedro Jose Lee • Martin Jacobs • Alexander Hayes • Mike McGuigan • Laurent BOSC • Karl Ansell • Anthony Christopher Hackett

Shogun

Rms • David J Williams • Kang Liedong • James Aukett

Ronin

Paul 'Moggie' Morrough • Fabrice Gatille • Pete Wood • Ashley Hall • Emma Owen • Anton Killin

Mechageddon

Battlefield Bangkok

Kaiju

Nicholas Chin • Dan Kaiwarrior Schell • Judykins •
Duncan Lenox, Blaine Lenox and Jason Lenox •
Stephane Bechard • Benjamin Wicka • Y. K. Lee •
Jason Vince a.k.a. 'Dream Walker Spirit'

Daikaiju

Our Games Trading Co Ltd • Andrés Rodríguez Rodríguez

About the Author

Jonathan Green is a writer of speculative fiction, with more than seventy books to his name. Well known for his contributions to the Fighting Fantasy range of adventure gamebooks, he has also written fiction for such diverse properties as *Doctor Who*, *Star Wars: The Clone Wars*, *Warhammer*, *Warhammer 40,000*, *Sonic the Hedgehog*, *Teenage Mutant Ninja Turtles*, *Moshi Monsters*, *Lego*, *Judge Dredd*, *Robin of Sherwood*, and *Frostgrave*.

He is the creator of the ***Pax Britannia*** series for Abaddon Books and has written eight novels, as well as numerous short stories, set within this steampunk universe, featuring the debonair dandy adventurer Ulysses Quicksilver. He is also the author of an increasing number of non-fiction titles, including the award-winning ***YOU ARE THE HERO – A History of Fighting Fantasy Gamebooks*** series.

He occasionally edits and compiles short story anthologies, such as the critically-acclaimed ***GAME OVER***, ***SHARKPUNK***, and ***Shakespeare Vs Cthulhu***, all of which are published by Snowbooks.

To find out more about ACE Gamebooks and his other projects, visit **www.JonathanGreenAuthor.com** and follow him on Twitter **@jonathangreen**, or Instagram **@jongreen71**.

Ingram Content Group UK Ltd.
Milton Keynes UK
UKHW011311180623
423619UK00003B/63